CW01512074

The Wrong Brother

IONA ROSE

Author's Note

Hey there!

Thank you for choosing my book. I sure hope that you love it. I'd hate to part ways once you're done though. So how about we stay in touch?

My newsletter is a great way to discover more about me and my books. Where you'll find frequent exclusive give-aways, sneak previews of new releases and be first to see new cover reveals.

And as a HUGE thank you for joining, you'll receive a FREE book on me!

With love,

Iona

Get Your FREE Book Here:
https://dl.bookfunnel.com/v9yit8b3f7

CHAPTER
One

JENNY

Every time I blink, it's like flipping through a magazine, each page showing a different perfect scene. They don't look real, any of them. This entire night feels like a fantasy...a place too beautiful, with its sprawling garden around the lake, all wrapped up in starlight and soft music. The whole scene glows with all the golden lights strung from the tree branches, shimmering in the lake's reflection.

I'm tucked up in my perfect hiding spot, curled up on a sturdy branch on one of the estate's many trees. From here, I can see it all...the glimmering water, the guests in their finery drifting across the lawn like they're in a movie.

This whole night is some kind of enchanted scene, and I'm just a spectator on the edges, looking in.

But I'm not here for them. Yes, they are beautiful and glamorous, but my eyes are glued to the shining star of the movie...Brett Jackson.

His blond hair practically glows in the crowd, bright and

golden. He sticks out like a beam of light among a sea of dark-haired men. He's laughing, that perfect laugh of his, and every time those marvelous teeth flash, I feel a jolt in my chest, like I can't breathe right. It's like he's lit from within. He is completely at ease. For he was born to be in this kind of crowd. And all around him, the women giggle, hanging on his every word, leaning in close to touch his arm. Their eyes sparkle with interest, and I feel a tight, hot knot of jealousy twist in my stomach. He isn't that funny…he's never been that funny.

I hate the way they look at him. The way they laugh, practically swooning, their eyes eating him up. I know he's charming, but they don't know him like I do. They don't know about the time he lifted me into his arms when I was little, scooping me up to protect me from that cranky dog everyone thought was harmless. They weren't there that day… weren't there when he smiled down at me and promised I'd be safe as long as he was there. They don't understand that he's been mine ever since. My heart's been his from the moment he rescued my stuffed animal from that dog's slobbery mouth and handed it back to me like it was nothing in the world.

Ever since then I've been biding my time.

One day… when I turn eighteen, I'll be ready, and he'll see me as more than the chauffeur's daughter who lives above the garage. I'll finally be part of this world, part of his world. But right now, all I can do is watch from the shadows, feeling like my heart will burst just seeing him laugh with someone else. It's torture, pure torture, knowing he's so close yet so far away, and all I can do is stay hidden up in this darned tree.

Just then, he glances away, moving from his little circle of admirers, and for a second, it feels like he's looking right at me. My breath catches, and I freeze, feeling my whole body go still as if by some miracle he's finally noticed me. But then

I realize...he isn't looking at me. His gaze has slipped past and is scanning the crowd. My heart sinks, realizing I've just imagined it.

But someone else is looking.

A darker, heavier presence, like a shadow passing over the ground. I spot Brett's older brother, Zack, watching from across the lawn, his eyes scanning the crowd with that intense gaze of his. My heart speeds up for a different reason now. Zack isn't exactly evil, but there's something about him that feels heavy, like he knows more than he lets on, and he's always watching, always lurking on the edge of things. I shrink back into the shadows, hoping he doesn't see me up here. He makes me feel like he knows my every little secret, like he sees everything I'm trying to hide.

Before I can sink any lower, I hear my father's voice calling out from below.

"Jenny! Jenny! Why on earth haven't you been answering your phone?"

I clench my teeth, trying to blend into the branches, willing him not to notice me. But his voice comes again, sterner this time. "

Jenny! Stop trying to hide, you brat. I know you're there. I can see you. I've told you to stay out of that tree. Get down here right now!"

My stomach twists with a sinking feeling as my father's voice echoes again, stern and unyielding. I know there's no hiding now. With a reluctant sigh, I begin to climb down, inching my way carefully from one branch to the next. The bark scrapes against my palms, rough and uneven, and I cling to each branch as though it might save me from the lecture I know is coming.

The leaves brush past my cheeks, whispering against my skin like a secret. I'm only a few branches from the ground when my foot slips and my hands lose their grip on the rough bark. Before I can even gasp, I'm tumbling through the branches.

The world blurs into a swirl of leaves and twinkling lights, my heart pounding in my chest as gravity pulls me down. I feel the sting of branches scratching against my arms and legs, snagging at my clothes as I tumble faster towards the ground.

And then…thud.

I land flat on my back, the impact jolting through my spine. For a moment, everything is still, the breath knocked out of me as I stare up at the sky, stars scattered like glittering shards in the vast darkness. My heart is racing, my pulse pounding in my ears as I lie there, feeling every inch of me throbbing from the fall.

The sounds of the party fade around me, muffled by the ringing in my ears. Slowly, I become aware of my father leaning over me, blocking out the stars. I blink, disoriented. His expression is a mix of worry and irritation. The world snaps back into place, the voices and laughter of the ball swirling faintly around us.

"You're going to break your neck one of these days," he says with a frown.

CHAPTER
Two

ZACH

T he night is perfectly orchestrated...at least, it should be.

Guests cluster around the gardens, champagne in hand, their laughter drifting lazily in the night air. My brother, Brett is as ever, surrounded by a bevy of admirers, each one with eyes full of the ridiculous fantasy that he will choose her. Most of them have come with their parents, who are also hoping Brett might finally show interest in one of their daughters. They won't approach me; they know better. My patience for small talk is nonexistent. The ball may look like a social event, but it's meant to keep the Jackson family's business running at full throttle.

I weave through the garden, catching the attention of a few key executives who have gathered in small groups, each one is here tonight for more than the champagne. I stop by one of the circles, and almost immediately, Richard Lawson, one of our lead architects, leans in.

"So, Zack, about the Manhattan project," he begins, his

voice loud to compete with the sound of the live music. "We're making quite the statement with this one. Have you seen the latest foot traffic numbers? We're going to be smack in the middle of it all. Tourists, locals...they will have the Jackson name in front of them daily."

"Exactly the plan," I say, nodding. "We're not just adding another high-rise. We're creating something that draws people in. Floor-to-ceiling glass, strategic lighting that highlights every inch. This building won't blend in. It'll stand out, even in the middle of Manhattan."

Lawson's eyes light up, clearly energized by the vision. "We've run simulations on it already. It's going to be one of the most noticeable structures on the skyline...right up there with the best of them."

Andrew Barron, another executive, chimes in. "And it's not just the aesthetics. With a space like this, we're also setting the standard for high-end office rentals in the city. Companies are already reaching out about securing floors. We're creating a brand in itself."

"Which is why we're carefully curating the tenants," I reply, my tone sharpening slightly. "We need long-term contracts, names that add prestige. We're Jacksons...this isn't a revolving door for anyone who can pay the rent."

Just then, the mayor strides over, extending his hand.

"Zack," he says, shaking my hand firmly. "I hear your new project is going to change the face of Manhattan."

"That's the goal," I respond, meeting his gaze. "But we could use a little cooperation with zoning."

He raises an eyebrow, clearly expecting this part of the conversation. "You know how it is...city council likes to see benefits for the community."

"Of course," I reply smoothly. "To that end we're building green spaces on the lower levels. A terrace accessible to the public, featuring local art facilities. We're not just putting up a building. We're creating an experience for the city."

He nods, pleased. "And air rights? How are you managing that?"

"We've already bought additional air rights from the surrounding lots," I say. "And as a show of goodwill, we're allocating a portion of the budget to refurbish the nearby subway entrance. It'll be safer and more modern."

Lawson jumps in, enthusiastic. "And by the way, we're aiming for a LEED Platinum certification. Eco-friendly design all the way. This building will be a model for sustainable urban development."

The mayor's interest piques. "The council will like that. It's good press for everyone involved, myself included."

I nod, knowing that's exactly the response we need from him. "We're hoping to submit final plans soon. I'd like to keep this moving on schedule, if possible."

The mayor's gaze is steady, calculating. "I'll make sure your plans get a proper review. And Zack—don't hesitate to call if you need anything expedited."

"Much appreciated," I reply, smiling broadly.

At that moment there's a sound of something crashing through the leaves and a sudden thud from somewhere beyond the garden. A few heads turn, confused, but no one knows what to make of it. No one's expecting someone to fall out of a tree at an event like this. I glance over, catching a flash of auburn hair through the shadows and shake my head.

It's her…Jenny, the chauffeur's daughter. I've caught her sneaking around like this before, hiding in places she shouldn't be.

It's only a brief disturbance, barely noticed by most. I move toward Brett, catching him just as he reaches for another glass of champagne. Without a word, I pull him aside to the champagne bar, handing him a fresh bottle.

"How nice of you Mr,.." he kids as usual.

"Maybe it's time to keep your admirers in line, or take them somewhere out of sight," I tell him, keeping my tone even. "This is still a business event, not a dating circuit."

He glances at me, unfazed. "What's the harm? Which one are you worried about...one or both?" he jokes, nodding to two women nearby, their eyes following his every move.

"The tall brunette is Harrington's daughter...major construction investor. The redhead? Millie Devereaux. Senator Devereaux's kid. So, you might want to consider carefully."

Brett raises an eyebrow, then smirks. "Harrington and Devereaux. Quite the pair." He pauses, considering. "Why not both?"

I roll my eyes, pushing the champagne bottle into his hands. "Whatever you do, make sure it's discreet. This is a serious event. Dad's going to notice sooner or later, and then you'll be hearing about it for months. He'll probably ban you from next year's ball too."

Brett frowns, though there's a playful glint in his eye as he accepts the bottle. "Fine, whatever keeps the peace," he says, rubbing my arm and giving a mock toast.

"Oh, and one more thing," I add. "Check on that girl...the chauffeur's daughter, Jenny. She just fell from a tree. Again."

"Again?" Brett's expression shifts, a flicker of concern mixed with surprise. Then he shakes his head, a faint, fond smile on his face. "She'll never stop climbing into trees and falling out of them. Sometimes I tell people I grew up with two brothers instead of just you. He turns around to look towards the trees and turns back to grin at me. "No worries there. Her father's got her. I on the other hand have two beautiful women to get to know a bit better if you know what I mean."

He wiggles his eyebrows as he makes his way over to

them with a bottle. I do know what he means and once again it worries me that he's not focused at all on fostering connections or participating in the company's enhancement. My father is the one who's most displeased with this but my mother in her immaculate kindness keeps insisting that we should let him be.

He walks away and I turn to watch Jenny's father more or less chase her back towards their home above the garage.

CHAPTER
Three

JENNY

"Jenny! Jenny!" My father's voice echoes down the hall.

I walk faster, pretending I can't hear him. He's close on my heels, furious with me for storming out in the middle of his latest lecture on "knowing my place." As if I don't know it well enough.

And of course, as I turn the corner, there is Brett, coming in my direction with his usual, lazy charm, a woman on each arm. They hold champagne glasses in their manicured hands, laughing like they'd already won him. I know where he's taking them. To the bloody indoor conservatory, where... No, I can't even think about it. About what he wants to do to them and with them. I'll lose my mind if I do.

· · ·

"Jenny, you okay?" Brett asks. "Zack says you fell out of a tree."

My pulse races as he addresses me but the hysterical giggles from the women hanging onto his arms makes me race ahead even faster to hide from the shame consuming me.

"Be careful!" Both Brett and my father yell after me, but I ignore them both and run home.

I shove open the door to our little apartment above the garage and storm into my room, pulling the blanket over my head as if it can block out everything...the party sounds, the music, the laughter, all of it. But it seeps through, filling my room and my head like poison. Sometimes it feels like I'm trapped in some kind of prison, surrounded by all this wealth, yet always just on the outside. It's like I'm taunted with it, reminded every single day that I'll never be part of it, and that Brett... would never see me as anything other than the chauffeur's kid.

Below me, in the garage, are more luxury cars than most people see in a lifetime. Brett loves them. I don't even care about cars, but I know every damn model because he's obsessed, talking about them with the kind of focus he never shows on anything else. Once, when I was fifteen, I tried to kiss him, back when we were both in the garage, just him and me in his sleek, cherry-red Ferrari. But he was so wrapped up in some smudge on the windshield, he barely noticed. I thought he'd feel something, just a flicker of what I feel, but...

nothing. He tossed a rag over his shoulder, not even looking at me, and I had to swallow back my embarrassment, pretending I was helping him with the damn spot on the glass.

Now, that memory burns in me, and my heart aches at the thought of what he's doing in the conservatory, with those two women laughing and fawning over him, probably already melting under his touch.

I've walked in on him before, wrapped around some woman like he couldn't get enough, and it was horrible. She was panting like an animal. Ugh!

A knock on the door breaks through my thoughts, and my father's voice follows, low and firm.

"Jenny. We need to talk."

I squeeze my eyes shut, hoping he'll leave, but of course, he doesn't. I hear the door creak open and his heavy footsteps as he comes in, pulling a chair to my bedside. The mattress dips slightly as he sits beside me, sighing in that way he does when he's about to start in on me.

"You can't keep doing this," he says, voice softer now. "I know what you're feeling, Jenny."

. . .

"No, you don't," I whisper, biting down the lump in my throat.

"Believe it or not, I know," he insists, his voice gentler but unyielding. "But I keep telling you that it's because you're young. It will pass. This infatuation will pass. You'll come to your senses soon enough to understand how this world works."

"Please stop," I plead. "I've heard you. I know I'm not good enough for the likes of the Jacksons. So please go."

He doesn't listen, and as always, he is adamant on trying his best to get me to come to my senses.

"Look at him, Jenny. Brett's not for you. You'll never be part of their world...you're not even in his orbit. These people... they're different. They don't live by the same rules. And Brett, he's the life of the party. Do you think he even knows you exist in the way you want him to?"

"Stop," I hiss, but my voice breaks. "Dad! I hear you. You don't need to remind me again that we are nothing. I get it."

He sighs, his hand resting on my blanket. "Jenny, I have been trying to get you to understand and to listen to me for the longest time, but you haven't. So now, I think it's best I take matters into my own hands and fix this problem."

. . .

At this, my heart nearly sinks into my belly. "What do you mean?" I ask. "What are you planning to do?"

"Virginia," my father replies. "I'm sending you to your grandparents. They'll be more than happy to have you. You'll stay there for a while, work on the farm. I think it'll be good for you to get away, to have some time, some distance."

I cannot believe the words coming out of his mouth. I'm in so much shock that for the longest time, I just stare right back at him, open-mouthed.

"No," I say, my voice barely a whisper, but my whole body stiffens. "No. You can't do that. I can't leave… I can't… No!"

"You don't have a choice. Plus, you always loved the fields and working in the gardens. There'll be plenty of trees for you to climb there, but please be careful."

He sounds casual, like this is just a discussion, but there is a finality in his tone that I know makes it clear this is not up for discussion.

"It's what's best for you, sweetheart," he says. "This crush, this obsession…it has to stop. You need to see this for what it is."

. . .

The words sear through me, leaving me raw and open. I clench my fists, fighting back the scream bubbling up inside me. I can't stand the way he looks at me, like I'm some naive girl with foolish dreams, like he knows everything, and I know nothing.

"Just... go away," I whisper, my voice shaking. "If you don't leave right now, I'll scream."

For a moment, he stays where he is, a heavy silence stretching between us. Then he sighs, standing up slowly.

"Alright, Jenny," he says, his voice quieter, sadder than before.

I hate to hurt him. I hate to be rude, but right now my heart is breaking. He's sending me away, and who knows if I'll ever return. He's talked about moving back to Virginia as well, so what if... what if I never get to see Brett again?

He leaves, closing the door softly behind him, and as soon as he's gone, I feel the tears well up, hot and unstoppable. I bury my face in the blanket, sobbing as I clutch my pillow, the pain ripping through me like nothing I've ever felt before.

. . .

He's right. There's no hope. There's no way out of this. Brett will never see me. I'm nothing more than the chauffeur's daughter, and that will never change. And now that he's shipping me off, there's no longer any time to fix this. I imagine the farm, spending my days there, wallowing…and it hurts too much. I make up my mind then. It's not a sudden thought. Frustration and despair have seeped in over and over again through the years, and the thought has crossed my mind countless times. But maybe now, it's time to find peace.

Sniffling, I reach for my journal, my hands shaking as I flip it open. I press the pen to the page, but I can barely see through the blur of my tears, my hand trembling as I start to write my suicide note.

CHAPTER
Four

ZACH

I'm making my way back into the house, planning to speak to the catering staff, when I catch sight of her running down the stairs, clutching something in her hand. Jenny. I watch, hidden in the shadow of the hallway, as she dashes across the entryway, looking pale and frantic, almost as if she's being chased by her own thoughts. She doesn't see me, too caught up in whatever dark path she's set her mind on, and I realize something's wrong.

She's holding a piece of crumpled paper in her hand…she's gripping it like it's her last lifeline. Her expression is twisted, almost feverish. It's not curiosity that keeps me watching. There's something desperate about the way she's moving, about the determined look on her face, and it pulls me forward without a second thought.

. . .

She's making a beeline for the garage, her steps quickening. I know she doesn't notice me following her, but I stay close enough to see her shoulders tense, her breaths coming fast. I usually wouldn't care but given that she's one to fall out of trees, I've trained myself over the years to pay closer attention to her…if only to avoid an unfortunate accident on the estate. I cannot count how many scrapes, injuries, and near-death experiences she's had, from encounters with wild dogs to incidents at the pool. She has always been so careless, just like a boy. And so, we all look out for her, never assuming she knows what she's doing, for the estate's continued peace and tranquility.

She reaches the final turn toward the garage, and then something in her snaps, and she breaks into a full run.

"Jenny," I call out, my voice low and steady. "Jenny, stop."

She doesn't hear me…or pretends not to. Her hand tightens around the letter, her knuckles white, her face drawn. I pick up my pace, sure now that she's set on something reckless. I reach her just as she whirls around the corner, heading straight toward the cars. She's too focused, too lost in whatever dramatic exit she's planned, to see me coming.

Before either of us can react, we collide, her body slamming into mine with a force that sends her stumbling backward. The letter slips from her fingers, fluttering to the floor as she loses her balance, her arms flailing. She reaches out as if to catch herself, but it's too late. Her head strikes the cold tile with a sharp, sickening crack, and she goes completely still, her eyes fluttering closed.

For a moment, I just stand there, my heart pounding, staring down at her motionless form. Her face, usually so full of that intense, restless energy, is now quiet, fragile even. A part of me feels an unexpected stab of worry, something I can't quite brush off. Especially now… that she's just lying there, small and pale, looking like the child she still is, even if she doesn't realize it.

I lean down, lifting her gently, cradling her close as I carry her up the stairs and into her room. The paper lies crumpled on the floor, but I ignore it for now. Her head rests against my shoulder, her breathing soft and shallow, as if she's suspended in some kind of fevered sleep. I try not to think too much as I take her down the hall, just focus on the steady weight of her in my arms.

As I reach her room, I spot her father in the small library corner in their apartment. The place is filled with more books than furniture, and it's the one place where I know he finds his peace.

When he sees us, though, his face goes ashen, and he rushes over, panic in his eyes.

"Jenny… what happened?" he asks, voice trembling.

"She'll be all right," I say, as reassuringly as I can manage. "But you should call a doctor to check her over."

.   .   .

He nods, hurrying to make the call, his hands shaking slightly as he dials. I settle Jenny onto her bed, brushing a stray lock of auburn hair from her face, my expression softening despite myself.

It's unsettling, this feeling creeping in, this strange weight in my chest as I look at her lying there, so still. Her father returns, hovering by her side, his worry palpable, and after a little while, the doctor arrives. In the meantime, I read the contents of the letter, and my blood completely runs cold.

The examination is brief, the doctor assures us that she's only sustained a mild concussion.

"She'll need rest," he murmurs, glancing from Jenny to her father. "Keep her comfortable, and she should be fine."

The doctor leaves, and her father exhales deeply, his shoulders sagging with relief as he thanks me again. I explain to him why I found her, but that's it. I don't mention the contents of the letter; he doesn't need to know that I didn't just step in to protect her. With what she had planned to do in that letter, she could have dragged our family's name down with her. I'm stunned and furious. But in that moment, seeing her father's gratitude, I can't bring myself to say anything. I give him a nod and step back, lingering in the corner of the room, my gaze drifting to the letter I picked up on the way back to her room.

I smooth it out, glancing over her words again, letting them sink in. She wrote that she couldn't live without Brett, that she'd rather die than see him with someone else. I shake my head, frustration mingling with a strange, unbidden sympathy. How could someone so young think her life is over just because she can't get what she wants? It's foolish. Reckless.

The faint strains of music drift up from the garden, a reminder of the party I should be overseeing, yet I find I can't leave, can't bring myself to move. I watch her, lying there so still, a girl caught in the whirlwind of her own feelings, her own illusions. I receive a phone call then from the party, and after it's completed, I turn to her father, who's still watching over her, his face softened with relief.

"During the commotion, one of the guests took notice of Jenny," I tell him quietly. "She mentioned that Jenny would make a perfect model for her daughter's fashion company in Paris. It's a three-year contract…school included, if she wants it. I think it could be the best thing for her. Some distance. Some perspective."

Her father is shocked by the sudden offer, his gaze flicking back to her, worry mingling with something else…hope, maybe. "This is good," he says. "She hasn't really ever mentioned wanting to be a model, but it's what a lot of young girls love these days, right? Maybe she'll be excited about it as well. She… she could use a fresh start. Somewhere she can find herself without all of this…" His voice trails off, but I know what he means.

"Can you leave me alone with her for a little while?" I ask.

• • •

Her father is startled by this but he seems to need the relief himself and so he nods and takes his leave.

When the room empties, I step forward, looking down at her pale face, her auburn hair spread across the pillow like flames. About ten minutes later she suddenly stirs, and her eyes slowly open, widening when she realizes I'm there. I'm just as surprised but relieved while she looks incredibly concerned and confused.

She probably has no idea what I'm doing in her room. To be honest neither do I but knowing now how unstable she is I cannot bring myself to leave just yet.

"Where were you going?" I ask. "Why were you in such a rush?"

She continues to stare up at me but doesn't respond.

I know now that she is not going to tell me anything, but she doesn't have to. For a moment I consider leaving the letter by her side so that she will understand that I know just how foolish she was about to act. However, at the last moment and at the pain in her eyes I decide against it.

It's so easy to completely dismiss her frustrations and sadness because of how young she is. I understand it even though I despise it but for today, for this moment I decide to cut her some slack. She'll be going to Paris. Perhaps she'll get the chance from there to become more independent. To gain perspective and get rid of these nonsensical fantasies about Brett.

And so, I turn around without a further word and walk away.

CHAPTER
Five

JENNY

I don't even realize when I fall asleep again after Zack leaves, but when I finally come to, I'm met with a gentle murmur of voices around me. My head feels heavy, throbbing with a dull ache, and it takes a few moments for the room to come into focus. I blink, and the familiar face of Mrs. Finnigan, the housekeeper, leans over me, her warm hand brushing a stray lock of hair from my forehead.

"Oh, Jenny, sweetheart," she says softly, her voice full of relief. "We've all been so worried about you."

I shift slightly, feeling the ache radiate through me, not just from my fall but from the heaviness that's settled in my chest. Mrs. Finnigan's hand stays on my forehead, her fingers gentle and warm. I try to give her a small smile, but it barely holds together.

As my eyes adjust, I realize that the room is filled with familiar faces…Mr. Collins, the butler, standing at the doorway with his usual quiet presence; Auntie Mae, the cook, sitting beside me with her hand on my shoulder; even a few of the younger maids lingering just beyond the door, all of them watching with expressions of worry and relief. They're all here, surrounding me, their faces filled with concern.

"You gave us all quite the scare," Auntie Mae murmurs, her voice thick with emotion. She pats my shoulder gently, like she always does when she thinks I need comforting. "You have to be careful, love."

Mr. Collins nods from the doorway, his usual stoic expression softened. "We're just glad to see you awake and all right," he says quietly. "Just... please, take care of yourself."

Their kindness wraps around me, warm and soft, almost like a real family. They don't know what I was really planning, don't know the darkness I was slipping into. I wonder where the letter is... where it fell. I hope no one ever finds it. But it worries me that they might have, so I try to get up to find it, but they don't let me.

"No, no, no more movements for you," Mrs. Finnigan says. "You're staying in bed for the foreseeable future, resting."

I try to work up a smile, but all it does is send shame prickling up my spine, knowing that they all care so deeply, while I was willing to throw it all away. I nod slightly, feeling my heart twist as each of them takes turns speaking, their voices gentle, almost like a chorus of quiet, loving scolding.

My father steps forward, clearing his throat. I can see the lines of worry etched on his face, and it breaks my heart all over again. He doesn't deserve this; none of them do. "Jenny, love," he says, his voice softer than usual, "I'm really glad you're okay, but for once there's a silver lining to you wanting to give me a heart attack."

I frown at his words, wondering what he's talking about. He explains, "You've been given a chance. Paris. A fresh start."

"What do you mean?" I ask, my voice croaking. My throat

is so dry. Instantly, he reaches for the jug of water by my side, fills up a glass for me, then hands it over.

"Apparently, in all the commotion of Mr. Jackson... Zack..finding you and bringing you here, one of their guests noticed you. She thinks you'd make the perfect house model for her daughter's fashion company in Paris. You'll be abroad, and you can attend an English-speaking school if you want as well. You'll be there for three years, and then you can come back. You'll also be able to take the time to travel around Europe. This is wonderful, isn't it?"

I stare at him.

Yes, it is wonderful, but... Brett.

Once again, he's sending me away, but at least it's not to a farm. I turn my head away and shut my eyes. By the time I return, Brett will probably no longer be available. I would likely have missed my chance. Well, I can't do what I had felt so distraught enough to do earlier, so I guess I have no choice but to bear it.

"Jenny," Mrs. Finnigan beams, her face lighting up. "Aren't you so happy? This is amazing! Just think, Jenny! You'll be off to see the world! Paris! It's such a great chance for such a young, gorgeous girl. You'll do great, sweetheart."

The room fills with gentle laughter, murmurs of encouragement, their voices weaving together, wrapping me in warmth. They're all so happy for me, so relieved that I'm safe and that I have this new opportunity. But deep inside, I feel a hollowness growing, a quiet sorrow that none of them can reach.

I force myself to nod, to give them the smile they want to see, but inside, I feel as if I'm already fading, slipping away from everything I know.

Auntie Mae squeezes my shoulder. "You'll have the chance to be someone, Jenny. To make us all proud." Her voice is soft, warm, and her hand lingers there, like she's offering me all the strength she has. I can see the brightness in her eyes, the hope she's holding onto for me, and it makes something deep inside me tighten, a bittersweet ache I can't shake.

I look around the room, at all these people who have loved me like family, who've watched me grow up, who've been there for every scraped knee and tear-filled day. They've seen me at my best and at my most foolish, and yet they still look at me now like I'm someone worth caring about, worth supporting. Mrs. Finnigan, with her gentle, motherly ways; Mr. Collins, ever so formal but steady as a rock; Auntie Mae, who's filled every gap in my heart with her warm meals and even warmer hugs. I see the younger maids watching from the doorway, their smiles shy but genuine, and even the gardeners who've come all the way up here just to make sure I'm all right.

And all of them, every single one, has nothing but hope in their eyes. Hope for me. And the realization fills me with a soft, aching sadness, because leaving them I realize now as well, feels like a loss I can barely comprehend. I cannot believe what I had planned to do. I would have hurt them all. It was truly beyond foolish.

I think beyond Brett now as my mind begins to truly consider Paris, and it feels like I'm being pulled away from the only family I've ever known.

I take a shaky breath, feeling the weight of it settle inside me, a quiet acceptance. Maybe, with enough time and distance, I can forget Brett, forget the way he looked right through me last night, his smile meant for everyone but me. Forget the hollow ache in my heart that whispers how he'll never be mine, no matter how much I wish for it. Maybe, in Paris, I can find something else, someone else.

One by one, they leave, each offering me a gentle smile, a nod, a quiet word of encouragement, like they're leaving me with pieces of themselves to take along. Auntie Mae is last to go, her hand squeezing mine just a bit tighter before she steps back, her eyes lingering on me like she's memorizing my face.

As the room finally empties, I lie back, staring up at the ceiling, the weight of their kindness settling over me like a blanket. They've given me all the love they can, wrapped me in it as if it could heal every bruise on my heart. But it doesn't change the pain pressing in on me, the heartbreak I carry like a secret, a burden I can't share. I wonder when it will end. In fact, I'm hoping now for Paris because at this point, I would give anything not to feel like this.

CHAPTER
Six

JENNY

THREE YEARS LATER

As the train slows into the station, I catch a fleeting glimpse of my own reflection in the window...sleek hair framing my face, lips painted in a muted rose, and clothes that practically announce Paris. I tug at the collar of my leather jacket, feeling the softness of the designer material beneath my fingers, grounding myself. I've come back a different woman, one who knows her way around a high-fashion studio and the vibrant streets of the Champs-Élysées. Yet here I am, heart pounding, as if I'm still sixteen, about to step into a world that's seen me only as the tomboy daughter of the chauffeur.

I scan the crowd for my father. He promised to be here on time, ready to see the version of me that Paris has polished and refined. But there's no familiar face in sight. I tap my foot impatiently, the strappy heels clinking softly on the polished floor, hoping to spot him any second.

My phone buzzes, and a message from him lights up the screen: *Stuck in traffic, love. Just wait a few minutes, and I'll be there.*

With a sigh, I slip my phone back into my jacket pocket and look around for a place to sit. Just then, my eyes land on something even more familiar than my father…a cherry-red sports car parked at the curb. My heart stutters. Brett's car? The same one I almost… I push the thought away, a cocktail of nostalgia and dread tightening in my chest.

The last time I saw that car; it had been a symbol of my own foolishness and despair. But now, I'm back, and I'm not the girl who would sit in the shadows hoping for a glimpse of Brett. I'm here with my own ambitions, my own purpose. Modeling isn't just a whim anymore; it's something I want, something I can build on. Maybe, if I'm lucky, it could even give me a way into the Jackson world…but on my terms.

I take a deep breath and steel myself, but my pulse quickens all the same when I do see him. I'm in shock. What are the freaking odds? And once again, I cannot pull my eyes away.

Brett, standing by the hood of his car, casual as ever, exuding that effortless charm. He's laughing, his arm slung over the shoulder of a woman stepping out of the passenger side, her laughter mixing with his as if they share a secret I'll never know. And just like that, the years between then and now slip away, and I'm back to being that girl up in the tree, watching him from a distance.

I'm frozen in place as he kisses her on the mouth, and then she walks away as though she owns the entire world. I cannot believe the grief and rage that fill me up. It starts slow, as envy, and then I'm irritated and furious all at once. I thought I had changed. I thought I was better. I thought I would feel better.

I think of what to do now. Ignore him altogether and wait for my dad or…

In an instant, I'm up on my feet and hurrying out of the arrivals hall. I look gorgeous, even more beautiful than the bimbo he was with. I really want to see if he ignores me. And so, I stare directly at him as I stroll over with my luggage, and of course, he notices. He's just about to return to the driver's side when he stops.

I walk past, but a few seconds later, the blare of a car horn jolts me out of my thoughts. I freeze, my heart hammering as I turn around to see Brett leaning out of the driver's seat, a playful smirk lighting up his face. "Hey! Need a ride somewhere, gorgeous?"

The word gorgeous hangs in the air, and for a moment, I can't move, can barely think. He doesn't recognize me. But I let him look anyway, let him really see me, hoping he'll realize who I am. His eyes roam over me, clearly intrigued, and I feel a thrill of satisfaction as his gaze lingers a little longer than it should.

I step closer, my heels clicking on the pavement as I approach him. The thrill is mixed with a strange, heady confusion. I'm right in front of him, and he doesn't know it's me. The thought is intoxicating, exhilarating even, as I watch him try to place my face. And I have to admit as well, annoying. It dawns on me now, more than ever, that I truly meant nothing to him.

There's no risk in going with him, so I put my luggage in and get in, and as always, he is the perfect gentleman, helping me all the way through.

"So," he drawls, leaning back in his seat, his smirk widening. "What's your name?"

My heart skips a beat, a mix of surprise and nerves bubbling up. For a moment, I wonder if I should tell him who I am, let him figure it out himself, or let him keep guessing. I hold his gaze, savoring the moment before finally saying, "Jenny."

"Jenny…" he murmurs, letting the name roll off his tongue as if trying it on for size. He squints, a flicker of confusion flashing across his face. "You know, I used to know a Jenny." His voice is softer now, as if he's remembering something distant, something half-forgotten.

"Oh?" I ask, keeping my voice light. "And who was she to you?"

He doesn't answer right away, just looks at me with a sort of quiet intensity that makes my heart beat faster. For a second, it feels like he's about to say something important, something that might finally make me understand what I meant to him—or if I ever meant anything at all. But instead, he just shrugs, breaking the moment.

"So," he says, clearing his throat, "where to?"

The question pulls me back to the present. I hesitate, feeling the weight of what I'm about to say.

"Home," I finally answer, giving him my father's address.

He nods, turning to start the car, but then stops, his hand hovering over the gear shift. I watch as the familiarity of the address sinks in, his brows drawing together in surprise. "Wait… home?" He looks back at me, realization dawning on his face. "That's my home."

I nod, watching as shock turns to recognition, his eyes widening as he finally sees me. There's a beat of silence, heavy and electric, and then he leans back in his seat, studying me with a mixture of disbelief and wonder.

"Jenny…" he says it again, softer this time, like he's seeing me for the first time.

I hate him but I can't help my smile at the shock on his face.

"Jenny? Holy shit! Jenny!"

Brett's jaw goes slack as he takes in my face, the disbelief flickering over his features like he's struggling to reconcile the girl he remembers with the woman sitting beside him now. I watch him, waiting, letting him feel the impact of who I am now…no longer the kid he knew but someone with her own life, her own purpose. He shifts, his gaze dipping down to my heels, then back up to my jacket, and finally resting on my eyes.

"Jenny?" he repeats, his voice barely more than a whisper, as if saying it louder might break the spell. He lets out a low laugh, shaking his head in stunned disbelief. "Wow… unbelievable." For a moment, the years seem to melt away, and all the resentment, the foolishness, the hope I carried for so long…everything just dissolves as he leans over, pulling me into a tight, almost desperate hug. I let myself sink into it, feeling the warmth of his arms, the solid strength of him surrounding me. This is what I had dreamed about in quiet moments, what I thought would make everything I felt back then worth it.

But there's something new now, something thrilling and bittersweet, knowing he's seeing me differently. When he finally pulls back, his hands still rest on my shoulders, holding me at arm's length as he studies me with something close to awe.

"Our Jenny. Look at you," he murmurs, and there's an unmistakable admiration in his eyes, a spark that wasn't there before. "What happened?"

I manage a nonchalant shrug, trying to play it cool despite the rush of emotions threatening to overwhelm me. "Paris," I say, brushing it off like it's no big deal.

He chuckles, shaking his head as if he still can't quite believe what he's seeing. "Didn't think you'd come back like… this. And no, it's not just Paris. Time happened to you as well. You're gorgeous!" His eyes linger on me, warm and unguarded, making my pulse quicken. "So… what have you been up to? Tell me all about your experience. It must have been amazing?"

"It was," I say, my voice steady as I lean back into the seat, crossing one leg over the other casually. "I actually loved it more than I expected. Got into modeling. Worked with some small agencies, went on a few shoots, met some… interesting people." I let the word linger, watching him react. "Turns out, I might just be good at it."

"Modeling, huh?" He raises an eyebrow, a glint of intrigue sparking in his gaze. "I never thought our Jenny would end up… walking runways."

I laugh softly, leaning in just enough so he catches the subtle fragrance of my perfume. "Well," I say with a teasing smile, "I'm not your little Jenny anymore, am I?"

His laugh is nervous, his gaze flicking to my lips before shifting back to my eyes. "Guess not. You're all grown up." His voice has a rough edge, and I savor the thrill that races through me, the realization that he's seeing me not as the kid who used to chase after him but as someone new, someone captivating.

Silence settles between us, thick with possibilities and unspoken questions. The car begins to move, the quiet hum of the engine filling the space between us. I glance out the window, watching the familiar streets pass by, trying to ground myself, to keep my heart steady.

Brett breaks the silence first. "So, what was it like… Paris?" He glances sideways, a hint of curiosity, maybe even jealousy, in his eyes.

"Vibrant. Alive," I reply, my voice soft, almost dreamy. "The city just pulls you in. I spent so many days walking those streets, getting lost and finding myself in ways I never imagined." I look over at him, a sly smile playing on my lips. "And the boys… they're different there. More… attentive, in some ways." I let the words linger, watching the faint flicker of surprise on his face.

"Attentive, huh?" He echoes, trying to sound nonchalant, but I can see the tension in his jaw. "So, you... met a lot of guys?"

I laugh, the sound light and airy, enjoying the way his eyes narrow slightly. "Turns out," I say, leaning back with a grin, "most guys my age don't really know what to do with a woman. At least, not in the way I'd like."

He shifts in his seat, his gaze turning more intense, almost guarded. "Wow. You really have changed. Never thought I'd hear these words coming out of your mouth."

This moment turns awkward, but I don't allow it to stop me from making my point. "Paris does that to you," I reply, letting the words hang in the air. The tension between us is thick, almost electric, and I can tell he's struggling to reconcile this new version of me with the memories he has. He wants to keep the image of that girl he once knew, but now he's faced with a woman who won't let herself be seen that way anymore.

The city fades behind us, replaced by sprawling fields and winding roads as we approach the Jackson estate. When we finally pull up to the grand gates, he parks the car, but he doesn't immediately get out. Instead, he turns to me, his gaze soft, yet filled with something new...something almost hesitant.

"I'm really happy you're back today because we're having a party tomorrow, and guess who's now going to be the special guest of honor?"

This makes me smile.

"What was the party for?" I ask.

"No reason, just because...you know how I am. But now we definitely have a reason," he says with a playful grin. "I can't wait for everyone to see the new, stunning Jenny. Not the little sister who used to follow me around. My circle of friends knows you; you know. I used to say I have two brothers, you and Zack. They'll be thrilled to see you again."

I raise an eyebrow, refusing to let him get too comfortable with that old narrative. "I'm not your brother, Brett, or your sister."

He laughs, holding up his hands in mock surrender. "Okay, not my brother or sister. My... hot model friend, then?"

His words send a shiver down my spine, but I keep my composure, my voice steady. "Not your friend either."

He pauses, his gaze holding mine, a question lingering there. "Then... what are you?"

I lean in, letting my perfume drift between us, feeling the thrill of having his attention, of watching him question what he thought he knew.

"You're being... flirty," he says with a teasing smile. "You've never been flirty before."

I shrug, smirk widening. "Maybe I have been, but you just didn't notice?"

His eyes twinkle as they lower down to my cleavage and then back up to my face. "Maybe."

Blushing, I lean away and push the door open. "I'll be at the party. Can't wait to see you."

"Can't wait to see you too," he says.

With a final glance, I step out of the car, my heels clicking against the gravel as I make my way toward the grand doors of the estate. I can feel his eyes on me, watching every step, his fascination thick in the air between us. As soon as I'm inside, closing the door behind me, I lean back, letting the thrill of it all wash over me.

For the first time, he's really seen me. And this... this is only the beginning.

CHAPTER
Seven

JENNY

As I make my way up to my room, my heart races with a mixture of anticipation and disbelief. I catch a glimpse of myself in the hallway mirror…flushed, breathless, and more alive than I've felt in ages. Brett's reaction plays over in my mind, his shock and awe, the way he looked at me like he was seeing a stranger he couldn't quite understand.

Inside my room, I set my bags down, taking in the familiar yet somehow distant surroundings. It's strange being here again, knowing everything has changed…not just in me, but in how the people around me see me.

Moments later, I hear a knock at the door. It opens before I can respond, and in walks Mrs. Finnigan, the housekeeper who practically helped raise me. Her face breaks into a warm smile, her eyes lighting up as she takes in the sight of me.

"Jenny! Oh, look at you!" she exclaims, pulling me into a tight hug. "Paris did wonders for you, didn't it?"

I laugh, hugging her back, feeling a wave of nostalgia and

comfort. "It's good to see you too, Mrs. Finnigan. I missed you."

She steps back, her eyes glistening with pride and perhaps a hint of awe. "We all missed you, dear. You're like family to us, you know." She glances around, as if expecting someone, then adds, "Everyone else will be here in a moment. They've been so eager to see you back."

True to her word, the staff I grew up around trickles in… Mr. Collins the butler, Auntie Mae the cook, and a few of the maids. They all greet me with smiles, kind words, and small tokens…a scarf, a little journal, a piece of chocolate…all things that remind me of home. Their warmth fills the room, melting away any lingering nerves.

Once everyone has said their goodbyes and left me with my gifts, I turn to unpack my luggage. I'm already thinking ahead, imagining tomorrow night, the thrill of walking down the grand staircase, of seeing Brett's face light up when he sees me dressed to impress.

As I stand in my room, taking in the familiar space after years away, there's a gentle knock on the door. My heart skips, knowing it's him…my father, who I haven't seen in three years. The door opens, and he steps in, a hesitant, almost apologetic smile on his face.

"Jenny," he says, his voice softened with relief, his eyes taking in the sight of me as though he can't quite believe it. "I'm so sorry for being late, love. Traffic was… well, you know how it can be." He chuckles, rubbing the back of his neck. There's a warmth in his gaze that makes me want to run into his arms and let him hold me like he used to when I was a little girl.

"It's alright, Dad," I say, offering him a reassuring smile. "I managed just fine."

He nods, stepping closer, his eyes filled with both pride and wonder as he takes in the woman standing before him.

"Look at you… Paris did something, didn't it?" His voice is soft, and I can tell he's proud, even a little in awe.

"It was great Dad. Thanks for letting me go. I learned a lot."

He looks at me, his eyes shining. "You'll have to tell me all about it. Every detail. I've missed so much."

I swallow, feeling a swell of emotion. "I missed you too, Dad. We'll talk…about everything. I have lots of stories to tell you."

He glances around the room, noticing my open luggage, the gifts the household staff left, his gaze softening even more. "They all missed you, Jenny. The house isn't the same without you around."

He hesitates, then lets out a quiet sigh. "I have to go out right now to pick up the Madam, but I'll see you later this evening for dinner."

"Sure, Dad," I nod, watching him retreat from the room.

With renewed energy, I turn to my suitcase and start to unpack. I'm already preparing for the party tomorrow. It's my one chance to impress because all his other usual girls, I'm sure, will be there, and I need to stand out…need him to see that none of them can compare.

My fingers pause over a few dresses…each one glamorous, but I need something just as sexy. Something that stands out, that radiates confidence and allure. Something that will make Brett's jaw drop.

Finally, my eyes land on the dress. Blood red, daring yet elegant, with a neckline that plunges just enough and a slit that rides high up my thigh. I hold it up, admiring the way the fabric catches the light, and I can already imagine the looks it will draw tomorrow night.

I try it on, smoothing the fabric over my hips, watching my reflection in the mirror as the dress transforms me. It's bold, almost dangerously so, but it feels like exactly the statement I want to make. I add the final touches...matching red lipstick, delicate jewelry, and strappy heels that elongate my legs. For a moment, I stare at myself, hardly recognizing the woman looking back.

With my heart pounding, I know Brett won't be able to ignore me in this.

After slipping out of the dress, I carefully hang it back up, smoothing out any wrinkles. Just trying it on has left me buzzing with anticipation. Tomorrow night is going to be unforgettable...I can feel it. I wipe off my makeup, setting the cloth down, and head to the bathroom, feeling the cool tile under my feet.

As the warm water cascades over me, I let myself drift into thoughts about the party and everything that could happen. I imagine the stares, the whispers, the way people will look at me in that dress.

I'll walk in, and they'll see me not as the chauffeur's daughter, but as someone who belongs. And Brett... he won't stand a chance. The way he looked at me today, stunned and barely able to believe it was me...I want to keep him there, captivated, breathless.

But I still need to decide how to do my hair. It has to match the dress...sleek but a bit wild, maybe pulled back with a few strands framing my face to highlight the red lipstick. Something that says elegance with a hint of rebellion. I smile to myself, savoring the image. Tomorrow, I won't just blend in with the crowd. I'll command the room.

After the shower, I towel off and head down for an early evening dinner, the excitement tingling just beneath the surface as I close my eyes.

The next evening arrives quicker than I expect, and soon I'm standing in front of the mirror, my heart racing. I smooth the dress over my hips, taking in the way the blood-red fabric clings to every curve, dipping low at the neckline and sliding up high on my thigh. It's bold, almost scandalous, yet sophisticated. I paint my lips the same shade of red, watching as the color transforms me into someone even I barely recognize...a woman who's unafraid to take what she wants.

As I finish my hair...sleek and slightly tousled, framing my face just right...there's a knock on my door. It's my father, his voice muffled but warm. "Jenny, don't be late. The party started an hour ago."

I glance at the door, sensing his worry, but I'm too exhilarated to let it dim my mood. "I won't be, Dad, plus I'm a guest, not the help. I'm not supposed to be the first one there," I call back, trying to keep the thrill from spilling into my voice. Once he leaves, I give myself one final look in the mirror. The girl who once hid in trees to catch a glimpse of Brett is gone, replaced by a woman ready to face him head-on. With one last breath, I head downstairs.

The party is in full swing by the time I step into the grand hall. Music drifts through the room, and people laugh, sipping champagne beneath the glittering chandeliers. As I walk in, heads turn, eyes trailing over me, some even pausing mid-sentence to stare. The sensation is intoxicating.

I catch sight of Brett across the room, talking with a group of men and a few women hovering nearby. When he glances over and sees me, his expression shifts...he barely notices when the woman beside him tries to regain his attention. It's like I'm pulling him toward me without a word.

But just as he starts to move my way, one of his friends turns, catching sight of me. A smirk stretches across his face, and he nudges another guy beside him. "Well, if it isn't little Jenny," he says loud enough for the others to hear, his tone playful but edged with mockery. "Look who's all grown up."

Heat floods my cheeks, but I keep my expression calm, my head held high. I flash him a polite smile, not letting his words rattle me. The whispers around us don't matter. Only Brett's gaze does…and it's locked on me.

Eventually, I drift toward the bar, needing something to steady my nerves. I order a glass of champagne, letting the bubbles fizz on my tongue as I survey the room. I don't have to wait long; Brett sidles up beside me, his presence electric.

"Jenny," he says, his voice low, a hint of amazement still lingering. "I have to say, you are breathtaking."

I tilt my head, raising an eyebrow. "So you've said already. Several times in fact."

I let my voice hold a teasing edge, watching his reaction.

He laughs, but there's something serious in his eyes. "Yeah, I have, haven't I? You make me slightly nervous now, I have to admit."

I give him a slow smile, holding his gaze, almost unable to contain how happy that makes me.

"Oh?" He leans in slightly, intrigued. "Well, maybe you should tell me explicitly how you want me to treat you?"

I take a sip of champagne, my heart pounding. "Like you treat the women you take to that conservatory," I reply smoothly, a glint of challenge in my eyes.

The words make him pause, his glass hovering mid-air as he registers my meaning. He slowly sets it down on the bar, his gaze sharpening. "Alright, Jenny," he murmurs, his voice lowering. "Let's… discuss that. But not here."

He takes my hand, guiding me away from the bar and leading me toward the indoor conservatory. My pulse races, my hand warm in his as he leads me through the crowd, away from the noise and distractions.

This is it. The moment I've dreamed of, only now it's real, and I'm no longer the girl hoping for Brett's attention. I'm the woman who has it.

CHAPTER
Eight

ZACK

I stand in the shadows of the grand hall, my eyes following the red dress that moves through the crowd, impossible to miss. Jenny. I've barely seen her since she arrived, and even now, I have to admit she's transformed. She's no longer the awkward girl who lurked around the estate, hoping for Brett's attention. Instead, she's blossomed, a woman with curves that draw attention, poised in that bold dress as if she was born to wear it. It's no wonder Brett's caught up, oblivious to everything else.

But it's clear from one look at her that she's still chasing something, and her stubborn foolishness is plain to see. This time, though, it's more than just a juvenile crush on my careless brother. It's a dangerous game she's stepping into, one that could cost us all more than she realizes.

"Yet another party?" my mother's voice comes from behind, pulling me from my thoughts.

I turn slightly, catching the raised eyebrow she gives as she surveys the scene.

"It's the second this month," she remarks, her tone laced with dry amusement.

I shake my head, a weary sigh escaping. "You all told me to indulge him. Let him be…well, here you have it."

"Don't be so stuck up," she says with a smile. "He livens up the house, plus there's a valid reason this time at least, since Jenny's back. I hope she's having fun."

She takes in the scene once again, and I know she sees it just as I do. "He has to be more careful though," she murmurs, folding her hands in front of her. "He's engaged now to Elizabeth, and her family won't tolerate anything that undermines it."

This is my concern as well. Elizabeth's family, the Crawfords, are the linchpin in a real estate empire that can catapult us to untouchable status in this world, so we were more than pleased to hear of Brett's growing interest in her. Now that things have been set in stone, the last thing I want is for their impending marriage to implode. It's the final step in securing a deal that's taken years to cultivate. One reckless move from Brett, and the Crawfords could pull back, leaving us exposed, vulnerable.

I glance at my mother, who meets my gaze, her expression sharp. "He can't afford to make mistakes now. Elizabeth's father has watched Brett closely; he won't approve if he sees… this," she says, with a slight nod toward the conservatory. "And neither will Elizabeth."

"Exactly," I mutter, barely containing my irritation. My eyes shift back to the conservatory, where Brett and Jenny are heading, her red dress swaying as she moves, Brett practically leading her into the lion's den. I tighten my jaw. It's more than just a risk…this could unravel everything if they're seen together. With Elizabeth out of town, Brett's likely forgotten the weight of this arrangement. He thinks he's untouchable.

I pull out my phone, scrolling through to Brett's contact

and dialing, but the call rings through unanswered. Typical. He's too wrapped up in his own world to even pick up. I look back at my mother, whose eyes have narrowed. "Brett's not answering," I tell her, frustration seeping into my voice. "I'll have to go myself."

Her eyes flicker with worry. "Zack... handle this delicately. He's a free agent, and he volunteered to do this. If he feels he's being boxed in, he'll call it off himself. Just... just make sure he understands what's at stake."

With a stiff nod, I turn, leaving my mother's watchful eyes behind as I stride toward the conservatory. Each step fuels my annoyance, a quiet fury building beneath the surface. I know Brett; he's impulsive, and right now, he's entangled in his shallow attraction to this "new" Jenny, blind to everything else.

I reach the conservatory entrance and hesitate for a moment, glancing through the glass. Brett and Jenny are standing by the far end, framed by the sprawling indoor plants, their laughter soft but lingering in the air. Jenny's leaning in, her eyes sparkling with the same mixture of naivety and boldness that I recognize too well. Brett's got his gaze locked on her, an amused grin on his face, oblivious to the danger of being seen with her tonight.

I push open the door and approach, my presence going unnoticed until I clear my throat. Brett looks up, his expression shifting from surprise to irritation. Jenny's eyes flick to me, widening slightly, but she quickly composes herself.

"Zack." Brett's voice carries an edge, his easygoing grin faltering. "What's with the interruption?"

I keep my expression controlled, arms crossed as I glance between them.

"Jenny," I call out to her. "It's nice to see that you're back."

She doesn't quite seem to know how to respond to this, and Brett seems amused.

"You're making her uncomfortable, Zack," he says.

My eyes rove down her gorgeous frame, and then I turn to him.

"A word?"

Nodding, he hands his glass over to her and excuses himself.

Before I can even say a word, he jumps to his defense.

"We're just talking, Zack. Relax."

"Talking?" I let out a short, humorless laugh. "Brett, if you wanted a casual conversation, you wouldn't have brought her in here. You do know what you're risking, right?"

His jaw tightens, a defensive glint in his eyes. "I know exactly what I'm doing. And Jenny and I—"

"Jenny and you?" I cut him off. "There can't be a 'Jenny and you.' I need you to tell me that you understand this. And this is no longer just about the marriage between you and Elizabeth. The entire deal is at stake now. Remember, you agreed to do this... to contribute. Do you want to renege on that now?"

Brett's face hardens, and I can see a flash of irritation in his eyes. "It's not that simple, Zack. I never said I'd—"

"It is that simple," I interrupt, my tone cold, my patience wearing thin. "You've been given a position in this family, responsibilities that come with it. This isn't the time for distractions." My gaze flickers toward the conservatory door, and then back to him. "You know exactly what you're risking here."

He runs a hand through his hair, clearly frustrated, but I don't let up. Brett needs to hear this, and he needs to understand it fully.

"If you're not ready for this, say so now," I continue. "But don't put the family in jeopardy because you can't control a passing interest."

He sighs, looking away, then nods reluctantly. "Fine. I get it, Zack. I'll control myself."

Satisfied, I hold his gaze a moment longer, watching him process my words, before stepping back. "Good. I'm heading out."

However, he stops me, grabbing my arm and shutting his eyes. I can tell he's conflicted deep within and doesn't quite know what to do.

"I understand," I tell him. "You've been called away to my office. There are urgent matters we need to discuss and an urgent phone call waiting for you."

He releases a heavy breath at this and sighs. "Yeah, thanks, I'll wait for you there."

As Brett heads back to Jenny to deliver his excuse, I lean against the doorframe, watching her through the conservatory's glass. She's radiant in the dim light, her red dress hugging her figure, her presence a striking contrast against the soft glow of the evening. The transformation in her is startling, almost magnetic, and for a brief, unsettling moment, I can understand why Brett is so easily swayed. But that moment passes quickly; my focus is on the consequences.

Brett emerges, his expression faintly conflicted as he closes the door behind him. He takes a deep breath, eyes a bit unfocused, before he turns toward me.

As we step away from the conservatory and make our way toward my office, Brett's silence breaks. "I know you're against this," he starts, his voice quieter than usual. "But I can't shake this feeling. Maybe I've been blind to it all these years. She's different now, Zack. Maybe... maybe I'm just seeing her for the first time."

I don't react outwardly, though my mind races, noting his tone...earnest, like he genuinely believes he's found something real with Jenny. I keep my face neutral, giving him room to continue.

He hesitates before speaking again. "Look, I know I'm engaged to Elizabeth. I know what's expected. But I can't help but wonder if Jenny came back at this exact moment for a reason. Maybe this is some kind of sign. Maybe Elizabeth was never really..."

"Stop," I say, my voice firm but quiet. I don't let him finish, don't give him the satisfaction of letting this become a discussion about "fate" or "signs." He needs to know his pattern, that I see right through it.

"You didn't even recognize her at the airport, Brett," I remind him, allowing a slight edge of irritation to color my words. "She walked right past you, and you only noticed her because she looked like some gorgeous stranger. Now, just because she's in a red dress instead of her old tomboy clothes, you're ready to throw away everything we've built...all for a whim?"

He opens his mouth, a flicker of defiance in his eyes, but I press on before he can interrupt. "This isn't about some romantic revelation, Brett. You have responsibilities...to the family, to the merger, to Elizabeth. You wanted to be a part of this, to finally step up and contribute. You think breaking an engagement now, jeopardizing the entire deal, is the way to do that?"

He lets out a breath, frustration clear on his face, but there's an underlying uncertainty as well. "I don't want to jeopardize anything. But I can't look past Jenny now. Not this time. I... I just want a chance, Zack. A chance to see where it might go with her."

I sigh, a weighty, sympathetic sound, masking the calculation behind it. "I understand, Brett. Really, I do. But you have to tread carefully. Let's talk this through."

As we head back to my office, I notice he's got a single champagne glass tucked into his back pocket...a careless habit he's picked up over the years. I shake my head, a hint of amusement breaking through. "Why do you still do that?" I ask, gesturing to the glass.

Brett shrugs, grinning in that nonchalant way of his. "It's practical, believe it or not," he says. "When I've got my hands full, it's easier to tuck the glass in my pocket. Then, when it's time to pour, it's right there."

I raise an eyebrow, shaking my head. "You know, they do make trays. And of course you can also use your hand."

"Yeah, but where's the charm in that?" he replies, giving a wink.

He's clearly in better spirits, and as we walk, he grows more animated, his thoughts wandering back to Jenny. "You know, it's crazy," he says, almost to himself. "I didn't even recognize her at first. Just saw this gorgeous woman at the airport, had no idea it was Jenny. She turned around, and... there it was. That spark. The same one she used to have as a kid, but... different now. More confident, like she's finally found herself."

I say nothing, letting him continue as he tries to make sense of his own fascination. "It's funny, right? She was just that tomboyish kid, always darting around the estate like she belonged everywhere and nowhere all at once. But now... she's something else entirely. She walks into a room, and it's like everything just stops."

He chuckles, almost in disbelief. "Makes me wonder if she's always been like this, and maybe I just never saw it. Or maybe she really has changed, like... she knows who she is, and it's refreshing. No games, no pretense."

We reach my office, and by now, he's lost in his reverie, oblivious to the glass in his back pocket.

"Have a seat," I say, and without a second thought, he drops into the chair, mid-sentence, leaning back with that same easy confidence. There's an immediate crack, a sharp shatter of glass, followed by his yelp as he jerks upright, eyes wide with pain, hands flying to his back.

"Damn it, Zack!" he exclaims, wincing as he gingerly reaches around, fingers coming back with blood. "The glass... it shattered!"

I step forward, barely containing my smirk. "Well, that 'practical habit' of yours just caught up with you." I grab a pair of scissors and carefully cut the fabric around the shards, revealing pieces embedded in his backside, spots of blood already visible on his pants.

"You're going to need a few days lying flat for this to stop hurting," I tell him, struggling to keep my tone sympathetic. "And maybe it's time to drop that little habit."

Brett lets out a frustrated groan as he lowers himself face-first onto the couch, resigned. "Just my luck," he mutters. "Please call the doctor. It's fucking hurting, and I don't want any scars or infection. It's bleeding, right?"

"Sure is," I reply.

"Hell!"

I lead him over to my couch where he settles horizontally and then head out of the office to call the doctor.

CHAPTER
Nine

JENNY

The conservatory is still, the air thick with the scent of blooming flowers. I can hardly think straight, my mind buzzing with everything I've heard tonight about Brett's engagement. I shouldn't care. I should turn away and let him go, but a part of me isn't ready to give up so easily. The door creaks open, and I tense, expecting Brett... ready to face him, maybe even to demand answers.

But it's Zack who walks in, not Brett.

I stiffen, thrown off by his unexpected presence. My heart picks up, both wary and puzzled.

What is Zack doing here? Where's Brett?

He moves with his usual calm confidence, dark eyes fixed on me as he approaches with a bottle of champagne and two glasses in hand. My heart beats faster.

Zack's dark eyes meet mine, unreadable and intense, like he can see through any façade I might put up. He doesn't break eye contact as he approaches, stopping just close enough that I feel the weight of his gaze.

"Jenny," he says, his voice low, almost too casual. "Brett won't be joining you tonight. He's had… an accident."

A wave of worry hits me, sharp and immediate. "An accident?" I ask, my voice tight despite my attempt to stay composed. "Is he hurt? Where is he?"

Zack raises a hand, his expression calm and steady, as if to keep me from spiraling. "He's fine, Jenny. Nothing too serious," he assures me. "He just needs to stay off his feet and rest for a few days."

Relief washes over me, though it's quickly replaced by lingering concern. "But… what happened? How did he get hurt?" I press, needing to know more.

Zack hesitates, glancing away briefly before meeting my gaze again. "Brett asked me not to share the details," he says evenly, almost too controlled. "He's resting, that's what matters."

He pauses, watching me closely as he uncorks the bottle, pouring a glass of champagne and handing it to me. "It seems you're left with me tonight."

I take the glass, eyeing him warily. "And I suppose you're here to tell me I shouldn't be around him," I say, meeting his gaze directly. "Because he's engaged, and that's what's expected of him."

Zack's expression shifts, a flicker of something unreadable crossing his face. "You're right. Brett does have obligations, Jenny," he replies, his tone careful, controlled. "Ones he can't afford to ignore."

I feel a surge of frustration and hurt, the tension between us thickening. "So, is that why you're here?" I say, my voice sharper than I intended, refusing to look away. "You've come to offer me money to walk away? That's how these things work with families like yours, isn't it? The girl gets paid off, told to disappear quietly."

A hint of amusement flickers across his face, and a small,

almost daring smile plays at the corners of his mouth. "A million," he says smoothly, his tone deceptively calm. The number is ridiculous, thrown out so casually, but there's something in the way he says it...like he's daring me to take the bait...that sends a chill down my spine.

My grip tightens around the champagne glass, fighting against the surge of emotions within me.

"No, Zack," I say, keeping my voice steady despite the turmoil churning inside. "None of this has anything to do with money. I've loved Brett all my life... and I still do."

For a second, his gaze flickers, a hint of something inscrutable passing through those dark eyes of his. Then, just as quickly, he gives a faint smile, shrugging slightly as if the whole conversation were trivial, a throwaway moment.

"Well," he says smoothly, almost dismissively, "lucky for you, it wasn't a serious offer."

His tone is casual, almost too light, as though he's trying to set me at ease. I don't quite trust it, but I feel the tension between us slip just a fraction, the sharp edge blurring as he shifts, glancing around the conservatory. He picks up his glass, takes a sip, and then looks back at me, studying me with that calm, assessing gaze of his.

"So, Paris..." he says, his voice trailing slightly. "It must have been an incredible experience."

I stiffen, caught off guard. Paris was indeed an experience but I'm in no mood to discuss it with Zack of all people. I shake my head, trying to deflect. "There's really nothing to say about it right now."

His eyes narrow slightly, not with anger but with a kind of piercing curiosity, as if he's trying to read between my words. "Nothing at all?" he presses, not letting me sidestep. "You came back a different person, Jenny. It's hard to believe you wouldn't have a few thoughts about the place."

I sigh, exasperated, but he doesn't back down. He holds

my gaze, his persistence disarming in a way that's almost maddening. "Honestly, Zack, I don't feel like talking about Paris." I bite the inside of my cheek, trying not to lose my patience. "I just want to see Brett… to make sure he's alright."

Something in his expression tightens, and for the briefest second, his eyes flash with a dark intensity that makes me want to step back. But he recovers quickly, his voice smooth and steady.

"You'll have to respect Brett's privacy, Jenny. He'll reach out to you when he's ready."

A spark of frustration flares inside me. "How convenient that he's disappeared and I won't be able to see him for a few days…especially when you just saw him a few minutes ago," I say, my voice edged with irritation. "You can't keep me away from him."

He tilts his head, his gaze never leaving mine. "I'm not keeping him away from you," he says quietly, though there's a subtle undertone to his words. "I'm just asking you to consider that Brett might need a little space. Not everything revolves around you."

Just as I open my mouth to retort, a familiar, haunting melody fills the conservatory, an old song I've loved since I was young. My anger wavers, caught off guard by the sound, and Zack notices immediately. He glances at me, one eyebrow raised, a trace of amusement in his expression.

"Shall we?" he says, extending his hand, his tone gentler than before. "It's the least I can do since you were expecting… someone else."

I hesitate, every instinct screaming at me to refuse, to pull away. But his hand is already outstretched, and the soft music wraps around us, a quiet invitation. Almost without thinking, I reach out, letting my fingers slip into his. He pulls me in close, his grip steady, almost comforting, as we begin to sway to the music.

"You never struck me as the dancing type," I say quietly, trying to keep the mood light, though there's an undeniable tension in the air between us.

His mouth curves into a small, sardonic smile. "There's a lot you don't know about me, Jenny," he replies, his voice low and measured. "But I'd wager you're used to that by now."

His words sting, and I can't help but look down, a strange mix of emotions swirling inside me.

He leads with an unexpected grace, guiding me across the conservatory with an ease that makes me feel as though I'm stepping into another world. The music fills the silence, each note weaving between us, breaking down the guarded distance I've tried so hard to maintain.

Just as the song begins to fade, Zack's hand shifts to my lower back, pulling me closer, his gaze intense and unwavering. I don't know why I can't look away, why I can't pull back...but there's a power in his eyes that holds me captive.

And then, without warning, his mouth is on mine.

The kiss is overwhelming, pulling me in like nothing I've ever felt before. My mind goes blank, my pulse racing as his lips press against mine, firm yet somehow... gentle, a strange combination of control and warmth. It's nothing like I imagined a kiss would be...so intense, so consuming that I feel as though the world has fallen away, leaving only the two of us.

And then, just as suddenly as it began, reality crashes back. The meaning of this kiss hits me like a cold wave, a reminder that this isn't right, that this isn't Brett. I break away, shocked and breathless, and before I even know what I'm doing, my hand flies up and I slap him, hard, my palm stinging from the impact.

He doesn't flinch. Instead, he looks at me with an expression I can't quite decipher, his eyes dark and steady, a trace of something almost... vulnerable flickering there for just a moment.

"I'm sorry," he says softly, his voice barely above a whisper. The apology sounds genuine, though I can't make sense of the way he's looking at me, like he's somehow lost in the same confusion I'm feeling.

My heart hammers in my chest, every beat echoing with the intensity of what just happened. I nod stiffly, accepting Zack's quiet apology, though my mind is a whirlwind of disbelief and confusion. I'm still reeling from the feeling of his lips on mine, the shock of it... something I'd never expected, something I'd never thought I'd want.

He steps back, his gaze lingering on me for a heartbeat longer than it should. There's an unspoken tension, a current running between us that leaves me breathless and unnerved. And then, without another word, he turns and leaves, his figure slipping out of the conservatory as if he'd never been here at all. I stand frozen, the silence closing in, my thoughts spiraling, tangling around what just happened.

A part of me feels robbed, wondering how it would feel to share something so intense with Brett, the person I've wanted for so long. It should have been him, it's always been him in my mind... but now, with Zack's kiss lingering on my lips, I don't even know what to think.

The thought makes me shiver, filling me with a strange, almost painful longing. I close my eyes, imagining Brett instead, trying to replace the feeling, to picture his touch, his presence. But no matter how hard I try, I can't shake the feeling that Zack's kiss has left... a feeling that refuses to fade.

CHAPTER
Ten

ZACK

L ater that night, I head into my room, slamming the door behind me, but it's like trying to lock out a storm that's already raging in my mind. She's there, etched into my thoughts...the look in her eyes, that red dress clinging to her like a challenge. Every calculated step she took tonight is burned into my memory, as if she's been taunting me, daring me to come closer. Hell, she knew exactly what she was doing.

No bra. That much was obvious...the way her chest pressed against the fabric, nipples peaked and proud, practically demanding my attention. And she knew. She knew the effect she had, knew exactly how to fill the room with that defiant heat. Every curve, every line of her in that dress was a deliberate torment, something that's now impossible to shake. Even as I stand here, I feel my body react, hardening in response, and I grit my teeth, furious at the power she has over me.

Damn her for getting under my skin this way, for making me feel so completely… unhinged. I can still see her there, holding her ground, pressing my buttons, her words laced with challenge. All I could think about was reaching out, pulling her close, proving to her exactly what she does to me, and then I'd lost myself. I had just intended to talk some sense into her.

I try to shake the image, but it's impossible. My body's reacting, hard and insistent, with the ache of it pushing me right to the edge. I grit my teeth, furious at her for getting under my skin this way, for winding me up so tight that my whole body feels like it's on fire. She was standing there, pressing my buttons, her words spiking with challenge, and all I could think of was reaching out, pulling her close, feeling the heat between her thighs.

I breathe in sharply, fighting the pull, and turn on the shower, cranking the water to ice-cold. It does nothing to kill the tension, the throb of want that's making it impossible to clear my head. I strip down and step under the water, but it only intensifies everything…every nerve is alive, hypersensitive, and her image won't leave me.

My hand moves down, gripping my cock, every inch of it hard and pulsing as I stroke myself slowly, savoring the illicit thoughts of her. She's so clear in my mind…her hips, the curve of her waist, the way her nipples pressed against the dress. She's there, her body open, so close to mine, so soft. My hand tightens, pumping harder, faster, the tension coiling tighter. I let myself go deeper into it, imagining her under me, my hands on her, my mouth tasting every inch of her.

The sensation is unbearable, building, filling me, and I'm lost in it. She's there in my mind, her lips parted, her breath catching as I take her, feel her. My cock throbs in my grip, veins bulging as I pump, harder, faster, the pressure mounting until finally, it hits. I spill, the release hot and thick, her name slipping from my lips in a breathless whisper as I come, spilling everything, every thought of her, pouring out.

I stand there, the water pounding over me, her image still clear, still haunting. I dry off, my pulse still racing, her face and that damned look still in my head. I lie down, frustrated, the ache still there, and I know there'll be no rest tonight.

Still, I try because I have the most hectic day ahead of me tomorrow, however my body remains alert and humming from the release.

The frustration only deepens, twisting into something more insistent.

Viciously she latches on, occupying every thought, taking up more space than I'd ever intended to give her. My mind drifts, unwillingly, through memories of the estate, moments I didn't even know I'd stored, flashes of her from over the years.

· · ·

I recall seeing her, even when she was younger, always moving, never at rest. She was a part of the estate as much as the land itself - climbing trees, picking apples from the orchard, working in the gardens with dirt smudged on her cheeks, her hands scratched but determined. She was never, never content to sit quietly like her father, always filling the space with some energy that couldn't be contained. And even then, even when she was young, I could see the defiance in her, the need to prove herself, the resilience that made her push past her limits.

I was only 22 when I saw her dragging a basket of tomatoes across the garden, stubbornly refusing any help, despite her knees scraping against the rough earth. I remember her falling, the basket tumbling from her hands as she wiped at her bloody knees with a grimace. Her father had been watching, not with concern but pride, as if that struggle, that dirt on her hands, was somehow proof of her character. I couldn't understand it then, the satisfaction her father took in her resilience. But maybe it's because he knew, even then, that she was strong in ways the rest of us weren't.

But now... now that same resilience is turning her into a problem I can't ignore. If Brett doesn't snap out of this infatuation, it will completely ruin this arrangement with Elizabeth and all that the family can get from it.

I know my brother...he's weak, easy to sway, led by every new fascination. If I can just keep her away from him, distract her long enough, he'll go back to Elizabeth willingly, marry into the family that will secure our position, and all this chaos will finally settle.

I sit up, my mind buzzing with the beginnings of a plan. If I give her something that holds her attention, something she can focus on, I can steer her away from Brett. It's not as if she'd ever sit still...she's spent her life working, moving, even when she didn't have to. The house staff dotes on her, but she's always found a way to stay busy, as if she's afraid to sit still, afraid to let herself stop. Maybe it's that drive I can use, that hunger for purpose.

A modeling job. She's spent all this time in Paris so surely she's ready to build the foundation of her career.

I know just the people who can make this happen. And it's not just about getting her away for a day or two; no, if I play this right, she'll have to go somewhere...Rome, perhaps...for a while. If I offer her something big, a brand that she can't say no to, she'll be out of Brett's reach. Out of my reach, too, for that matter, and maybe that's exactly what I need right now.

I reach for my phone, dialing my assistant, and instruct her to contact one of our associates in Rome. A high-end brand, maybe Tod's, something that would turn her head, something she can't resist. The thought of it...of watching her disappear into that world, completely engrossed, too far away to interfere with anything here...settles the anger buzzing under my skin.

· · ·

But as I sit there, waiting for my assistant to confirm the arrangements, a thought claws its way to the surface. It's not enough. Just getting her to Rome isn't enough to keep her away from Brett. She'll return, just as she always does, and nothing will have changed. But what if... what if I make her focus on me instead? She's young, impressionable, and if I show her what real attraction, real desire feels like, she'll be too entangled in that to think of Brett. She'll be chasing after me instead, lost in the thrill, and by the time I step away, she'll be so consumed that Brett won't even be a thought in her mind.

I tell myself that this is just a means to an end, a way to handle a problem that's spiraling out of control. And yet, the memory of her against me, her lips, her body, the warmth radiating off her... it's something I can't push away, something I can't deny. I'll take her to Rome, charm her, make her see that Brett isn't worth her time. She'll be out of his reach, wrapped up in a game she won't even realize she's playing until it's too late.

I know it's calculated, ruthless, but I tell myself it's necessary. There's no room in my life for women, for romance, for any of this mess so I know that at the end when my goal with Brett has been achieved then I can withdraw my attention from her. My only focus is the family, the legacy, the business. This kiss with her... it's a distraction, a mistake, nothing more. But if I can use it to keep her away from Brett, then at least it serves a purpose.

. . .

I settle back into bed, the plan forming clearly in my mind, and finally, I feel a sense of control settling over me.

CHAPTER
Eleven

JENNY

I sit hunched over my bowl of oatmeal in the empty kitchen, stirring it mindlessly as I fight to keep my frustration in check. It's well past breakfast, but I'd barely slept last night, tossing and turning, worrying about Brett and his condition. Was he better? Was he recovering at all? When I finally drifted off, it was already morning, and now here I am, late to start the day, feeling adrift and alone.

I glance around the room, taking in the stillness, the air thick with quiet that only serves to press on my nerves. I look up at Mrs. Finnigan, the housekeeper, hovering near the stove. "How's Brett doing? Have you heard anything new?"

Mrs. Finnigan looks at me with sympathy, her hands busy with a cloth she's folding and unfolding. "From what I know, he's in his room. Just needs some stitches and needs to rest. That's what his butler told me," she says, her voice soft, as if trying not to upset me.

A wave of frustration crashes over me. Zack. I know he's keeping Brett away from me, longer than necessary, just to keep us apart. My hands tighten around the bowl, and I feel the sting of unshed tears as anger burns hot in my chest. It's so like him...always controlling, always scheming. I swallow back the tears, forcing myself to stay composed, but the bitterness lingers.

"I really can't see him?" I ask. "Even if it's for just a few minutes?"

Before Mrs. Finnigan can respond, my father strides into the kitchen, his expression hard as he catches the end of my question. He stands there for a moment, just watching me, and I feel his disappointment settling in the room like a heavy fog.

"Jenny," he begins, a sharp edge in his voice that he seldom uses, "You're getting on my nerves. You're like a dog with a freaking bone.You're still asking about Brett? Seriously? Do you even realize what you're doing?" He pauses, his tone growing heavier. "It's not just you who'll face the consequences here. You're putting both of us in jeopardy, you know that?"

The words sting, even though I know he's trying to get through to me, to make me understand his fear of losing everything he's built here. But it only makes the anger simmer hotter beneath my skin.

"So, that's it?" I murmur, looking down, not wanting him to see how much it hurts. "Zack gets to control everything just because... because he's Zack? Because he's in charge?"

"You're not seeing the bigger picture," he says, his voice softening just a little, but the sternness remains. "Zack's a good man. He knows how to handle things, how to make the right choices. He's done well by us, Jenny, and you need to show him some respect."

"Respect?" I echo, bitterness creeping into my voice. "You think it's respectful to let him decide who I can see or where I can go? To keep me from seeing Brett like I don't even matter?"

"You don't matter," my father replies. "Why don't you get this? This is their world, and Brett is not powerless. If he wants to see you, he will send for you."

His words cut deep, but I force myself to stay quiet, clenching my jaw as I stir my cold oatmeal. He is right, though. This is their world, and as long as I remain in it, I'll never get what I want, and perhaps Brett won't even get the chance to choose me if we are both under Zack's thumb. I know my father cares about me, but he'll always put this family's needs and wishes first, even if it means dismissing mine.

Just as I put down my spoon, I hear the clattering of plates and hurried footsteps echoing through the kitchen. My stomach twists. This flurry of motion can only mean one thing…Zack has come down for breakfast.

I try to calm myself, focusing on the worn grain of the wooden table, but I'm aware of every movement, every quick step, every whispered instruction as the staff rushes to attend to him. Zack's presence in the house is magnetic, powerful, as if every object or person shifts subtly to accommodate him. He's been the head of the household for as long as I can remember, ever since his grandfather passed and his father started staying abroad. Zack took over everything, learned every aspect of the business with a ruthless determination that seemed bred into him. Now, the house is his dominion, his empire, and everyone…my father included…bends to his will.

I feel my pulse quicken, my heartbeat a relentless thud in my ears. I can't stay here, pretending to be the dutiful, obedient daughter. Zack may hold the reins, but I still have a say in my own life. I swallow, feeling the weight of my decision settle, grounding me. I rise slowly, ignoring my father's startled glance as I leave the kitchen and head towards the conservatory.

As I enter, the morning light filters through the glass panels, casting a warm glow over the room, illuminating the lush greenery with a soft radiance. And there he is…Zack, seated at the table, his tablet in one hand and a cup of coffee in the other. He's dressed impeccably, of course, in a sharp, tailored suit that seems as much armor as attire. His head lifts as I clear my throat, and his gaze shifts to me, assessing, cold, unyielding.

For a fleeting second, my mind flashes back to last night, to the dream that had kept me up for hours. I was in this same conservatory, Brett's hands sliding down my arms, his face inches from mine, his breath hot against my neck as he whispered my name. My heart had raced with anticipation, his presence like fire against my skin. But then, in an instant, his features had blurred, morphed into Zack's, his dark eyes burning into me with that familiar, calculating intensity. I'd woken drenched in sweat, breathless and disoriented, haunted by the vividness of it. And now, seeing him in front of me, my skin prickles, a reminder of how inescapable his presence is, even in my dreams.

I steady myself, taking a deep breath. "I'm moving out," I announce, my voice wavering but resolute. "I think it's high time that I make my own way, separate from your family."

He raises an eyebrow, his expression unreadable. Slowly, he places the cup down, a faint smirk curling at the edge of his lips as he studies me. "And where, exactly, are you going to go?"

"That's my business," I say, forcing myself to hold his gaze, even as my insides twist. "I'm an adult now, so… I'll figure it out."

A flicker of something…amusement, maybe…crosses his face, and he leans back, his fingers tapping rhythmically against the table. "An adult, you say?" he murmurs, the words laced with mockery. "Well, I guess you won't need me to pull any strings for you? Because, if I'm not mistaken, I heard of an opportunity from Tod's and wanted to arrange it for you. Glad to know now that I don't need to bother."

I blink, caught off guard. "Tod's? What are you talking about?"

He chuckles, low and almost amused, as he watches my reaction. "It's a modeling opportunity. You know, since you're so eager to spread your wings and leave the nest." He lets the words hang, his eyes glittering with an unreadable intensity. "I'm flying to Rome late this week, so you can hitch a ride if you want. They're not paying for your transportation until you get there. When in Rome, Tod's team will contact you with all the details." He raises an eyebrow, letting the silence stretch, as if daring me to object or perhaps fall to my knees in gratitude. I hate it even more because I'm so suddenly excited that I'm considering it.

The floor seems to shift beneath me. "This week? Already? So… I just show up and they take it from there?" I say, my voice barely a whisper.

"That's generally how these things work," he replies smoothly, taking a leisurely sip of his coffee, his gaze never leaving mine. "Or, you could choose to decline. You are an adult, after all."

The last words are laced with sarcasm, his smirk deepening.

A mixture of anger and confusion coils in my chest. It's exactly what I wanted…a chance to leave, to make something of myself, and yet… there's this nagging doubt, this sense that he's orchestrating everything, even this, pulling strings just to keep me at a distance, out of his brother's life.

"Isn't this you just trying to send me away?" I ask. "A

different city, a job. Maybe you hope it will make me forget Brett?"

"Jenny ", he calls. "Believe it or not I have very little interest in your ... attachment to Brett." He says this so seriously I'm almost compelled to respond.

His words cut deeper than I expect, but I swallow the sting. The truth is, I do need this. I want to build a modeling career, to make something of myself, and yes, the money would help. It would help me move back to the city and find my own place, far from all this tension, from the suffocating control Zack has over everything.

"What about Brett?" The question slips out, softer than I intended, betraying the raw edge of my worry. "I... I can't leave without knowing how he's doing."

Zack's eyes narrow slightly, the flicker of a smirk gone, replaced by something colder. "Brett?" he repeats, as if savoring the name on his tongue. He picks up his coffee and tablet once again and lets out a low sigh, the sound full of controlled irritation. "Let's be honest, Jenny. If Brett wanted to see you, he would have reached out by now. He knows exactly where you are."

The same thing my father said!

I feel my fists clench by my sides. "Fine. And about the contract?" I ask, trying to steer the conversation back to something I can control, something concrete. "How long would it be for?"

He shrugs nonchalantly. "That's up to Tod's but from what I hear may be a month or two. You can choose to accept it or reject it when we arrive. No one's forcing you, Jenny." His gaze pierces into me, his words hanging in the air like a challenge.

I hesitate, my resolve weakening under his scrutiny. This is the opportunity I've been waiting for, but it feels like a poisoned apple, tempting and dangerous.

"Okay," I say.

For a moment, he's silent, his gaze flickering with something unreadable, something almost... admiring? But it's gone in an instant, replaced by that cold, calculating expression. He nods, a faint smile playing at the corner of his lips.

"Good," he murmurs. "I'll let them know and they'll reach out to you."

He turns back to his tablet, dismissing me with a flick of his hand, but I stay rooted to the spot, the weight of our exchange pressing down on me. Determined, I turn on my heel, leaving the conservatory, my heart pounding. I've made my choice, and no matter what Zack throws at me, I'll find my own way, on my own terms.

CHAPTER
Twelve

ZACK

I have never met anyone as aggravating as her. This isn't new…Jenny's always had a way of getting under my skin. But what is new, or at least what I'd like to pretend is, is the fact that she's driving me out of my mind. Once again, she's left me rock hard, and all she did was stand there in the conservatory, arguing, defiant as ever. Watching her, I couldn't shake last night's image, that intoxicating scene in the conservatory playing out in my head over and over.

All I could think about was how perfect she'd look bent over, her anger fueling something darker, something primal. Damn it. This should be easy…she's a distraction, nothing more, a current thorn in my side. But every time I'm around her, that restraint gets harder to hold on to. I can barely stand to sit through breakfast, each bite reminding me of how she tasted in that kiss, of the scent that lingered in my head far longer than it should have.

Finally, I push the plate away, barely touched, and get up, striding out of the house without so much as a backward glance. I don't need to be surrounded by her scent, her memory, this entire house I'm realizing now more than ever, is filled with memories of her. We were worlds apart, but the fact is that we both grew up here so memories of brief glances and sightings daily reels through my mind. In the car, I dial my secretary, needing something concrete, something to snap me out of this absurd state.

As soon as she picks up, I don't waste time. "Update me on the Tod's contract," I say, my tone clipped.

"Yes, Mr. Jackson," she replies smoothly, the sound of clicking keys filling the brief silence as she pulls up the file. "The modeling contract is a six-month initial term with options to renew every three months. It includes a minimum of four campaigns for their upcoming collection. They're covering accommodation expenses, a monthly salary, and a significant bonus based on performance."

I absorb the details, settling into the comfort of business strategy. Part of me knows this arrangement serves my purpose...keeping her occupied, focused elsewhere, away from any risks she could stir up here. But despite my original plan, I can't shake the need to ensure she's treated well.

"Add a stipulation," I say, my voice softening slightly, though I mask it with a cough. "Make sure she isn't over-worked. I want scheduled breaks, enough to allow her travel time back to New York once a month."

There's a pause on the other end, but my secretary quickly masks her surprise. "Understood, Mr. Jackson. I'll also add a termination clause, allowing her the option to end the contract at any time."

"Good," I murmur, clearing my throat as if dismissing the sentiment beneath my instructions. "And ensure she has everything she needs. No skimping on accommodations or resources."

"Yes, Sir," she responds, her tone efficient. I can hear her typing, finalizing the amendments.

As I end the call, I lean back, exhaling slowly. It's just business, I remind myself. I'm doing this to ensure she is properly occupied enough to forget about her nonsense infatuation with Brett. But deep down, I know I'm not as indifferent as I pretend to be. And that, more than anything, is the problem.

"What's my schedule like for the rest of the week?" I ask, already calculating.

My secretary's voice is crisp, unfazed by the urgency in mine. "Tomorrow, you have back-to-back site meetings in Manhattan, starting at 9:00 a.m. The first is with Richard Lawson and his team to review updates on the Midtown project's architectural details. They're pushing hard to finalize the floor-to-ceiling glass specifications and lighting strategy."

I nod, recalling the vision I'd laid out…the building's glass exterior designed to capture light from every angle.

She continues, "At 1:00 p.m., there's a scheduled walk-through with potential tenants. Andrew Barron will be present. He mentioned interest from three high-profile companies, all looking for long-term leases. He'd like your input on tenant selection to ensure we're aligned with the brand's prestige."

I lean back, already anticipating the types of questions these tenants will ask. They'll want the best, and that's exactly what we're delivering…bespoke spaces that elevate their brands by association with ours.

"The mayor's office also reached out regarding the zoning cooperation we discussed. They're expecting you at City Hall on Wednesday. They'd like an update on the green spaces and public art facilities you proposed. The mayor's keen to see this move forward…he sees it as a win for the community and good press for his office."

"Good. We're buying goodwill with that terrace. The press

won't miss the green space angle," I say, picturing the public terrace we'd designed to break up the commercial density with open-air access and commissioned art. It's another layer of appeal, not just for tenants but for the city, reinforcing our image of urban responsibility.

She hesitates briefly before adding, "There's also the matter of air rights, as you mentioned to the mayor. We're expected to finalize those agreements by Friday, assuming you want them completed before submitting the final plans next week."

"Make sure everything's aligned with the city's expectations, and get me an update on those air rights," I say. "We don't want any hitches."

As she wraps up, I consider shifting a few items around. The thought of taking time off feels foreign, but Rome calls. I clear my throat. "Push everything that isn't critical to next week," I say. "I'll be out starting Thursday."

There's a pause. "Of course, Mr. Jackson. Should I move the zoning follow-up as well?"

"Yes, everything," I confirm. Rome was originally scheduled months down the line, but it's convenient to bring it forward. There's more to handle there than just business, and the sooner I address it, the better.

"Understood," she says, noting down the adjustments. "I'll make sure everything is coordinated for next week."

As I end the call, I look out the car window, catching a glimpse of the mansion's conservatory as we pull away. The memory of her standing there lingers…fierce yet uncertain, a blend that gnaws at the edges of my thoughts. She's reckless, stubborn, and clearly blind to the mess she's stirring. But for the first time, sending her off to Tod's feels more strategic than cold…a way to give her the opportunity she craves and keep her from entangling herself any further here.

And if flying to Rome to oversee the start of her contract is what it takes, well, it's simply part of the arrangement.

CHAPTER
Thirteen

JENNY

I n the cramped, familiar space of my closet, I fold and refold clothes, barely believing that I'm about to leave this tiny apartment above the garage once again…my whole world since I was a kid. The scent of fabric softener mingles with the faint aroma of oil and car grease wafting up from below, grounding me in the familiarity of home. My fingers brush over the worn edge of my favorite sweater, one I know I won't take with me. It's not "fashionable," not the polished image Tod's would want from me now, but it represents everything about who I've been.

This time, packing feels different. Paris was my first step, working for a local brand, posing for quaint boutique campaigns. There was charm in it, but it felt limited, small. Tod's is something else entirely…a giant, a name people know everywhere. It's intimidating, thrilling, and maybe even the first time I'll have to really prove myself on a stage much larger than I've ever been on.

I consider each piece I place in my suitcase carefully, choosing clothes that project a polished, professional image. Jackets with sharp lines, blouses that fit just right, pants that speak sophistication. I feel a mix of pride and nerves, knowing that every piece I take has to tell the story of someone who belongs in a high-end, international world.

Beside me, Lila, Mrs. Finnigan's niece, hovers in awe, her wide eyes drinking in every piece I lay out. She's only thirteen, but there's a fierce curiosity in her, a spark I remember having myself once. She runs her hand over a neatly folded blouse and sighs, a wistful smile creeping onto her face.

"Do you know how lucky you are, Jenny?" She says, her voice a mix of admiration and longing. "You get to live here. You get to go to Rome."

I pause, looking at her, and the reality sinks in. Lila probably thinks I'm living some kind of fairy tale, getting to live on the estate, going off to model in Rome. But she doesn't see the flip side…the lingering feeling of not quite belonging, of knowing that everything could vanish in an instant because it's not truly yours.

"I'm lucky, yeah," I say softly, tucking a pair of jeans into my bag. "But it's not as perfect as it looks." I don't want to disappoint her, though. She's too young to see all the rough edges.

. . .

She gives me a small smile, her fingers brushing the hem of a dress. "I wish I was Mrs. Finnigan's daughter, sometimes, you know? So, I could live here too."

The words hit me harder than I expect, reminding me that despite being the chauffeur's daughter, I've been treated with warmth and kindness. I've had chances that most in my position wouldn't. The Jackson household itself may be distant, but the staff...Mrs. Finnigan, the cooks, the gardeners... they've embraced me like family. They've looked out for me, even encouraged me, and never made me feel like I was "the help."

That's why the thought of possibly interfering in Brett's engagement, of stirring up tension with Zack, weighs on me. Yet, standing up to Zack still feels right. He may have the power, the influence, but he doesn't control my heart. I love Brett, and I have to hold onto that, no matter what Zack thinks or how intimidating he makes himself out to be.

After Lila leaves, I run my fingers over the open suitcase and realize I haven't even booked a flight yet. I glance at the Tod's contract lying on my desk, the email from their office stark and professional. Zack had been right; they'll cover everything once I'm in Rome. But until I'm officially signed, any travel is my responsibility.

I feel a pang of embarrassment. I don't have the money for an international ticket on such short notice. It's absurd, being so close to a dream and yet staring down a logistical wall because I'm just... me. With a grimace, I realize I'll have to accept Zack's offer to hitch a ride on his private plane.

．　．　．

I know his routine, so the next morning, I head downstairs toward the gym, hoping to catch him at a moment when he might actually listen to me. As I step inside, I'm met with the sight of him, striking the heavy bag with an intensity that makes my breath hitch.

Zack is a force, each punch steady, controlled. Muscles bunch under his skin, his shirt clinging to his back, damp with sweat, accentuating the solid lines of his body. I'd always thought Brett was attractive, with his easy smile and boyish charm, but Zack... he's something else. His form is more intimidating, less playful...intense in a way that makes something unsteady flutter in my chest.

I stand there, mesmerized, as he throws another punch. His brow is furrowed, beads of sweat trailing down his temple. He takes a step back, grabs a bottle of water, and notices me standing at the doorway.

"Well?" His gaze flicks over me, eyes sharp and unamused. "What are you doing here? Why are you up so early?"

I swallow, caught off guard by the intensity of his presence, and force myself to look directly at him. "I wanted... I mean, I need a favor." My words come out softer than I intended, almost hesitant, but I don't let myself back down.

．　．　．

He raises an eyebrow, clearly not amused. "A favor?" He repeats, the skepticism unmistakable. "At this hour?"

"Yes," I reply, steeling myself, trying to hold onto my resolve. "I… I need a ride to Rome. Since Tod's isn't covering travel, not until I'm officially signed on. You said I could go with you."

His gaze lingers on me, unreadable, but there's something behind his eyes…a flicker, almost too fleeting to catch. He sets the water bottle down, and I watch as a bead of sweat trails down the side of his face, catching in the hollow of his collarbone before disappearing beneath his shirt. I feel my pulse quicken, and I hate that my eyes follow the movement.

A part of me expected him to refuse, but in the end, and I am certain to get me out of the way, he agrees.

"Sure."

CHAPTER
Fourteen

ZACK

In the early morning light, my sleek black Mercedes pulls up onto the tarmac, the plane looming ahead, an impressive sight as always. I let myself exhale, feeling a rare flicker of anticipation…though it's not entirely because of the trip. I'm on the phone, wrapping up a call with a client who has been dragging on about petty contractual details. As the door opens, I step out, my gaze briefly flicking toward the jet where I spot Jenny already seated, looking, surprisingly, on time for once. I nod to the flight attendant waiting at the bottom of the stairs, allowing my bag to be whisked away as I stride up.

"Let's finalize that on Tuesday," I say into the phone, a little impatient now, my eyes fixed on Jenny's profile through the window. She's scrolling through her phone, seemingly oblivious to my arrival. Good, I think, as I finally end the call and slip my phone into my pocket, heading up the stairs.

. . .

Inside, the attendant greets me, her smile perfectly trained, and I settle into the seat opposite Jenny…luxuriously spacious, and, regrettably for the moment, too comfortable. Jenny barely glances up, lost in whatever she's doing, her legs tucked up on the seat as she scrolls.

After a moment, she notices me watching her and turns. "Hi," she says simply, looking slightly wary, as if unsure what to expect.

"Hi," I reply, letting a small smile curve at the edges of my mouth. She blinks, looking caught off-guard, and I can almost see the wheels turning in her head, wondering why I'm being civil.

Seeing that little frown on her face doesn't escape me. I lean back, letting an idea take shape.

"Your father reads all the time, doesn't he?" I say, raising an eyebrow as I nod toward her phone. "But I'm guessing you're just scrolling through social media?"

She narrows her eyes, irritation flashing across them. "Actually, I am reading," she replies, tone defiant, tilting her phone toward me so I can see the text on display. "See? But, of course, you'd assume otherwise."

. . .

I can't help the slight smirk that forms as I observe her, watching how her posture shifts, chin lifting a fraction in that way she does when she's proving a point.

Amused, I let my gaze linger on her, taking in the way she sits, almost smug, chin tilted slightly, that little look daring me to push her buttons just a bit more. But as my eyes drift lower, my amusement fades into something darker, something I can't quite restrain. That cropped top clings tightly across her chest, pressing against the fullness of her breasts, and there's no hiding the way her hard nipples push against the fabric, taunting me with what lies underneath.

She's ditched her usual prim outfits for jogger pants and that tight little top, and, damn it, it's doing something to me I hadn't expected. Those curves look different in this light, in this setting. My eyes trace the shape of her body, taking in every line and dip, the thin fabric hinting at what I'm not supposed to be noticing.

"You're really not a kid after all," I remark, my voice dropping a notch, and her cheeks flush almost instantly, though she holds her ground, meeting my gaze with steady defiance.

"And you're still judgmental, apparently," she says, smirking a little as she crosses her arms. "Guess some things don't change."

. . .

"Not everything," I concede, leaning back, unbuttoning my cuffs and rolling my sleeves up as casually as I can, feeling her eyes drift over my forearms, the hint of exposed skin drawing her attention. I can tell she's noticing, taking in the way I'm easing into a less formal posture. "Tell me, then, Ms. Professional…how serious are you about modeling? Or is this just a way to kill time until something more… 'respectable' comes along?"

She bristles, clearly taking the bait. "What, you don't think I'm serious?" Her voice sharpens, her lips pressing into a line. "I've been working at it for years, even in Paris. I was modeling for a local brand there."

I nod, letting my eyes linger on her as I contemplate her words. "So you want to take this further. Internationally. Aiming high?"

Her gaze meets mine, almost challenging. "Of course. This is my chance to do something for myself. Not just to be… here."

Interesting. I keep my expression neutral, but inside, I feel a strange satisfaction at hearing her say it—that she wants more than just lingering around Brett, more than this small world she's known. But I keep my tone casual as I ask, "So, no plans for college or anything outside of this?"

She hesitates, eyes flicking down before meeting mine again. "Modeling is what I want right now. College… maybe one day. But this feels like something real, something I can actually achieve."

She's watching me now, her eyes a little softer, searching, like she's gauging my reaction, hoping, maybe, for some kind of approval. But I give her none, not yet. I let the silence linger, the hum of the plane surrounding us, her every subtle shift under my gaze drawing my attention.

The attendant appears, placing our trays before us, the elegant plates with poached eggs, smoked salmon, fresh croissants, and fruit artfully arranged. I catch her watching me as I start to eat, eyes flicking from my hands to my mouth, before she quickly looks away, focused on her own plate.

There's something raw, almost palpable, in the tension simmering between us, an energy that's as intoxicating as it is dangerous.

"So, what about you?" She asks finally, breaking the silence, her voice hesitant, as if she's treading on unfamiliar ground. "Why Rome?"

"Business," I say simply, cutting into my food with deliberate precision, savoring the pause. "It's always business. This is just… another project."

"Oh." Her voice is soft, a little lost, and I sense her trying to piece together what drives me, what keeps me bound to this endless rotation of deals and contracts.

. . .

She tilts her head, curiosity lighting up her eyes. "Do you enjoy your work?"

I let a slow smile creep across my face. "Enjoy it?" I pause, letting the weight of the question settle. "I enjoy the benefits," I say, watching her reaction. "The power that comes with it."

Her eyes narrow a bit, a hint of wariness mixing with intrigue. "Power to control everyone, right?"

I don't hesitate. "Yes. Power to control... and the power to take someone nobody knows and get her an international modeling contract by twenty."

Her mouth opens slightly, clearly caught off guard. For a second, she's stunned into silence, and then...she laughs. Loud and genuine, the sound surprising even her. "Touché," she says, nodding, clearly amused. "Guess I owe you a thanks for that."

I watch her laugh, the sound so unexpected that it catches me off guard. I'm used to defiance and arguments...but this? This open, amused reaction? It makes me pause.I raise an eyebrow, still leaning back, intrigued. "Doesn't sound like a thank you," I say, just enough edge in my voice to keep things interesting.

. . .

She stops laughing, but a smirk remains. "Yeah?" she says, lifting her chin, a spark in her eyes. "Thank you, Zack. For giving a 'nobody' like me a shot."

There's a challenge in her voice, but underneath it, there's something real, something unguarded. I realize she's holding her ground but, strangely, meaning it. And it's that honesty, that little crack in her defenses, that keeps my gaze locked on her.

"You're welcome," I murmur, watching her closely. "Even if you don't need anyone's help... I still think you'll make the most of it."

CHAPTER
Fifteen

JENNY

It's after breakfast and I can't stop sneaking glances at him. The way the sunlight filters through the plane window and hits Zack just right, illuminating his profile—strong jaw, focused gaze, his dark blue eyes on his tablet. He's in a tailored suit, but there's this raw intensity to him, like he could just tear out of it any second. I can barely breathe. Every glance I steal makes my heart pound harder, and I feel the heat crawling up my cheeks. He's Brett's brother, and yet he couldn't be more different.

Unable to hold back, I pull out my phone and text Camille, my best friend from Paris boarding school. If there's anyone who'll understand how twisted up I feel, it's her.

Me: I'm losing it.
    Camille: Why?

Me: I'm with Zack. We're on our way to Rome, and this plane is suddenly too hot. I think I want him to kiss me again.

Camille: What? Zack! Brett's brother?

Me: Yes, exactly. It's insane. It's not even like I really fancy him... but I can't stop thinking about that kiss. I'm still hung up on it, and I can't get it out of my mind.

Camille: It must be because you hate him.

Me: Maybe... but it's different with Brett. With Brett, I'm usually excited... but with Zack, it's... intense.

Her reply comes with a string of laughing emojis.

Camille: You're in a tough spot, my dear. But I'm at work, so no more texts. Call me if you want."

I glance over at Zack, gauging if he understands any French. He looks deeply focused on his tablet, so I clear my throat. "Do you uh by any chance speak French?"

He glances up and gives a brief shake of his head. "No."

Relieved, I press the call button, my heart racing as soon as Camille picks up. I drop my voice low, and the words spill out in French, as if confessing something I can barely admit to myself.

Me: He's so... attractive, and I can't help it. It's insane, Camille.

Camille: You're talking about Zack, Brett's brother? But I thought you were crazy about Brett!

Me: I thought so too, but with Zack, it's... different. I can't stop thinking about him, and not in the same way I thought about Brett. This is just physical attraction, I think, and it's his fault. He was the one who kissed me instead of Brett.

Camille: So, what is it? What are you imagining?

I hesitate, glancing over at Zack. His focus on the tablet is unwavering, completely unaware of what I'm about to confess. I bite my lip, a reckless thrill pulsing through me.

Me: I dream of him almost every night... I wake up in a sweat. Every detail of our kiss in the conservatory... it was... God, Camille, it was incredible. And he didn't even really touch me like that.

Camille: Wait, wait... tell me in detail. What happened in that kiss to drive you this crazy? You mentioned it, but it's been days now and you're still talking about it.

My cheeks flush just remembering it. I lower my voice further, almost as if whispering it makes it more real.

Me: He looked at me like... like I was the only thing that mattered. Then he leaned in, and I felt his arms around me... And when his lips touched mine, it was like... God, I could have given him everything right there.

Camille: And since that kiss, it's all you think about?

Me: Yes... and more. I wonder what he'd do if he really touched me, if he decided to take control.

I pause, glancing at him again, feeling that reckless need building.

Me: I think about him when I go to bed, Camille... if I could... I'd let him do whatever he wants to me, here in Rome. Just to feel him.

Camille: Oh my god, you're completely screwed. And I love it.

I laugh under my breath, feeling bolder with every word.

Me: You know, he's so strong. I saw him working out a few days ago and I couldn't look away... his shirt was soaked with sweat, and he kept going without even catching his breath.

Camille: So? Tell me, what were you thinking while spying on him like a little pervert?

I close my eyes, remembering that exact moment, the way

he'd looked when he took a breath, muscles taut, sweat glistening on his skin.

Me:I thought he could lift me with one finger... that if he really wanted me, I wouldn't stand a chance resisting.

Camille: That's exactly what you want, isn't it? To have no choice. Just you, at his mercy.

Me: Yes, and that every move he makes, I feel it everywhere... like every fiber of my body is under his control.

Camille: And you wake up thinking about all that... sweating and ready to scream his name?

My pulse races, and I laugh softly.

Me: Fuck, yes.

Camille: Then what are you waiting for, darling? This trip to Rome is your chance.

Me: Oh, no, I love Brett. Zack is just a fantasy, Camille.

Camille: So you say—

Me: Yes, he's... strong, and... darker, but Brett, he's like... a ray of sunshine. Zack, he stirs things in me, but it's nothing real. Plus, you know I'm still a virgin... I'm not about to mess that up like this. I have a career to focus on, and Zack's still an ass, even if...

I trail off, glancing over at Zack, reassuring myself that he is not hearing any of this. But just as I let myself feel that relief, he suddenly lifts his gaze from his tablet and catches me staring. My heart stops. His eyes hold mine for a beat, long enough that I feel exposed, like he's seeing right through me. I snap my gaze away, feeling my cheeks burn.

Me: Camille, he just looked at me. Why would he do that? I'm scared. I think he might understand French.

Camille: Oh my God, girl, you're screwed... do you really think so though? Maybe all rich guys understand second languages...

Panic seizes me, my pulse racing out of control. I feel my face turn red, and my mind jumps to every single word I've just said. God, if he caught even a little bit of that… Then he sighs, lowering his tablet with an irritated look, and his voice cuts through the air, sharp and commanding.

"Stop staring at me. You're distracting me," he says. He says this in English, each word clipped and impatient. I release the breath I didn't realize I was holding, a wave of relief washing over me.

Me: I don't think he understood… Thank God. I think I would have thrown myself off this plane if he did.

Camille: Oh, poor Jenny. You're doomed. But I love seeing you in this mess.

I hate it, but still I laugh softly, still shaken but feeling a little more grounded. I lean back in my seat, closing my eyes, letting the relief settle in, knowing that this is a game I shouldn't play too seriously—but somehow, I just can't stop.

Me: I have to hang up… if I keep going, I think he's going to throw me off the plane. He's busy and I'm distracting him.

Camille: Alright, but remember… have fun, and if you ever find yourself in a situation where you don't know what to do, call me.

I laugh softly, the tension easing just a bit, but I still feel my heart racing.

Me: Love you, Camille. Talk soon.

Camille: Love you too. Call me soon, okay?

With that, she ends the call, her laughter still echoing in my mind. I lean back, letting out a long sigh. I can't stop thinking about everything we talked about, her words looping in my head. Finally, the exhaustion pulls me under, and I drift off.

CHAPTER
Sixteen

ZACK

I know now that I can stare at the screen of a tablet and not read a single word in ten minutes. And it's not because I'm tired. No, it's because the girl next to me... who's oblivious to the fact that I understand every word...is busy on the phone with her friend, whispering in French as if it's some secret code. But it's not. I catch every single word.

I'm not even sure what to make of it...her "fantasies," as she calls them, spilling out in a low, embarrassed rush. Her words replay in my head, one after another, and I can barely process them.

I try not to look at her as she finally drifts off. There's a strange mix of disbelief and... something else, gnawing at me. Because for all her rambling, all her innocent denial of these feelings for me, she wants things from me she couldn't bring herself to admit out loud if I asked her directly. She wants intensity. She wants to be consumed. I never truly thought she had that kind of fire in her.

And maybe... maybe she'd be easier to win over than I

thought. It was a simple enough plan, to have her infatuated with me, so she'd leave Brett alone. But now, I find myself watching her, maybe longer than I should. There's something interesting about her…stubborn and completely unaware of herself, like she doesn't see just how clearly she shows everything she feels. But I shake the thoughts away, forcing myself to focus back on the screen, on the numbers waiting for me.

The plane touches down in Rome as the sun begins to set, bathing the runway in a golden light. Jenny, of course, is buzzing with excitement, practically bouncing in her seat. From the windows, she scans the tarmac, clearly looking for her own way out, as if she's forgotten I'm even here.

Once she collects her bags, I point her toward the black sedan waiting for us. "Your ride's this way."

She frowns, glancing past me. "Actually… I already booked a hotel for myself. I can find my way there from here. It's a little place on Via Maggio. It's affordable, and you've already done more than enough for me, so I'd like to handle it from here."

I feel my jaw tighten, but I manage to keep my voice calm. "Affordable?" I repeat. "Jenny, we're in Rome. It's a big city, and I'd rather know you're safe. I have a suite at Hotel de Russie. You'd be comfortable there."

She shakes her head, crossing her arms. "Thank you, but no. This is my trip, and it's work-related, so I'd really like to handle it on my terms."

I take a slow breath, forcing myself to stay patient. "Alright," I say, meeting her eyes. "But if anything feels off or you change your mind, call me. Don't take any chances."

Her mouth quirks up in a small, triumphant smile. "Noted," she replies, clearly feeling victorious.

We step off the jet onto the quiet tarmac of the private terminal, where a sleek black sedan is waiting nearby, the chauffeur already holding the door open. However, she doesn't get in.

"What is it now??" I ask and her hand tightens around the handle of her suitcase.

"Actually," she starts, meeting my gaze with that same defiance, "I'd rather handle this myself as well. Just drop me at a main area nearby, where I can catch a cab."

I raise an eyebrow. "You don't need to call a cab, Jenny. I can drop you off. I need to at least know where you're staying."

She shakes her head, her stance firm. "Thanks, but no."

I sigh, resigned, and signal the chauffeur to take us to a central location near the commercial terminal where taxis are available. As we pull up, she gives a quick, triumphant nod.

"Thanks for the lift," she says, stepping out with her suitcase.

I watch her disappear into the city, both exasperated and reluctantly impressed. This trip might be more challenging than I'd planned.

The drive to the hotel is quiet, though I can't shake the irritation gnawing at me. Once we arrive, the concierge shows me to the suite, a sprawling setup with an adjoining door... planned for Jenny to be next door. It was supposed to be perfect, but now she's off at some questionable hotel, stubborn as always, and I'm stuck with an empty room beside mine. I grind my teeth as the door clicks shut, feeling the frustration settle deeper. Stubborn doesn't even begin to describe her.

CHAPTER
Seventeen

JENNY

The evening sky over Rome casts a warm, orange glow as I finally step into the modest hotel I booked for myself on Via Maggio. It's not much, and definitely not anything like the Hotel de Russie Zack had insisted on, but it's affordable and it's mine. I feel a little spark of pride, walking in here on my own terms, ignoring the concierge's surprised look when I confirm my single night's stay in what must be one of the cheapest rooms they offer. It's tiny, but I'd expected that.

As I close the door and set down my bag, I glance around the room. The bed takes up most of the space, with only a small dresser on one side and a narrow bathroom tucked into the corner.

There's a lingering, stale smell in the air, but I ignore it. It's just one night, and I wanted this…a chance to prove I could manage things on my own.

. . .

I take a quick shower and change into a loose T-shirt and shorts, determined to get a good night's sleep.

I turn off the lamp and settle into bed, my phone resting nearby, just in case.

At first, it's almost peaceful, the sounds of the city just a murmur through the thin walls. But then, faintly, I hear raised voices…a couple arguing somewhere down the hall. I tell myself it's none of my business, focusing on the cracked paint on the ceiling instead, tracing the lines in the dim light from the street. But the voices don't go away; they get louder, moving closer. A woman's voice cuts through, muffled but sharp, followed by the thud of something heavy against the wall.

I sit up, suddenly tense, straining to hear. I can't make out the words, but the sound itself is disturbing. She yells again, something shrill, and there's a slam that makes the headboard tremble against the wall. I pull the covers tighter around me, glancing nervously at the door. My mind wanders to the pristine, quiet halls Zack had promised at his hotel, with thick walls and a concierge on every floor. Somewhere, he's probably enjoying every detail of that expensive place without a care in the world.

Another thud pulls me out of my thoughts, and this time, the sounds coming through the thin walls are unmistakable.

. . .

It starts low and muffled, a woman's voice rising, a breathless laugh echoing, and then another, deeper voice, slow and thick. My cheeks warm, and I try to brush it off, but the sounds continue, soft gasps and then a thud against the wall, as if someone's being pinned or pressed. The laugh returns, this time too wild to be friendly.

They're not arguing or shouting. They're... they're definitely fucking. Oh my god.

My face heats up as I lie there, frozen, listening in spite of myself.

The bed on the other side of the wall creaks with each movement, every thud matching the quickening beat of my own heart. There's an intimacy to it, something raw and unrestrained, and I know I should look away, or at least try to block it out, but I can't seem to move.

I clutch the pillow tighter, feeling an odd, uncomfortable heat pooling in my stomach, spreading to my skin. They're completely lost in each other, their voices intensifying, merging together in a way that makes me feel like an intruder. And yet... I can't stop listening. There's a tension in the air that draws me in, and each moan, each breath, somehow heightens the silence in my room, making me hyper-aware of how close I am to it all.

None of this is what I signed up for. I just needed a place to crash and rest in time for work tomorrow but here I am perhaps living through an episode of the Addam's family.

. . .

The noises are relentless, shifting from one thing to another, a loud argument, then a woman's quiet cries, until I don't know if I should be worried or just annoyed. I glance at my phone, debating if calling my dad would be ridiculous or completely reasonable. Perhaps both because he is sure to be worried out of his mind and with no way to help me.

It's past midnight now, and my patience is running thin. The space feels too close, too suffocating, with every sound pressing in on me from all directions. My heart races, and I clutch my phone, fingers hovering over Zack's number. I hesitate, swallowing the strange mix of shame and pride at the thought of calling him. But the muffled argument and sounds of fucking aren't stopping. I can't ignore the pit of fear settling in my stomach.

The walls are bloody paper thin. I'm horrified.

Finally, I press call.

The phone rings once before he answers, his voice low and laced with an edge of alertness. "Jenny?"

"Zack… I know it's late, and I really wanted to handle this myself," I whisper, feeling a flush of embarrassment creep up my neck, "but… I just don't feel safe here." I take a shaky breath. "There's yelling, and… I think it might be a fight, or I don't know what... I'm sorry for calling you about this."

There's a pause, and I can almost feel him absorbing my words, irritation and worry mingling on the other end.

"Send me the address," he says, his tone firm but steady. "I'll be there soon."

I hang up, curling up on the edge of the bed, straining to block out the noises coming from all sides.

Every single one feels more heightened, louder, and I flinch, clutching my phone like a lifeline, listening intently for the faintest sound of a knock.

It's not long...maybe fifteen minutes...before there's a firm, unmistakable knock on the door. I rush over and peek through the peephole, my heart pounding when I see Zack, his expression hard and unreadable. Taking a steadying breath, I open the door a crack, unable to hide my relief as he looks me over, his gaze assessing the narrow, dim hallway, the flickering lights, and the thin, grungy walls.

"Rough night?" he asks dryly, his gaze finally landing on mine.

I nod, feeling foolish but relieved. "It's... noisier than I expected."

. . .

"Clearly," he mutters, his eyes sweeping over the cramped room behind me, the faint smell of stale smoke and something else. He barely contains his disdain. "Let's go."

I grab my bag, cheeks burning with a mix of embarrassment and relief, and follow him out of the room. I expect some kind of smug remark, maybe a hint of "I told you so," but he says nothing as we head to the G-Wagon. The luxury of the leather seats feels like an escape, a world away from that cramped, uncomfortable hotel, and I exhale slowly as the door shuts, finally feeling safe.

Zack's gaze is fixed forward, his expression unreadable, jaw set. The silence stretches between us, heavy and thick, and I realize with a pang of surprise that he isn't gloating, not even a hint of it. I study his profile, the way his brow furrows slightly, how his hands grip the steering wheel. He's focused, frustrated maybe, but there's something else...a quiet concern I hadn't expected. I find myself wondering what he's thinking, almost as if I'm starting to understand him, despite knowing I shouldn't be able to.

He could so easily make this about him, about being right, about me not listening. But he doesn't, and that restraint, that silence, tells me more about him than anything he could say. It's unsettling, and oddly reassuring, and I can't help but feel something shift slightly, a deeper sense of him that I hadn't noticed before.

. . .

As we pull up to the Hotel de Russie, the grandeur of the place steals my breath, but it's Zack's steady silence that lingers with me. We walk through the lobby without a word, and it's only when we reach the elevator that he finally looks at me, his expression softer, almost unreadable.

"You should learn to listen."

There it is. I'm disappointed, yet somehow not surprised. But I'm grateful, so I hold back from snapping back.

When we reach his room, I stop short in the hallway, surprised he doesn't have a separate one for me. Zack opens the door, and I follow him in, finding myself in a small, elegant foyer with two doors on opposite sides and I am immediately relieved. He hands me a key, studying my reaction with that unreadable look.

"Did you eat?" he asks, his voice steady, almost neutral.

"Yes, I got some pizza earlier," I manage, feeling strangely exposed in his presence.

He nods, giving the slightest hint of a polite smile. "Goodnight," he says simply, and then he's gone, disappearing through his door and leaving me alone with my thoughts.

. . .

I turn to my room and step inside.

The space opens up in soft, warm lighting, casting a glow over walls painted in a deep, serene ivory. High, ornate ceilings rise above me, creating an airy, almost ethereal sense of space.

Underfoot, the marble floors are cool and smooth, polished to a mirror-like sheen that reflects the ambient light. A lavish, king-sized bed dominates the room, its rich, cream-colored linens spilling over the edges like clouds, each layer inviting and impossibly soft, topped with oversized pillows and a luxurious velvet throw in shades of deep sapphire. The scent of fresh linens and delicate lavender fills the air, making me feel instantly calm.

To my right, floor-to-ceiling windows open to a sweeping view of Rome, the city lights glittering in the distance like scattered stars. The curtains, thick and intricately woven, frame the scene, adding an intimate touch to the breathtaking panorama. Every detail is exquisite, from the carved wood dresser adorned with fresh white lilies to the plush armchair in the corner, draped with a soft, cream-colored cashmere blanket. Each element speaks of elegance and comfort, yet with an effortless beauty that doesn't try too hard to impress.

A sense of ease fills me, every inch of the room crafted to make me feel as if I've stepped into another reality, one where I belong here, surrounded by luxury.

· · ·

Setting down my bag, I can't help but feel a strange pull toward the adjoining door. Zack is just on the other side, probably getting ready for bed, his presence almost palpable, even through the walls. My mind wanders to the memory of him earlier in the evening, his expression unreadable, yet somehow softer than I've seen before. He'd been dressed down in a crisp dress shirt, the top buttons undone, giving a glimpse of his toned chest. The shirt flowed over his tailored slacks, fitting him perfectly, while his hair, usually so meticulously styled, fell in soft waves around his face, slightly tousled from the flight.

There's an almost forbidden thrill at the memory of him, in control… concerned for me. I feel a rush of warmth between my legs, the quiet solitude of the room amplifying every sensation. I stare at the door, feeling my pulse quicken, a bit reckless, a bit daring.

I slide under the covers, slipping my hand slowly down my body, my fingers grazing over my bare skin. A slow warmth builds as I imagine his gaze, intense and unflinching, those gray eyes fixed on me with a knowing look that sends a thrill down my spine. I can picture his lips, always pressed into that firm line, controlled, like he's holding back so much more.

I try to push him from my mind, to replace his face with Brett's but it's impossible; the image of him keeps flashing back, and I feel the heat building in my body, a restlessness I can't shake.

I close my eyes, one hand slipping beneath my shirt, brushing over my stomach as I try to breathe, try to convince myself that this is nothing, that he's nothing to me. But my body isn't listening. I can already feel a warm dampness between my thighs, my body betraying the thoughts I don't want to have. A soft gasp escapes my lips as my fingers slide lower, grazing over the sensitive skin, and I bite my lip, fighting against the rush of sensation.

The tension only builds as my fingers slip over my clit, rubbing slowly, tentatively, as if testing myself, daring myself to go further. My body feels raw, every nerve on edge, and I let out a shaky breath, trying to stifle the small moans that keep slipping out, pressing my face into the pillow to muffle the sounds.

Each touch feels like it's pulling me closer to the edge, and my mind races, the friction against my skin sending waves of heat through me. My fingers move faster, the slickness only adding to the intensity. The more I try to fight it, the harder it is to stop, my body betraying me entirely as I finally let go, my hips arching as a shuddering release crashes over me, leaving me breathless and flushed.

I lie there in the quiet aftermath, my heart still racing, my cheeks burning with embarrassment and a bucketload of shame.

I thought I hated him. I should hate him because, currently, he is standing in the way of everything I want. So why, then, is my clit throbbing once again at the very thought of him, needing more… hungry with need? Grabbing one of the pillows from my side, I slam it down over my head and resist the urge to scream with all my might into it.

CHAPTER
Eighteen

ZACH

The night feels endless. I'm lying in bed, staring at the ceiling, and I can't get the image of her out of my head…Jenny, standing there, calm as you please, talking about that godforsaken hotel as if it weren't a hellhole. As if the noises, the fights, the danger she was surrounded by were just an inconvenience.

She could have been hurt. Hell, she could have been killed.

I clench my fists against the memory of her voice when she'd called me, trembling but trying to sound composed. It had done something to me…an immediate, instinctive response I couldn't stop. I'd leapt out of bed like a lunatic, my heart pounding so hard I could barely see straight. The sheer terror that something might happen to her had made me reckless.

I'd called the police, fully prepared to unleash hell if I didn't find her within minutes.

But she's fine now. Of course, she's fine. Probably asleep in her plush, safe suite without a care in the world while I'm here, losing my goddamn mind. I'm furious at her stubbornness, furious that she's still so damn naive. And even angrier at myself for letting her get under my skin like this. She's just a girl, I remind myself. A girl I'm supposed to be controlling, not obsessing over.

I don't blame her though. Not really. How could I? She doesn't realize the effect she has on people. On me. It wasn't like this before. I've known her since she was a child, wild and free, running around the estate like she owned the place. Back then, I never thought twice about her...never allowed myself to. But there was always a softness, a quiet affection. I've spent years protecting her without her ever knowing. Stepping in when things could have gone wrong. Making sure she was safe, smoothing over the rough patches her father couldn't fix on his own.

That was different. Simple. But now, it's like she's become someone else entirely...a woman. It's difficult to handle. I feel lust for her, undeniable and consuming, but it's not the same as romance. And that's the problem. I want to indulge in it, to let myself feel it fully, but a part of me worries if I can ever truly remain detached. I've always been detached with other women; it's how I've kept control. But Jenny isn't just any other woman. And now, I'm not sure if I can let her be just another fleeting indulgence...or if I even want to.

· · ·

My stomach growls, breaking the spiral of my thoughts. I skipped dinner in my irritation, and now it's catching up with me. I throw the sheets back and sit up, running a hand through my hair. I'm still wound up, still restless, but hunger wins out. There's a bottle of wine sitting on the small bar cart near the balcony. I grab it, twisting off the cork and pouring a glass as I step outside.

The night air is cool, carrying the faint hum of the city. Rome sprawls out before me, glittering and alive even at this hour. I lean against the railing, the wine glass dangling from my fingers, and let out a long breath. The view is stunning, sure, but it does nothing to distract me from the lingering knot of frustration in my chest.

And then I hear it…the soft click of a door opening beside me.

Jenny steps out onto her balcony. My first reaction is anger, a sharp spike of irritation cutting through the quiet. Of course, she'd be here. Of course, she'd ruin the brief moment of solitude I'd been desperate for. I don't turn, don't acknowledge her, hoping she'll go back inside. But even as I try to ignore her, my body betrays me. Lust rises, unrelenting and immediate, like a fire catching on dry timber.

She hasn't noticed me yet, and for a brief moment, I let myself watch her. She's wearing the thinnest slip of a nightgown, the fabric whispering against her body, clinging in all the right places before it flows down over her frame. Her hair falls loose and tousled, as if she just rolled out of bed. And yet, she looks like she belongs in a dream…something untouchable, something I shouldn't want but can't stop craving.

. . .

My cock hardens instantly, throbbing in time with the heat coursing through me. The sound of her soft footsteps, the faint hitch of her breath, the way the air seems to shift around her…it all lights a fire under my skin.

My eyes drag lower, catching on the way the soft glow of the city outlines her breasts. Her nipples press against the fabric, two faint peaks that I can't help but notice. My throat tightens, and my jaw clenches as my hands grip the railing. All I can think about is how she'd feel in my arms, the weight of her body pressed against mine, her breath hitching as I—

Stop. For fuck's sake, stop.

I drag in a sharp breath and force my gaze upward, but it's no use. The damage is done. She's invaded my thoughts again, and I know it'll take hours to shake the images she's burned into my mind. She's trouble, I remind myself. Pure trouble. And yet, every time I'm near her, I'm torn between wanting to pin her against the nearest wall and walking away to preserve whatever's left of my sanity.

She moves closer to the railing, still oblivious to my presence, and I feel the tension coil tighter in my chest. Her hand brushes the metal, her fingers delicate but sure, and I notice the slight shiver that runs through her as the cool night air hits her skin. It's ridiculous how something so simple makes me want her even more.

. . .

And then she notices me.

Her eyes widen in surprise, and her hand flies to her chest, pressing against her breasts in a way that only draws my attention there again.

"Zack!" she gasps, her voice breathy and startled. "I didn't realize you were out here."

I bite back the sharp reply on the tip of my tongue, my frustration barely leashed. "Yeah," I say, my tone clipped as I raise the glass of wine to my lips. Anything to give my hands something to do other than reach for her.

A long stretch follows as I wonder what she will do. Head back into the room, or be definitive and engage, and remain out here.

She of course chooses the latter like I expect.

I force myself to take another sip of wine. "Couldn't sleep?"

She shakes her head slightly, her hand still resting on her chest, toying with the necklace against her skin. "No, I... I just needed some air," she murmurs, her tone quiet. There's no defiance here, no sharpness. Just her, standing there, unsure of how to fill the silence.

I don't reply, letting the quiet stretch between us. But my eyes betray me, dragging down once again to her breast.

I imagine my palm replacing her hand, the way her skin would feel against mine, and the thought sends a jolt of heat straight to my core.

Her gaze flicks to the glass in my hand, breaking my train of thought. "Is that wine?" she asks softly, her tone curious but cautious.

I nod, swirling the glass lazily. "It is."

"Care to share?" she ventures, her voice gaining a bit more confidence.

I let out a low laugh, though it's rough with the effort of restraint. "I don't think it's suitable for minors."

Her lips part slightly, surprise flashing across her face, but it's gone as quickly as it came. Her eyes narrow, and with measured grace, she straightens her posture, holding herself with quiet strength. "Minors?" she repeats, her tone calm but laced with unmistakable challenge. "Do I look like a minor to you, Zack?"

Her words are deliberate, each one cutting with restrained anger. She's not raising her voice, but the weight of her indignation is impossible to miss. It's not just a question...it's a reminder that she's no longer the kid I once thought she was.

I ignore her, but she takes a step closer, closing the gap between us. Her eyes meet mine, searching, and I know I should step back. My mind goes back to the conversation she'd had with her friend, and I straighten away from the railing. My intention is to return to the room before I find myself pinning her against the wall or her, down on her knees with my cock in her mouth. But instead, I stand there, for some reason unwilling to leave, the tension between us tightening with every passing second.

I let out a low laugh, though it's rough, barely masking the strain I'm under. "I don't think it's suitable for minors," I say, the words sharper than they need to be.

Her lips part slightly, surprise flickering across her face, but it quickly hardens into something else. Offense. She straightens her back, her posture composed but tinged with quiet anger. For a moment, she just looks at me, and I feel the weight of her thoughts before she even speaks.

"I'm not a minor," she says softly but firmly, her voice steady. "I'm nineteen. Almost twenty."

· · ·

Her words land with more impact than they should. Nineteen. It shouldn't make a difference, but somehow, it does. She's not that little girl running around the estate anymore, and she wants me to know it. Wants me to feel it. And damn it, I do.

She pauses, her hazel eyes searching mine, looking for something I'm not ready to give. "Do I really seem like a minor to you, Zack?" she asks, her tone quieter now, less sharp but no less piercing. Her words are calm, but her eyes... they dare me to answer, to acknowledge the obvious.

I don't answer, not immediately. How the hell am I supposed to? I look away, swirling the wine in my glass like it holds some kind of escape. But there's no getting away from this. From her.

She takes a step closer, the soft shuffle of her bare feet on the balcony tiles pulling my attention back to her. The moonlight frames her face, her hair glowing like something out of a dream. Or a nightmare. She's close now...too close...and every nerve in my body is on fire. I grip the glass tighter to stop myself from doing something stupid, but all I can think about is the way her lips would taste if I closed the space between us.

"Zack," she says again, her voice softer this time, hesitant, but her eyes flick to the wine glass in my hand. She tilts her head slightly, her loose waves catching the light. "Will you share? Is there any more left? I can't sleep… it might help."

. . .

I glance at the glass, then back at her, measuring my response. She's asking, not demanding, but there's a challenge in her tone, an invitation almost. She's too damn close. Too calm for someone who was inches from danger just hours ago.

I swirl the wine slowly, buying myself a moment. "Can you handle it?" I ask, my tone light but edged, deliberately baiting her.

Her brows knit together, just slightly, enough to show her irritation. "Really? You're extremely condescending you know this right?"

The corner of my mouth twitches despite myself as her pride and stubbornness once again rear their ugly heads.

"Being an adult is not just about being able to handle wine," I say, my voice dropping as I tilt the glass toward her. "It's about everything it requires...for instance, ensuring your safety, especially as a woman, is your priority at all times."

She frowns at me deeply, clearly not interested in being scolded.

She hesitates for a beat, her eyes holding mine, searching for something I'm not sure she'll find. Then, without a word, she steps closer and takes the glass from my hand, her fingers brushing mine. The touch is brief but electric, and it takes every ounce of control I have to stand still, to let her set the pace.

She lifts the glass to her lips, her movements slow, deliberate. I watch as she takes a sip, the wine staining her mouth a deeper red. She licks her lips once, catching a stray drop, and something inside me twists, sharp and primal. My cock throbs painfully, and I have to clench my fists at my sides to keep from reaching for her.

She hands the glass back, her gaze steady. "Is there anymore, or was that all you had left?" she asks softly, her tone careful but curious.

I gesture toward the bar cart near the balcony doors. "There's more," I say. "Come inside, and I'll pour you some."

She hesitates for a moment, as if considering, before nodding and slipping back into my suite. I follow the sound of her bare feet on the floor blending with the faint hum of the city outside. The room feels smaller now, the air is thick with something I can't name but can feel all the same.

At the bar cart, I pour half a glass for her, the deep red liquid swirling like blood under the light. I turn and hold it out, watching as she takes it, her fingers brushing mine again. This time, the contact lingers, just for a second, but it's enough to send another jolt of heat through me.

· · ·

She drinks, slower this time, savoring it. I can't look away, my eyes fixed on her mouth as it moves. A drop spills over the edge, sliding down the curve of the glass and onto her hand. She catches it instinctively, licking it off her skin in a single, unthinking motion.

The room tilts slightly, or maybe it's just me. I'm losing it. I'm losing control, and I know it.

I watch her, my gaze heavy, lingering on the curve of her lips, the line of her throat as she swallows. Her lashes flutter briefly, and she sets the glass down on the edge of the bar cart. Her eyes meet mine again, and for a moment, neither of us speaks.

The memory of our kiss in the conservatory flashes through my mind. The taste of her, the way her body had felt against mine, soft and warm and yielding. My chest tightens as the desire to take her again claws at me, stronger now, almost unbearable. But I can't. Not yet. Not like this.

I step back, needing the space to breathe, to think. My hands move automatically, unbuttoning my shirt as I force myself to calm down. The cool air hits my skin as I shrug the fabric off, tossing it onto the bed. She watches me, her gaze flicking briefly to my chest before darting away, her cheeks flushing faintly.

"You should sleep," I say finally, my voice rough but steady. "It's late."

.   .   .

I sit on the bed and start to take off my watch. Next goes my belt, and I wonder just how audacious she is...whether she'll remain in that spot and watch me.

To my amazement, and perhaps a bit of relief, she doesn't.

Instead, she just watches me for another moment before turning and slipping back toward her room. The door clicks shut behind her, leaving me alone, shirtless, and still painfully hard. I drag a hand through my hair, letting out a slow breath.

This trip is going to destroy me.

CHAPTER
Nineteen

JENNY

The morning sun streams through the sheer curtains of my hotel room, casting golden light across the polished floors. I blink at the brightness, feeling a mix of grogginess and a faint excitement bubbling under my exhaustion. Today is the fitting at Tod's...a place I'd never dreamed I'd set foot in, let alone as part of their campaign. The thought brings a flicker of pride, but it's quickly smothered by self-doubt.

Am I here because of me, or because of Zack?

The question lingers, heavy and unwelcome, as I rub my eyes and stretch. I toss the blanket aside, the weight of last night pulling me back. Tossing and turning, my mind had refused to quiet, replaying the same scene over and over. Zack. The way he'd looked last night, standing on the balcony with that quiet intensity, his shirt slipping off his shoulders, revealing muscles that moved like liquid steel beneath his skin. It wasn't just his body that haunted me, though…it was his presence, the way he commanded the space around him without a single word.

And then there was the kiss.

The kiss from the conservatory has been etched into my memory, vivid and consuming. It wasn't just any kiss…it was my first. My very first. And it wasn't from Brett, the man I thought I wanted for so long. It was from Zack, the man I wasn't even supposed to be thinking about.

It had been overwhelming in its intensity, a force that pulled me under and left me gasping. The way his lips moved against mine; the way his hands gripped me like he couldn't let go... It had made me feel alive in a way I didn't understand. A way that scared me.

And now anytime I look at him it's nearly all that I can think about, I shake my head, forcing the thoughts away as I pull on a simple but comfortable outfit…a fitted blouse tucked into high-waisted jeans. Stylish enough for Tod's, but not so much that I'll draw unnecessary attention. As I glance in the mirror, I take a deep breath, trying to steady myself.

This morning isn't supposed to be about Zack. It's about proving I belong at the fitting, proving I'm more than just the girl handed an opportunity because of someone else's influence. But even as I pull on my clothes and run a brush through my hair, I can't stop wondering if I'll see him.

He's in the room next door. The thought alone sends my heart racing. Will I run into him when I leave? Will I catch him stepping out, impeccably dressed, his usual commanding presence impossible to ignore?

I hesitate for a moment, staring at the door, my pulse pounding in my ears. The idea of facing him again makes my chest tighten, but it's not dread. Not entirely. There's something else, something I don't want to name.

When I finally step out into the hall, I glance toward his door, half-expecting it to open. It doesn't. I breathe a sigh of relief as I make my way downstairs, my heart gradually settling.

But as I enter the dining area, the relief vanishes instantly. He's there.

Zack sits at a table near the window, bathed in soft morning sunlight that catches the sharp angles of his face. He looks flawless, as always, his suit perfectly tailored, his posture confident and relaxed. My stomach twists painfully, and for a moment, I consider walking away, pretending I haven't seen him. But it's too late. His eyes lift from his phone, meeting mine with a calm intensity that makes it impossible to look anywhere else.

· · ·

I have no choice now but to head over and it severely annoys me that suddenly and unnecessarily my knees feel wobbly.

As I sit down, I catch a glimpse of him out of the corner of my eye, his focus still glued to his phone. His brow is slightly furrowed, his posture relaxed yet commanding, as though even here, in this casual setting, he exudes control. He doesn't glance up at me, not even once, and it twists something in my stomach…part frustration, part something else I can't quite name.

My nerves bubble under the surface, making it impossible to sit still. The silence between us feels oppressive, heavy with things unsaid, so I push my chair back and stand abruptly. If he notices, he doesn't show it, his attention fixed entirely on his screen.

I make my way to the buffet, my palms damp as I grab a plate. The spread is impressive…fruits, pastries, eggs, juices… but I barely see any of it. My hands move automatically, placing a small omelet and a few slices of toast onto my plate, my mind elsewhere. The glass pitcher of orange juice feels cool in my trembling grip as I pour myself a drink, the faint clink of glass on glass making me flinch.

When I return to the table, he still hasn't looked up. I set my plate down carefully, easing myself into the chair, trying not to make any noise. My heart pounds, though I don't know why. He hasn't spoken to me, hasn't even acknowledged my presence, yet I feel his energy filling the space between us.

. . .

I pick up my fork, my hand unsteady as I take a small bite of the omelet. The eggs are warm, fluffy, and should be comforting, but they might as well be sawdust for all I can taste. My nerves make every chew feel labored, my throat tight as I swallow.

He shifts slightly, the sound of his chair creaking, catching my attention. For a brief moment, I glance up, but his gaze remains fixed on his phone, the faint furrow in his brow deepening as if whatever he's reading requires his full focus. The silence stretches, suffocating and thick, and I find myself hyperaware of every movement I make...the scrape of my fork against the plate, the faint clink of the glass as I take a sip of orange juice.

I try to focus on my food, but it's impossible not to notice him. The way his tailored suit molds to his broad shoulders, the subtle tension in his jaw as he sips his coffee, the way his fingers move deliberately across the screen...it's maddening. How can he be so composed, so unaffected, when my every nerve feels like it's on fire just sitting here?

We eat in silence, the tension between us growing heavier with each passing moment. My chest feels tight, my breath shallow, but I force myself to keep my head down, to focus on the simple act of eating.

. . .

All of this is because I'm exhausted, I tell myself. That's the reason I'm feeling so much more than I should. So much more tense, more nervous...plus Tod's. The fitting today. This morning could be the start of something big for me. A career. A future where I won't just be "Jenny, the chauffeur's daughter." A future where I'll be someone in my own right.

The thought steadies me, gives me something to hold onto. This could be my chance to stand on my own, to reach something closer to the Jacksons level. Not the same amount of wealth...they're in a league of their own...but acclaim. Recognition. Enough to step out from the shadow of my dad's station and into a light of my own.

I glance down at my plate, pushing the eggs around with my fork. I love my dad, but being around the Jacksons all my life has taught me one thing: I want more. Much, much more.

When I finish eating, I hesitate. My fitting at Tod's is coming up, and the thought of navigating Rome's unfamiliar streets alone fills me with unease. I want to ask Zack for a ride, but he looks so absorbed in his work. The idea of interrupting him, of admitting I might need him for something as simple as a ride, makes my stomach churn.

I push my chair back, standing quickly. Better to leave now than wrestle with the growing tension knotting in my chest.

· · ·

But before I can take a step, his hand shoots out, catching mine. The touch sends a jolt through me, an electric charge that leaves me breathless. So, he was aware of me. Hm. I try to pull away instinctively, but his grip is firm, warm, and unrelenting.

"Where are you going?" he asks, his voice low and commanding.

I turn to face him, my heart racing. His dark eyes lock onto mine, the intensity in his gaze pinning me in place.

"Work," I manage to say, though my voice betrays the storm inside me. My pulse is thundering, the heat of his hand wrapped around mine making it hard to think straight. His grip is firm, just tight enough to keep me there, to remind me that he has the upper hand.

"For Tod's," he states.

"Yes," I reply, my voice barely above a whisper.

"How are you getting there?" he asks, his voice calm but carrying an edge that sends a shiver down my spine.

"The bus," I say quickly, too quickly. I can feel his gaze tighten on me, like he's dissecting my words, my reasons.

. . .

His brow arches slightly, a flicker of disapproval crossing his face. "The bus?" he repeats, and there's a weight to the words, a quiet challenge that I can most defiantly place.

"Yes," I say again, firmer this time. But the tremor in my voice betrays my nerves. I can feel his eyes on me, heavy with judgment, the kind of look that makes me want to squirm. He's dissecting my answer, probably thinking about last night... about the trouble I got into for making the same decision. It's as if he's pinning me in place with nothing more than his quiet disapproval, daring me to admit I might need him.

I try to pull my hand free, but his grip lingers for just a moment longer before he finally lets go. The loss of his warmth feels sudden, jarring, but I force myself to straighten my bag on my shoulder and take a step back.

"You're sure?" he asks, his voice still calm but edged with something sharper. Concern? Frustration? I can't tell, and I don't dare look too closely.

"I'm sure," I reply, turning my back before he can say anything else. My steps are quick and deliberate, but each one feels heavier than the last. I know he's watching me as I leave, and the weight of his gaze presses against my spine like a hand I can't shake off.

. . .

I should've taken the ride. It would've been easier, safer, and far less chaotic. But the idea of being trapped in the car with him, so close, with his presence filling the air like some suffocating force, is more than I can handle. I need space. I need air. I need time to figure out what's happening inside my own head with my career and Brett before I let Zack Jackson invade it any further.

The bus stop is just down the block, near a line of small cafes and boutique shops that glitter in the morning sunlight. The street is alive with motion...pedestrians bustling past, scooters zipping by, and the faint hum of conversation blending with the clink of cups and plates from the cafe terraces.

The bus arrives with a loud hiss of brakes, and I step on, clutching the pole tightly as it lurches forward. The ride is bumpy, the city's cobblestone streets jarring the frame of the bus and making me tighten my grip. My thoughts swirl, a chaotic mess of nerves and doubt.

When I finally arrive at Tod's, I'm a mess. My blouse clings to my back, damp from the heat, and my hair feels limp, the loose waves I'd carefully styled this morning now frizzy from the humidity. I glance at my reflection in the polished glass of the building's facade and grimace. Not exactly the picture of a confident, polished model.

Inside, the air is cool and buzzing with quiet efficiency. A receptionist checks me in and leads me to the fitting area, where the other models are already gathered. My heart sinks the moment I see them.

They're stunning.

Tall, elegant, and so effortlessly beautiful it feels almost painful. One girl has a striking, angular face with cheekbones so sharp they could cut glass. Another has skin that glows under the soft light, her dark eyes framed by lashes that look like they belong in a mascara commercial. They're all so distinct, so memorable, the kind of women you'd never forget after seeing them once.

And then there's me.

I catch my reflection in a nearby mirror as I'm handed a sleek black dress with leather accents for the fitting. My features are softer, less defined. My lips are full, my eyes wide and bright, but there's nothing extraordinary about me. I'm just... pretty.

Pretty isn't enough.

My stomach tightens as I follow the stylist toward the main fitting area. The other models are already scattered around, chatting casually with assistants or posing in front of mirrors as their outfits are adjusted. They seem at ease, moving with the kind of grace that feels out of reach for someone like me.

. . .

The stylist leads me to a corner where a woman in a crisp white blouse and thick-framed glasses greets me with a polite smile. "You must be Jenny," she says, extending her hand. Her tone is warm, but there's a sharpness to her gaze that makes me feel like I'm being appraised.

"Yes," I reply, shaking her hand and trying to muster a confidence I don't feel.

"I'm Elena," she introduces herself. "I oversee all new campaigns for Tod's. We're excited to have you on board."

Her words should be comforting, but instead, they feel heavy. Like I need to prove I belong here, like being handed this opportunity isn't enough...I have to earn it.

"You're aware of the terms in your contract, yes?" Elena asks, motioning for an assistant to bring over a clipboard.

I nod, though my heart speeds up slightly. "Yes. Three months, covering a range of shoots and events, right?"

"Correct," she says, flipping through the paperwork as though double-checking. "It's important that you understand what's expected. Tod's prides itself on professionalism and precision. Your punctuality, attitude, and adaptability will all reflect on us, so we expect nothing less than excellence."

"Of course," I say quickly, though her words only make the pressure in my chest tighten.

She hands the clipboard to me, pointing to the last page. "Sign here to confirm everything, and then we'll get started with the fitting."

I scrawl my name across the paper, my hand trembling slightly, and hand it back. Elena nods and gestures to the stylist. "Let's get her into the first look."

The black dress is sleek and sophisticated, with leather accents that add just the right touch of edge. The stylist helps me into it, carefully adjusting the straps and smoothing the fabric over my shoulders.

"Beautiful," she says with a smile, stepping back to admire her work.

I turn toward the mirror, my heart sinking slightly as I take in my reflection. The dress fits perfectly, hugging my curves in a way that feels both flattering and foreign.

I shift uncomfortably as the photographer approaches, his camera hanging around his neck.

"Jenny, right?" he asks, his voice brisk but not unkind.

. . .

"Yes," I reply, trying to steady my voice.

"Great. We'll start with some simple poses to get a sense of your angles," he says, gesturing toward the backdrop.

I step onto the small platform, the bright lights overhead making my skin feel warm. The photographer gives quick, precise instructions as he begins snapping photos.

"Chin up. Relax your shoulders. Eyes here…perfect."

I do my best to follow his lead, but every movement feels stiff, unnatural. I catch glimpses of the other models out of the corner of my eye, their poses fluid and effortless, and it only makes me more self-conscious.

"Good," the photographer says after a few more clicks of the camera. "Let's try a smile. Not too much…soft and natural."

I force a smile, but it feels wrong, like it doesn't belong on my face.

I should be much better than this. Maybe it's the pressure because this is a much bigger gig… a much bigger opportunity?

.   .   .

I release a heavy sigh and try my best to keep my inner battle off my face.

After the first set of photos, I'm led to a small table where the creative team has gathered. They're deep in discussion, flipping through sketches and fabric swatches, but they pause as Elena introduces me.'

A man with salt-and-pepper hair and a thick Italian accent stands and shakes my hand. "Welcome," he says warmly. "I'm Marco, head of design. You'll be wearing a lot of my creations, so make sure you bring them to life, sì?"

"Of course," I reply, my smile faltering slightly under his expectant gaze.

Another woman, younger and with a clipboard in hand, nods toward me. "We'll be shooting in different locations throughout Rome. Villa Borghese, the Spanish Steps...iconic spots. Be ready to work hard, but I think you'll do great."

"Thank you," I say, my voice barely above a whisper.

As the meeting wraps up and I'm ushered back toward the fitting area, the weight of everything presses down on me.

The expectations, the comparisons, the constant feeling of being out of place.

I think of Brett. His easy smile, his endless optimism. If he were here, he'd tell me not to worry. He'd tell me I'm beautiful, that I have nothing to be afraid of. And for a moment, I wish I could hear his voice, feel his reassurance.

But then, unbidden, Zack's image creeps into my mind. His sharp eyes, his commanding presence, the way he looks at me like he knows exactly what I'm thinking. What would he say if he were here?

He wouldn't coddle me, that's for sure. He wouldn't tell me everything's fine or that I'm perfect as I am. He'd challenge me. Push me. And for some reason, that thought sticks with me longer than it should, sending a faint shiver down my spine.

Why does he make me feel this way?

I shake the thought from my head as the flash of light nearly blinds me. It's just the reminder I need to scrape all of this nonsense out of my head and focus solely on my work.

CHAPTER
Twenty

ZACH

The vaulted ceilings of the palazzo seem to press down as Mark clicks through slides, his voice a steady drone against the backdrop of a room humming with possibility. Frescoes overhead, their colors softened by time, hint at the stories this place has already witnessed. I lean back in my chair, fingertips grazing the edge of the polished table, my focus shifting between the presentation and the view through the arched windows.

The Spanish Steps rise in the distance, a reminder of the property's prime location and the stakes riding on this venture. Months of consideration have brought me here, but it's the newfound connections through Elizabeth's father that make this moment feel within reach. The right contacts. The right leverage. The right time.

"This valuation aligns with projected growth in luxury development," Mark says, his tone careful, almost reverent.

I don't look at him. My gaze is locked on the sun-drenched courtyard below, where tourists mill about, their laughter rising faintly through the open window. "And the permits?"

Mark hesitates. "Expeditable, with the relationships we've cultivated."

I nod once, slow and deliberate, the weight of the potential filling the silence between us. This is mine to claim, my vision to build. It's not about Elizabeth's family...not directly...but their influence hangs over this deal, an invisible thread weaving opportunity into my hands. I tap my pen against the table, a slow rhythm that matches the pulse of the city outside.

Mark clears his throat, continuing the pitch, but his words fade into the background. My mind drifts, unbidden, to another image...hazel eyes that flash with defiance, a slip of a dress catching the moonlight. Jenny. Even now, miles away and focused on her fitting, she's still here, threading through my thoughts like she belongs there.

I exhale sharply, dragging my attention back to Mark, the room, the deal. Focus. There's too much at stake to lose sight of what matters. Too much to let anything...or anyone... distract me.

After the meeting comes to an end, though, my mind once again drifts to her. This trip is a good chance to handle business, but the fact is that the focus is on Jenny. I find, however, that I'm doing what I can to avoid my focus being on her, and it aggravates me that I'm so concerned about getting close that I'm dodging this. I should be bold, uncaring, and as usual, determined to take what I want and bend everything to my will.

However, when it comes to her, I feel exhausted and conflicted. Sighing, I decide that now is the time to take control and do what I have to. Perhaps slowly, with the time we have here, a way will open up. Perhaps we wouldn't even have to get intimate at all, and I can just talk some sense into her…getting her to let go of her fantasies with Brett and focus more on her career.

I step outside onto the terrace overlooking the city. The view is breathtaking…Rome sprawling out beneath me, a mix of ancient ruins and modern elegance. But it doesn't hold my attention for long. I pull out my phone and call Simone, one of the executives at Tod's and the person who helped secure Jenny's spot in the campaign.

She answers on the second ring, her tone light and curious. "Zack, to what do I owe the pleasure? Not often I get a call from you during working hours."

"Simone," I say, leaning against the railing, my voice steady. "How's the fitting going?"

"Finished a little while ago," she replies smoothly. "Thanks for recommending her, by the way…she's an interesting choice."

"Interesting?" I echo, the word tugging at my curiosity. "What does that mean?"

"She did well," Simone continues, her tone thoughtful. "Better than I expected, actually. She's got something…fresh, unpolished, but in a good way. She just doesn't know it yet."

That gives me pause. "Doesn't know it?"

"Impostor syndrome," Simone explains, her voice softening. "It's not uncommon, Zack. She's new, trying to find her footing. She's got potential, but she doesn't see it yet. Honestly, she's holding herself back more than anyone else is."

I press my thumb against the railing, the rough metal grounding me. That shouldn't bother me, but it does. I can picture her now…hesitant, unsure, doubting herself in a room full of women who have no idea what doubt even looks like. And yet, she's still standing.

"Keep me updated," I say, my voice more curt than I intend.

"Of course," Simone replies smoothly.

I nod to myself, ending the call without another word. As I slip my phone into my pocket, my gaze shifts to the streets below. She's done for the day, and if I know her, she'll be trying to handle the city on her own again.

I call my chauffeur to meet me downstairs, and within minutes, I'm on my way to her. It's not hard to find her... standing at a bus stop close to the Tod's office, looking slightly frazzled but no less beautiful. She's clutching her bag tightly, her shoulders tense as she waits. The sight of her, so stubbornly self-reliant, sparks equal parts irritation and admiration.

I step out of the car, my polished shoes clicking against the cobblestones as I approach her.

"Jenny," I call, my voice cutting through the ambient noise.

She turns, startled, and nearly drops her bag. Her eyes widen when she sees me, a flicker of something...relief... annoyance...crossing her face. "Zack," she says, her tone guarded. "What are you doing here?"

"I was nearby," I lie, gesturing to the bus stop. Its not a very good lie but yet she doesn't seem to notice or even care.

I step closer, noting the weariness in her posture, the thoughtful stillness in her eyes. She's calmer now, reflective, as if the day has settled something in her. There's no defensiveness, just a quiet uncertainty that makes her look even more vulnerable.

"Come on," I say, gesturing toward the car. "I'll take you back."

Her eyes linger on the bus stop for a moment before she speaks, her voice soft, reflective. "I thought I'd just walk around for a bit. I don't know when I'll get a chance to see Rome like this again."

There's a wistfulness in her tone, an unspoken worry threading through her words. It's not about sightseeing; it's about something deeper. She most probably had a nerve-wracking day. According to Simone she was most likely under a lot of performance pressure especially from herself.

I step closer, keeping my voice low and steady. "You'll see a lot more. This is just the beginning."

She glances at me, her hazel eyes flickering with doubt. "Is it?"

I nod, watching her carefully. "Of course. You're a model now. Travel comes with the territory."

She holds my gaze for a moment, something unreadable in her expression, then looks away. "Am I?" she murmurs, almost to herself. Then, without waiting for a response, she turns and starts walking, her bag shifting on her shoulder.

I follow her, matching her pace as the cobblestone streets of Rome unfold around us. The air is warm, the city alive with its usual rhythm...street performers strumming guitars, couples strolling hand in hand, the distant hum of Vespas weaving through traffic. For a while, we don't speak, the silence between us comfortable yet heavy with unspoken thoughts.

We pass a small piazza where a fountain sparkles under the evening light. I catch her glancing at it, her steps slowing slightly. "How was your first day?" I ask, breaking the quiet.

She exhales softly, her gaze fixed ahead. "It was... good," she says, though her tone carries hesitation. "Different. A lot to take in."

I nod, keeping my tone casual. "It'll get easier. First days always feel like that...like everything's too big, too much. But you'll find your rhythm."

She looks up at me, her brow furrowing slightly. "Why are you walking with me?" she asks, not accusing, just curious.

I pause for a beat, considering how to answer. "You're done with work for the day," I say finally. "I want dinner, and I thought of you."

The words feel strange even as I say them. I don't think about people like this, not normally. But with her, it's different. I actually mean it and I'm just as taken aback as she is. She doesn't press me for more, though I can tell the answer surprises her as much as it surprises me.

We continue walking, the city unfolding around us like a living postcard. We pass a gelateria, its bright awning spilling light onto the sidewalk. I stop, nodding toward it. "Gelato?"

She hesitates, shaking her head. "I'm fine."

I glance at her as we pass the gelateria, its warm light spilling onto the cobblestone street. The faint hum of chatter and the rich, creamy scent of gelato hang in the air. I stop, nodding toward the entrance. "Come on. Ice cream's always a good idea."

She hesitates, her arms crossing loosely over her chest. "I'm not really in the mood."

I step closer, lowering my voice slightly. "Hazelnut and chocolate. That's your favorite, isn't it?"

Her brows lift in surprise, and for the first time tonight, I catch a flicker of emotion breaking through her distracted calm. "How do you know that?"

I shrug lightly, a small smirk tugging at my lips. "It might be easy to forget this but I've known you since you were a baby. Come on. You've had a long day. Let's get something to take the edge off."

She hesitates, glancing toward the glowing interior of the gelateria, her expression softening but still tinged with uncertainty. "Okay," she murmurs finally, letting out a quiet sigh.

Inside, the cool air greets us, carrying the sweet scent of fresh cones and vibrant gelato. She stands at the counter, her gaze flicking over the endless choices, but I notice how her focus lingers...not on the flavors, but somewhere far away. Her posture is relaxed but distant, as though her mind is miles from here. The oversized black satin dress she's wearing flows elegantly down to her calves, paired with sneakers that make her seem both poised and playful. She's stunning, even now, caught in a moment of distraction.

"What are you thinking about?" I ask softly, leaning slightly closer.

She blinks, turning to me as if pulled from a dream. "Nothing. Just... everything."

Her answer makes me pause. I watch her carefully, struck by how vulnerable she seems, how real. For a moment, I forget the controlled, calculated version of myself I usually present.

"You're going to be fine, you know," I say quietly. "Today was just the beginning. You'll figure it out."

She looks at me, her hazel eyes softening, though doubt still lingers there. "You really think so?"

"I know so," I reply. "It's the same with business. Sometimes... the strain wears down on you. I hope, though, they didn't work you too hard today."

"No, no," she says. "They were fine. Kind. Patient. Very patient."

Her lips part once again, as though she's about to say something, but instead, she turns back to the counter, studying the flavors again. I step forward, nodding to the server. "Two scoops...hazelnut and chocolate for her, and pistachio for me."

When I hand her the small cup, her fingers brush mine, and for a brief second, something unspoken passes between us. She looks at the gelato, then at me, a hint of a smile pulling at her lips.

After a quick glance around I find a park bench and we head over to it.

She sits hesitantly, the soft fabric of her dress catching the light as she moves. Her sneakers tap against the cobblestones, and for the first time tonight, she looks more relaxed. She takes a tentative bite, her lashes fluttering slightly as the flavor hits her tongue.

Her eyes widen, and she lets out a quiet laugh. "Okay, this is… really good."

I lean back, watching her with a faint smile. "Told you. Sometimes it's the simple things."

For a while, we sit in silence, the hum of the city around us. I steal glances at her as she eats, struck by the way she seems to belong here, in this moment, more than she realizes. The air between us feels different tonight…not just charged, but… softer. Like something unspoken is starting to take root.

The bench we sit on is nestled under the shade of tall cypress trees in the Villa Borghese Gardens. The soft rustle of leaves swaying in the evening breeze mingles with the distant hum of Rome…its city streets alive yet softened by the sanctuary of this place. The gelato melts slowly in my cup, but I can't seem to focus on anything but her.

She's quiet, savoring each bite, her hazel eyes fixed on the scene ahead of us. A couple rides past on bicycles, laughing as they wobble along the path, their carefree joy oddly infectious. She follows them with her gaze, her lips twitching as if tempted to smile but holding back.

"It's beautiful here," she murmurs, breaking the silence.

"It is," I reply, though my eyes are on her. The way the fading sunlight catches in her hair, the slight tilt of her head as she watches the world go by…she looks so effortlessly captivating, even in this unguarded moment.

She finishes her gelato and sets the cup down on the bench beside her. "I've been thinking…" she starts, then trails off, her voice soft but uncertain.

"About?" I prompt, gently, leaning forward to rest my elbows on my knees. My tone is casual, but my curiosity is anything but.

Her fingers toy with the hem of her satin dress, the material slipping between her fingers. "Today, at the fitting. The other models... they seemed so confident, so sure of themselves. It made me wonder if I even belong in a place like this."

"You do," I almost say, but what's the point? Blind reassurance isn't what she needs right now. It wouldn't help her, and honestly, it wouldn't be true...not in the way she'd want to hear it. So, I choose something else, something more fitting for her.

"Do you want to belong?" I ask instead, keeping my voice steady.

She freezes, caught off guard by the question. Her head tilts slightly as she processes it, her eyes flicking to mine. I can see her turning it over, trying to find an answer, though she doesn't speak right away. The silence isn't awkward...it's thoughtful, weighted, and I let her have it.

After a moment, her gaze drops to her lap, her fingers fidgeting with the hem of her dress. "I don't know," she says softly, almost to herself.

Her vulnerability in this moment catches me off guard, the way she's willing to admit what most people would avoid saying. I lean forward slightly, resting my arms on my knees. "Figuring that out is part of it," I tell her. "Belonging isn't handed to you. You carve it out yourself."

"Right," she nods and continues with her ice cream.

"I used to ride bikes all the time as a kid," she says suddenly, her tone wistful. "I don't think I've been on one since."

The words catch me off guard. I glance at her, noting the faint smile tugging at her lips, the distant look in her eyes. She's not talking to me, not really...she's talking to a memory, something softer, simpler. I let the silence stretch for a moment, letting her have it.

Then she turns her gaze toward me, a flicker of hesitation

crossing her face. "I'd love to ride one now," she says, her voice quieter, like she's testing the thought out loud. "But you probably wouldn't be interested in something so… casual."

Pointless. I don't know if she's saying that because she believes it or because she's bracing for my rejection. My instinct is to brush it off…keep things structured, predictable. But something about the way she says it makes me pause.

For a moment, I don't respond, studying her instead. Her expression is guarded, but there's an undercurrent of longing there, like she's daring herself to ask for something just for the joy of it. And damn it, for some reason, I want to give it to her.

"You know what?" I say, my voice calm. "Let's do it."

Her eyes widen, surprise flickering across her face. "You're serious?"

I shrug, keeping my tone even. "Why not? There's a rental station down the path."

She looks at me like she doesn't quite believe it, like she's waiting for the catch. "You don't seem like the bike-riding type, Zack."

"I'm not but for once, why not," I reply, though I can hear the faint edge of self-amusement in my voice. Truthfully, I'm not sure what's come over me. It's been years…decades, even…since I've done anything as casual as riding a bike.

She glances toward the rental station, her uncertainty softening into something closer to excitement. "You're really going to do this?"

"Sure," I say, already walking toward the station.

She hurries to keep up, her sneakers scuffing lightly against the cobblestones.

At the station, she busies herself examining the bikes, running her fingers over the handlebars and testing the brakes. She's distracted, her brows furrowed as she tries to figure out how the rental process works. I watch her for a moment, noting the way her dress moves as she leans forward, the sheen of her makeup catching the dim light.

"You're stalling," I say, stepping up beside her.

"I'm figuring it out," she replies, her tone defensive but not sharp.

"Let me help," I offer, entering my details into the kiosk. She steps back, watching me as I select two bikes.

When the locks release, she pulls her bike free, testing it cautiously.

"You really don't seem like the type for this," she says again, her tone lighter now, almost teasing.

"I'm not," I admit, lifting my own bike and adjusting the seat. "But tonight's not about me."

Her expression shifts slightly, a flicker of something unspoken crossing her face. She doesn't respond, but the faint curve of her lips tells me enough.

We set off down the path, the crunch of gravel under the tires and the gentle hum of the wheels filling the quiet space between us. The Villa Borghese Gardens stretch out in every direction, the manicured lawns and ancient sculptures glowing faintly under the streetlights. The scent of blooming flowers lingers in the air, mingling with the faint sound of distant laughter and the rustling of leaves in the breeze.

She rides ahead of me, her movements cautious at first, but she quickly grows more confident, the bike weaving lightly as she experiments. Every so often, she glances back at me, her smile growing wider with each turn.

I slow my pace deliberately, watching her from a distance. There's a joy in her movements, something effortless and pure, and for once, I let myself just enjoy the moment. It's not something I've done in years…maybe ever. But tonight, it feels… right.

As we near a clearing, I pull out my phone to check the time and map our location.

"Twenty bucks says I'll get there first."

I shake my head, smirking. "Make it a hundred."

Her eyes widen briefly before she nods, determination flashing in her gaze. "You're on."

And with that, she takes off, her laughter trailing behind her as she gains speed. I linger for a moment, watching her figure disappear down the path, her hair catching the wind. The world feels lighter, freer, in her presence, and for once, I don't mind letting her take the lead.

With a soft chuckle, I start after her, the cool night air rushing past as I pedal, the sound of her laughter echoing in my ears. The city unfolds around us, ancient and alive, and for the first time in years, I let myself simply be.

The restaurant isn't far now…just a short ride through the park. An idea sparks, something unexpected but fitting for the lightness of the moment. "It's not far from here," I say, holding up my phone. "How about we make this interesting?"

She arches a brow, intrigued. "Interesting how?"

I smirk, slipping the phone back into my pocket. "Let's see if you can beat me there."

Her eyes light up with a mix of challenge and mischief. "Twenty bucks says I'll get there first."

I shake my head, my smirk widening. "Let's make it a hundred."

Her mouth opens slightly in surprise before she recovers, narrowing her eyes playfully. "Send me the directions."

I do, and she studies her phone briefly before tucking it away. "You're on," she says, kicking off and picking up speed instantly.

I watch her for a moment, her figure cutting through the fading light as she glances back at me with a grin. I deliberately slow my pace, letting her pull ahead.

The park unfolds around us in pockets of beauty…bronze

statues tucked into alcoves, gardens blooming even in the dim light, and the steady stream of people enjoying the evening. A group of children races past on scooters, their excited shouts ringing out, while an older couple strolls hand in hand, pausing to admire a rose bush. I've spent so much of my life rushing through moments like these, always focused on the next deal, the next victory.

It makes me sigh now, thinking of how many tiny, mundane, magical moments like this I've missed.

About forty minutes later, as the sun dips lower and the sky deepens into twilight, we arrive at Antico Arco.

Jenny beams with triumph as she slows to a stop, her laughter spilling out into the crisp evening air. Her chest rises and falls with exhilaration, her cheeks flushed from the ride, and the faintest sheen of perspiration glistens on her forehead under the soft glow of the streetlights. She leans forward slightly, gripping the bike's handlebars as she catches her breath.

"I told you I'd win," she says between gasps, her voice bright with satisfaction.

I can't help the small smile that tugs at my lips as I step off my bike. "You did," I admit, reaching into my pocket for my handkerchief. The white linen is crisp, my initials embroidered neatly in one corner. I hold it out to her. "Here."

She looks at me, her eyes flicking to the handkerchief before taking it. Her fingers brush against mine briefly, and then she dabs it lightly against her forehead. "Thanks," she murmurs, her voice quieter now, still breathless. She puts it away in her messenger bag.

The sight of her...radiant, glowing from the thrill of victory...renders me momentarily still. She's breathtaking. Not in the overly polished, put-together way the women I usually surround myself with are, but in a way that feels entirely her. Real. Unfiltered. Stunning.

My hand slips into my pocket, retrieving my wallet. I pull out a crisp 100-euro bill and extend it to her, my other hand resting casually on the handlebars. "Your winnings."

Her brows knit together as she glances at the note, then back at me. "Wait... this is a hundred euros. I meant dollars."

"When in Rome..." I reply, tucking the wallet back into my pocket with a faint smirk.

Jenny laughs softly, taking the bill from my hand with a shake of her head.

CHAPTER
Twenty~One

JENNY

The evening air feels lighter after the bike ride, the lingering exhilaration still tingling in my fingertips as I dismount and catch my breath. My chest rises and falls, the warm breeze brushing against my skin, carrying with it the faint, intoxicating scent of Rome. For the first time all day, the tightness in my chest has loosened, replaced by something softer…something that feels almost like hope.

I glance at Zack as he secures the bikes, his movements calm, efficient, and utterly self-assured. He looks up, his gaze meeting mine briefly, and there's something in his expression…something unreadable but grounding. I tear my eyes away, focusing instead on the soft glow of Antico Arco's lights spilling out onto the cobblestones ahead. The restaurant looks like something out of a dream, perched on a hill with views of the entire city twinkling below. I feel a pang of awe, quickly followed by the familiar ache of not belonging.

I smooth my satin dress, fingers brushing over the soft, flowing fabric that feels both luxurious and oddly childish paired with my sneakers. The thought makes me smile faintly, though the moment is fleeting. We step inside, and I'm immediately struck by the elegance of the place...the quiet hum of conversation, the faint clinking of glasses, the refined atmosphere that seems almost too perfect. It's not new to me, not really. Growing up with the Jacksons meant I spent more time in places like this than most people ever would. But tonight, it feels different. This isn't their world anymore. It's mine. Or at least, I want it to be.

The hostess leads us to a table by the window, where the view outside is breathtaking. Rome sprawls out in golden lights, the distant hum of the city muted by the glass. I slide into my seat, trying not to fidget as I glance around. The other women in the restaurant are striking...dressed to perfection, their every movement polished and effortless. My stomach twists, the same sinking feeling I'd had at the fitting creeping back. I don't belong here. Not really.

Zack settles across from me, and I steal a glance at him as he shrugs off his tie, setting it aside with deliberate ease. He unbuttons the top two buttons of his crisp white shirt, his sleeves rolled up to reveal strong, tanned forearms. His dark hair is tousled from the ride, and the soft lighting makes his pale grey eyes almost translucent. It's impossible not to notice him...breathtaking in a way that feels dangerous, as if he's too perfect to be real. Brett, I remind myself. Brett is approachable, warm, easy to be around. Zack... Zack is something else entirely.

I hate to compare them, but truly I cannot help it.

The brush of fabric against my skin brings me back to the moment, and I shift slightly, my nipples brushing against the satin of my dress. My cheeks flush as I force my gaze down to the menu, telling myself it's nothing. Just a reaction. Just a stupid, physical thing. It doesn't mean anything.

"What do you want to drink?" Zack asks, his voice low, calm.

I glance up, meeting his gaze. "Red wine," I say quickly, the words slipping out before I can think them through.

His brow arches slightly. "Wine?"

"Yes." I close the menu and sit back, trying to steady my voice. "I think I need it."

The corners of his mouth lift in the faintest hint of a smile, and for a moment, I think he's going to tease me. Instead, he nods. "Red it is."

When the waiter arrives, Zack barely glances at the menu before ordering with the kind of confidence that seems second nature to him. "The veal saltimbocca," he says, his voice smooth, "with a side of sautéed spinach and roasted rosemary potatoes." He hands the menu back with a nod, adding, "And a bottle of Brunello di Montalcino—2015."

The waiter nods appreciatively, as if Zack's choice carries a weight he respects, before turning to me. I glance down at the menu again, my fingers brushing the edge as I search for something that feels right. "The ravioli al tartufo," I finally say, my voice a bit softer, "with the garden salad on the side."

The waiter writes it down without missing a beat, and I hand him my menu, feeling a little unsure but masking it as best I can.

Zack speaks up again, this time his tone more deliberate. "And decant the wine for us," he adds, leaning back in his chair with an air of quiet authority. "Let it breathe."

I glance at him, surprised by the attention to detail. He catches my look and raises an eyebrow.

"What?"

"Nothing," I say quickly, shaking my head. "You just seem… particular."

"I am," he replies simply, as though that explains everything.

The waiter disappears, and I try to focus on the conversation, but the weight of Zack's presence and his easy command of the situation leaves me feeling oddly out of place...and yet drawn to him even more.

I reach for my glass of water, needing something to occupy my hands. But as I lift it to my lips, the memory of last night flashes unbidden in my mind...the wine we'd shared on the balcony, the tension that had hung heavy between us. The way he'd looked at me, like he could see right through every wall I'd ever built. My grip on the glass tightens, and I force the thought away.

The silence stretches between us, comfortable in a way I didn't anticipate, until I find myself speaking again.

"There are probably so many other people you'd rather be having dinner with right now," I say, the words slipping out before I can stop them. My tone is light, teasing, but there's a genuine curiosity beneath it. "Business partners. Girlfriends. I mean, just look around. There are so many beautiful women in this city."

His gaze doesn't waver, his expression unreadable. "What are you trying to say?"

I shrug, the movement small, almost self-conscious. "Nothing. I'm just... wondering. We've known each other for years, but we've never actually spent time together. Not like this."

He holds my gaze for a moment longer, the weight of his attention making my pulse quicken.

"Unless it's a business dinner. I don't like eating with unfamiliar people."

"Oh," I say, feigning nonchalance, though my heart skips a beat. "So I'm familiar, then."

His lips twitch, the faintest hint of a smile breaking through. "You could say that."

For a moment, the air between us shifts, something

unspoken lingering in space. I glance down at the table, my fingers tracing the edge of my napkin. The city lights outside blur slightly as my focus turns inward, the quiet realization settling over me: Zack isn't like Brett at all. The more time I spend with him, the more the difference between them becomes stark, and I cannot help but admit to myself that maybe, just maybe, I might prefer the dangerous heat that Zack stokes in me to the warm and sweet one that Brett does.

The silence stretches as our food arrives, each dish a work of art plated so beautifully it feels wrong to disturb it. Zack doesn't speak, but I can feel his presence like a weight in the air. He watches me as I take my first bite, the rich flavors melting on my tongue, but his gaze is so steady, so unreadable, it makes my pulse skip.

I try not to fidget under his scrutiny, but the longer we sit, the more I find myself wondering what's going through his mind. He seems so composed, so perfectly in control, but beneath that polished exterior, there has to be more. And for reasons I can't quite name, I suddenly want to know. I want to understand who he is beyond the commanding presence, the calculated looks, the unreadable silences.

"You came to Rome for business, right?" I ask, my voice breaking through the quiet. It's a simple question, but it feels like the first step toward unraveling him.

He pauses, his fork hovering over his plate before he answers. "Partially," he says, his tone measured. "I plan to take some meetings, but I'm treating the rest of the time here as… a sort of holiday."

A holiday? The word feels strange coming from him, like it doesn't quite fit. "You?" I tease, raising a brow. "Taking a holiday?"

He leans back in his chair, the faintest smirk tugging at his lips. "Right."

The corners of my mouth lift despite myself. "Well, you should. Rome's beautiful. I might just do the same."

"You should," he says, his gaze unwavering. "You've earned it."

I nod, setting my fork down and reaching for my wine. "I didn't plan much of an itinerary, to be honest. Everything happened so fast. Plus…" I trail off, hesitating as the words catch in my throat. I don't know why I'm saying this, why I feel compelled to bring it up. "It felt like you were just trying to send me away, so I didn't know how it was going to play out."

He freezes, his expression sharpening slightly. "But you still came," he says after a moment, his tone quiet but firm.

"I did," I admit, my voice soft. "I came because of the job. And as for you trying to send me away…" I sigh, forcing myself to meet his gaze. "Unless you ban me from the country somehow with your connections, I'm still going to head back eventually. Plus, you've forgotten what I said. I'm moving out."

"Moving out?" he repeats, his brow lifting slightly. "And where exactly do you plan to go?"

I shrug, swirling the wine in my glass. "Let's see after I get my paycheck from today."

He leans forward slightly, resting his elbows on the table, his eyes narrowing as they lock onto mine. "You shouldn't move out too soon," he says, his voice low, almost coaxing. "Your contract's for a few months. You'll be busy."

"Which is exactly what you wanted, isn't it?" I shoot back, though there's no real heat in my tone.

His lips curve into a slow, deliberate smile, the kind that makes my chest tighten. "You can't blame me for trying to exert my influence to get what I want. It's what I do. But ultimately, the choice is yours."

The way he says it, the weight in his words, sends a shiver

down my spine. It's not a threat…it's an acknowledgment, a reminder of his power but also of the fact that, for once, he's leaving something in my hands. The tension between us feels like it's vibrating now, filling the space with an electricity I can't ignore.

I hold his gaze, my pulse quickening as the silence stretches. For a moment, I don't know what to say. But then, a small, wry smile tugs at my lips. "Well, that's… surprisingly generous of you."

He smiles once again, amused, and my heart starts to race. What is it about him?

I want to see him unflustered, though I realize I want to see him completely lose his composure so that I know I'm not the only one.

This is lust, I remind myself. It's his fault for teasing me. All I have to do is control myself until I get back to New York, and then I'll take matters into my own hands and kiss Brett. I cannot be careless here the same way I almost was with him last night. Plus, if any accidents happen with Zack, I understand that automatically erases any future I could have had with Brett.

All my life, it was the one thing I was sure about, and now I feel somewhat uncertain. I love Brett, but now I wonder if the way Zack makes me feel isn't what I truly want.

"Where are your shoots going to be for the rest of the week?" Zack asks, his tone casual but his eyes focused on me in that way that always seems to strip away my defenses.

I hesitate for a moment, surprised by the question. "Villa Borghese tomorrow," I reply, my voice softer than I intend. "Then the Spanish Steps later in the week. After that, there's some indoor work at a historic palazzo… they want to capture the elegance of the architecture or something like that." I stop, glancing at him. He's still watching me, his expression unreadable but intent.

As I continue, I start to notice something in the way he listens. He's not just nodding politely or waiting for his turn to speak. He's paying attention, really paying attention. I'm not used to this…his focus, the way it feels like he's drawing every word out of me with his quiet, steady gaze.

The silence stretches for a moment before I blurt out, "Do you have a girlfriend?"

The question catches even me off guard. It's impulsive, thoughtless, but now that it's out there, I can't take it back. It's just that I'm realizing now, for the first time ever, that unlike Brett, I haven't actually ever seen him with a woman. My heart pounds as I wait for his reaction, and when he doesn't answer right away, I rush to cover my tracks. "I mean, not that it's any of my business. I just… I've never seen you with anyone. Not that I would know, but…maybe you're… maybe you don't like women?"

His frown deepens at this as he stops chewing entirely, and I want to bury myself in the sand.

"Jenny," he says his voice calm but firm enough to make me stop rambling. His gray eyes narrow slightly, and his lips twitch with the faintest trace of amusement. "Your interest in my personal life seems to be increasing."

My face flames.

"It's not," I say too quickly, the words tripping over themselves. "I was just… curious. That's all."

"Curious?" He echoes, his tone making it clear he's not convinced. He watches me for a long moment, his expression unreadable, before finally leaning forward, resting his forearms on the table. "No. I don't have a girlfriend. And no, I am most definitely not gay."

The admission shouldn't affect me as much as it does, but my stomach flips all the same. "Oh," I say, trying to sound indifferent, though I know I'm failing miserably. "I just assumed… someone like you…"

"Someone like me, what?" he asks, his voice low, challenging.

I look up at him, my heart racing. "You're Zack Jackson," I say, as if that explains everything. "Wealthy, powerful, and, well…" My cheeks burn as the rest of the sentence catches in my throat. I don't need to say it. He knows exactly what I mean.

"And?" he prompts, his voice edged with intrigue.

"And nothing," I mutter, turning my attention back to my plate. "Forget I said anything."

For a moment, he doesn't reply. The silence between us feels heavier, charged with something I can't name. Then, unexpectedly, he chuckles softly. "You shouldn't try so hard to hide your thoughts. It's not like you. You've always been honest and loud-mouthed, giving your opinions even when not asked."

This suddenly makes me laugh out loud because my dad, as well as a step-worker I grew up with, always says the same thing.

I'm reliving my time with him, I realize, even though I know I shouldn't be. And soon, I resolve to settle my nerves and treat this simply as what it is…two acquaintances sharing a meal together. I fill up my glass once again and turn my focus to the wine.

CHAPTER
Twenty~Two

ZACH

"Let's go dancing," she says suddenly, her voice light, her hazel eyes sparkling with just enough mischief to make my pulse quicken.

The words catch me off guard. I glance at her, taking in the faint flush on her cheeks and the slight tilt of her lips…a mix of challenge and playfulness. The wine has softened her edges, revealing a side of her I don't often see. It's disarming. And dangerous.

"Dancing?" I ask, keeping my tone neutral even as my mind scrambles to understand what's shifted.

"Yes," she says, leaning forward slightly, her fingers brushing the table as if her excitement can't be contained. Her dress pulls down her chest as she moves, revealing the swell of her breasts in ways that make it hard to focus. "There should be a club not too far from here," she says as she pulls out her phone.

I ignore this and her as I pick up my wine to drain, hoping she soon abandons this completely nonsensical idea. I glance around the restaurant, my gaze sweeping over the elegant women scattered at nearby tables. They're stunning, each one polished to perfection. Yet none of them hold my attention the way she does. Even in her understated satin dress and sneakers, she commands the room…effortlessly striking in a way that makes it impossible to look anywhere else.

However, a few minutes later she exclaims much too loudly. A few heads tun and my eyes go wide.

"Sorry," she says, her cheeks turning red. "I'm sorry."

"Here," she turns her phone screen to my face."

"There is one and it's not far. It's dark now…they should've started by now. I just want to dance for a little bit. Shake off the day."

I'm about to reject the idea outright. I don't do clubs. Loud music and sweaty crowds have never been my thing. But then I catch the way she looks at me, the faint glimmer of expectation in her eyes, and something inside me hesitates.

"You can leave, you know," she says, leaning back in her chair with an air of nonchalance, though I can see the challenge flickering beneath the surface. "Head back to the hotel. I'm just telling you what I'm doing."

Her words are a dismissal, but the thought of leaving her alone…vulnerable, even slightly intoxicated…grates against every instinct I have. My jaw tightens.

"Fine," I say finally, my voice low, deliberate. "Let's go."

Her face lights up instantly, her smile wide and unguarded, and for a moment, I forget why this is such a bad idea. She's radiant, and the light in her eyes is infectious. My chest tightens at the sight, the tension in me softening ever so slightly.

As she leans forward to pick up the wine bottle, her breasts once again presses against the edge of the table. My gaze flickers there despite myself, the sight stirring something primal that I force back. I glance away, shaking my head slightly as if to clear it, but when I look up again, she's already rising from her chair, the excitement practically radiating off her.

This was definitely a terrible idea. But as I follow her out of the restaurant, I can't seem to make myself care.

The drive is quick, the club pulsing with life as soon as we step out of the car. The music thrums through the air, vibrating in my chest, and I already regret this. Inside, it's a chaos of flashing lights, bodies pressed together, and a heat that's almost suffocating.

Jenny seems to come alive in the atmosphere, her head tilted back slightly as she takes it all in. I watch her, caught between irritation at the noise and an unexpected fascination with how the environment seems to suit her.

"I'll get us drinks," I say, raising my voice over the music. She nods, already making her way towards the dance floor.

At the bar, I order something simple…a whiskey for me and a lighter cocktail for her. When I turn back, I see her swaying to the music, her satin dress catching the light in ways that make my throat tighten. Men notice her, of course they do, their gazes lingering too long, some edging closer.

I grip my glass tighter, the coolness of it biting into my palm as my jaw locks. Across the dance floor, a man steps too close to her, his intentions written all over his face. He leans in, his hand hovering near her waist, trying to press into her space. She brushes him off with a polite smile, stepping back with a soft laugh that seems to only spur him on.

My chest tightens, a heat building inside me that I don't want to name. I force myself to look away, focusing on the amber liquid swirling in my glass. I take a long sip, hoping the burn of the alcohol will drown out the burn in my veins.

But it's futile. My eyes find her again as if drawn by a force beyond me. She moves with the music, her body fluid and effortless, the light catching the sheen of her satin dress as it clings to her curves. Her smile is soft, unguarded, and the way she loses herself in the rhythm is magnetic.

It's maddening…how much she commands my attention, how she doesn't even notice the effect she has. The pull of her is intoxicating, and I hate it. But no amount of rationality can stop the way my chest tightens every time another man circles too close, their gazes lingering far too long on what isn't theirs to admire.

I grip my glass tighter, my knuckles whitening. The irritation thrums low and hot beneath my skin, each laugh she gives them like fuel to a fire I can't seem to control. I want to step in, to end it, but I hold myself back. She's entitled to enjoy herself.

But I can't keep my eyes off her for long. The way her body moves to the rhythm, the curve of her smile, the sheer magnetism she exudes…it's intoxicating. And maddening.

When another man gets too close, placing a hand on her waist, I can't take it anymore. I down the rest of my drink and head for the bathroom, needing a moment to compose myself.

I shove the door open and head straight to the sink, gripping the edge so hard my knuckles ache. My reflection stares back at me…tense, flushed, and unrecognizable. The music outside is muffled but still pounding, each thump a reminder of her, of how she moves to it, how she lets them watch her like she's meant for all of them. She isn't. She isn't meant for me either, but my dick doesn't seem to think so.

My hands clench and unclench, and before I can stop myself, one drifts lower, palming the strain in my pants. My cock is thick, heavy, pulsing against my palm. The heat radiating from it feels unbearable, the veins pronounced and flushed, throbbing with every maddening thought of her. I squeeze, and the ache sharpens, driving me to the edge of control. My jaw tightens as I curse under my breath.

I squeeze hard, a sharp hiss escaping my lips, but it only

stokes the fire, the need crawling through me like a fever. The alcohol isn't helping...it's making everything worse. Or maybe it's just her.

I slam into one of the stalls, locking it behind me. My hands tremble as I yank at my zipper, freeing myself from the unbearable constraint. The cool air hits me, and I groan low, wrapping my hand around my length. It's rock hard, the head swollen and already leaking, greedy for something more than my touch. I stroke it roughly, the slickness of precum easing the movement, but it's not enough. The friction feels torturous, pushing me further into desperation.

I press my forehead against the stall wall, stroking harder, faster, imagining her...the way her dress clings to her, the sway of her hips, the teasing glance she threw over her shoulder earlier, like she knew exactly what she was doing to me. The thought of her lips, her skin, the way she moves, bold and intoxicating, has me groaning louder, my breath hitching.

Every pump is a struggle between release and restraint, the pressure building like it's going to rip me apart. My grip tightens, my strokes become brutal, and finally, with a guttural growl, I shatter. My body jerks violently as I come, hot and thick, spilling over my hand. My head tips back, eyes squeezed shut, and all I can see is her...her smile, her laugh, her body moving to the rhythm, claiming every corner of my mind.

The relief washes over me in waves, leaving me trembling, spent, and still wanting. She's inescapable, her presence a torment I can't seem to escape. I clean myself up quickly, my breaths still uneven. But even now, all I can think about is going back out there and claiming her...even though I know that I have absolutely no right to.

This is torture. She's torture.

Back on the floor, my eyes lock onto her immediately, drawn by the subtle tension in her posture. She's surrounded by two men now, their stances too close, their smiles too persistent. She's still smiling, but it's polite...forced. The way she shifts her weight, inching back ever so slightly, tells me everything I need to know. She's uncomfortable, trying to maneuver away without making a scene.

For a moment, I hesitate, forcing myself to assess the scene instead of barreling in. But when one of the men leans in closer, his hand brushing her arm as he murmurs something into her ear, I can't hold back any longer.

I push through the crowd, my stride deliberate, each step fueled by an anger I can't quite contain.

The music pulses around me, the bass thudding in time with my heartbeat. People part instinctively as I move, catching the sharpness in my expression.

By the time I reach her, she's taken another step back, her discomfort more apparent now as one of the men blocks her retreat. Without a word, I step between them, my hand closing firmly around her arm. The warmth of her skin against my palm is grounding, but my focus stays on the men.

"She's with me," I say, my voice low and even, carrying enough weight to make my intentions clear. There's no room for argument in my tone...just cold, unwavering certainty.

The men exchange glances, hesitation flickering in their eyes. One of them opens his mouth as if to protest, but I step closer, my frame looming over theirs, and the unspoken threat in my stance makes him falter. He mutters something under his breath...a weak attempt to save face...and then steps back, pulling his friend with him.

I don't move until they've retreated into the crowd, my gaze following them until I'm sure they won't be back. Only then do I look at her, my grip on her arm loosening but not letting go entirely.

"You okay?" I ask, my voice quieter now, but no less steady.

"Yeah," she says, her voice soft. I don't hear her much, though I make out the word from the movement of her lips. For my own sanity, I don't stay too long. But then she reaches up on her tiptoes for some reason needing to let me hear. Very bad idea.

Then her warm breath seeps into my ear, and my eyes shut for a moment.

I suddenly know that I cannot bear to leave her here. She needs to break away from these leeches around her. And so do I.

I don't let go of her arm, guiding her off the dance floor. "Let's get another drink," I suggest, needing something to ground me.

At the bar, I glance at her and signal the bartender, reordering something new light for her...cranberry juice. No alcohol this time; she's had enough for one night. When the drink arrives, she sips it absentmindedly, her hazel eyes scanning the crowd. It's not until she sets the glass down that she frowns, realizing the vast difference.

"There's no alcohol" she says, looking at me with mild disbelief.

"No," I reply calmly, sipping my own whiskey. "You've had enough."

Her lips purse in a small pout, and she waves the bartender back over, determined to rectify the situation. "Vodka. Double. Add it to this."

I turn to her sharply, arching a brow, but I say nothing. The bartender hesitates, glancing at me for approval. I sigh and nod, letting her have her way. She watches as the vodka is poured into her cranberry juice, and then, with a defiant lift of her chin, she takes a long, deliberate sip.

I lean back, sipping my drink as I watch her, my gaze

fixed on the way her lips curve against the glass. She finishes the concoction quickly, setting the glass down with a satisfied exhale.

"There," she says, her tone slightly smug. "Much better."

Before I can respond, she leans into me, her body swaying slightly from the alcohol. I'm seated on a barstool, and within moments, she's closer…too close. Her hips press against my knees, her hands lightly gripping the edge of the bar for balance as she tilts her head up to look at me.

"Why so serious?" she drawls, her voice soft but teasing. Her hazel eyes lock onto mine, her lips curling into a faint smile. "You should loosen up. Let's dance."

"No," I say firmly, my voice steady as I shake my head. I glance around for the bartender, intending to order another whiskey, but she's quick to intercept.

"Then buy me another drink," she demands, her tone playful but persistent.

"You've had enough," I repeat, my tone edging toward exasperation.

"Fine," she mutters, her lips quirking mischievously as her hand moves to rest on my chest. The sudden contact sends a jolt through me, her palm warm and soft against my shirt. My breath catches as her fingers linger, her touch light but charged.

"Jenny," I say quietly, reaching up to take her hand and pull it away. My voice is firm, though there's no edge to it. "That's not a good idea."

She frowns slightly, but she doesn't protest as I let go of her hand. Instead, she leans back against the bar, her gaze flicking between me and the now-empty glass on the counter. There's a beat of silence, and then she smirks, a teasing glint in her eyes.

"Still no dancing?" she asks, tilting her head slightly.

"Still no," I reply, my tone dry but amused.

She huffs softly, shaking her head before motioning to the bartender again. The playful challenge in her eyes lingers, but I can't help the way my gaze follows her every move. She's a contradiction...daring yet delicate, bold yet vulnerable...and it's driving me insane.

"Another, please," she orders, and I shake my head at the bartender.

"No," I say. "Water," I tell the bartender, and thankfully, this time she doesn't protest, just looks sourly at me and pouts, and I swear to God I nearly kiss her right there.

The air feels heavier, charged with the weight of unspoken tension. Jenny sits close, her hazel eyes bright with mischief and softened by the glow of the club's dim lighting. Her pouting lips, her playful challenge, the way her hair falls in loose waves over her shoulders...it's all maddeningly irresistible.

She leans back against the bar, swirling the water I insisted on ordering for her in the glass, her movements lazy yet deliberate. I should be relieved she's finally drinking something nonalcoholic, but the way her pout deepens with every sip almost makes me regret it. Almost.

I want to taste the alcohol on her tongue, taste the heat of her. Sighing once again, I shut my eyes for a moment and lean against the counter, but then all I can think of is what she would look like on her knees with my cock in her mouth as she sucks me off. Hungry, greedy, excited, radiant.

Fuck!

"Uh oh,"she suddenly says and eye yes flash open in alarm.

"What is it?"

Her gaze shifts past me, and I follow it to see one of the men from earlier making his way toward us, his posture cocky, his expression smug. My entire body tenses as he approaches, his intentions as obvious as the cheap cologne trailing behind him.

"Is she your girlfriend?" he asks, his tone laced with challenge. His accent is thick, his words sharp.

I force myself to remain calm, though my fingers curl tighter around the edge of the bar. "No," I reply evenly, my voice low and measured.

The man smirks, emboldened. "Then you have no reason to worry, eh?"

He steps closer to Jenny, leaning in as though I'm not even there. She stiffens, her cheeks flushing as she tries to step back, but the bar limits her movement. "I'm fine, thanks," she says quickly, her voice firm but polite.

"Come on," he presses, his hand reaching for hers. "Just one dance—"

That's it. Before I even realize what I'm doing, I've moved, stepping between them with deliberate force. My hand finds Jenny's arm, pulling her gently but firmly behind me as I plant myself in front of the guy.

"She said she's fine," I say, my voice dangerously calm. My eyes lock onto his, the challenge clear.

The man hesitates for a moment, taken aback by the intensity of my tone, but he recovers quickly, his smirk widening. "Relax, man," he says, raising his hands in mock surrender. "No need to get aggressive."

I don't respond, my glare enough to make him shift uncomfortably. He looks between us, clearly weighing his options.

The man doesn't back down. Instead, he steps closer, his hand moving toward Jenny's arm again.

The music pounds louder, a disorienting backdrop to the flash of heat that rushes through me.

The man's smirk only widens as I say coldly, "Let her go."

Instead of listening, he leans in closer, his hand brushing

Jenny's arm in a way that's too familiar, too deliberate. Jenny stiffens, stepping back instinctively, her discomfort evident. The man doesn't care; if anything, her reaction seems to spur him on.

"Come on," he says, his voice loud and slurred. "Just one dance."

My patience snaps. The music, the crowd, the flashing lights...all of it fades into the background. I step forward, my presence towering over his smaller frame. "I said, let her go," I growl, my voice low and deadly.

But the man doesn't heed the warning. Instead, he chuckles darkly, muttering something under his breath as he reaches for her again.

And then it happens.

The world narrows into a sharp, red-hot focus. My hand moves before I can think, curling into a fist that drives straight into his jaw with a force that sends him reeling. The sickening crunch of bone echoes louder than the bass of the club's speakers. He stumbles back, crashing onto the floor in a heap, clutching his face as blood spills between his fingers.

"Fuck! You broke my jaw!" he howls, his voice barely audible over the music. A ripple of gasps and murmurs spread through the crowd, and I can feel the weight of dozens of eyes on us. Jenny stands frozen beside me, her lips parted in shock as chaos briefly blooms around us.

The man writhes on the ground, his curses muffled by the pounding beat and the frantic energy of people scrambling to get out of the way. I tower over him, my chest heaving, fists clenched, daring him to move, to say something else, to try again. But he doesn't. He stays down, his groans of pain mingling with the music.

Jenny's hand closes around my arm, tugging gently but urgently. "Zack," she says, her voice barely above a whisper. "Let's go."

Her touch anchors me, pulling me back from the edge of my fury. My jaw tightens, but I don't move until I'm certain he won't get up again. Only then do I turn, my arm slipping around Jenny protectively as I guide her through the parting crowd, the weight of the moment still heavy in the air.

The night is cool when we step outside, but it does little to soothe the heat still coursing through me. Jenny's hand trembles slightly as it rests on my arm, and I glance down at her, my expression softening. She looks up at me, her hazel eyes wide and searching, and for a moment, neither of us speaks.

Finally, she breaks the silence, her voice shaky but firm. "You didn't have to do that."

"Yes, I did," I reply, my tone leaving no room for argument.

She doesn't respond, her gaze dropping as she swallows hard. I open the car door for her, ushering her inside before sliding in beside her. The tension in the car is palpable, the silence heavy with words unsaid. But I don't care about the stares or the whispers we left behind. All that matters is she's safe.

And I'll make damn sure it stays that way.

CHAPTER

Twenty-Three

JENNY

The silence in the car is suffocating, save for the low hum of the engine and the faint, distant thrum of my heartbeat in my ears. My body is buzzing…not just from the alcohol but from everything. The chaos of the club, the way he'd stepped in, the raw fury in his eyes as his fist connected with that man's jaw…it's all swirling in my head, too vivid, too intense. I press my fingers against my thighs, trying to steady myself, but it's useless. I feel like I'm trembling from the inside out.

In the dim, shifting lights that spill in through the car windows, Zack looks... otherworldly. His hair, tousled and wild from the commotion, falls across his forehead in dark waves. The sharp line of his jaw is taut, his lips pressed together in a grim line as he stares out of the window, his expression unreadable. The veins in his neck are still faintly visible, his hands resting on his knees clenched just enough to make the tendons stand out.

I can't stop sneaking glances at him, my gaze drawn to the

strength in his posture, the way he holds himself like nothing could ever shake him. And yet, he's silent. The distance between us feels like a chasm, and I'm not sure if it's because he's furious or because I've done something wrong. I shift uncomfortably in my seat, the lingering heat from the alcohol pooling low in my stomach, making everything feel heavier, sharper.

My skin feels too tight, my thoughts spiraling. God, why does he have to look like that? In the club, under the flashing lights, he hadn't seemed real…more like some untouchable hero out of a movie. The fury in his face, the way his hair had fallen into his eyes, the veins in his hands and neck…he'd been a force of nature, terrifying and breathtaking all at once. The memory sends a shiver down my spine, and I have to clench my hands together to keep from doing something stupid. Like touching him.

But I can't stop thinking about the way his body had moved, the sharp precision of his punch, the sheer power in it. It had been savage, raw, and impossibly arousing. I shift again, trying to ignore the ache building inside me, the heat that refuses to dissipate no matter how hard I try to focus on anything else.

"Are you hurt?" I blurt out suddenly, my voice breaking through the oppressive quiet.

He doesn't turn to look at me. "No," he says shortly, his tone clipped.

That's it. Just one word. No glance, no reassurance. I bite my lip, frustration curling in my chest. He's mad. He has to be. Why else wouldn't he look at me? The thought makes my throat tighten. I didn't ask him to do that, to step in like that…but he had, and the fact that he'd done it so fiercely, so completely, makes my heart twist in ways I can't quite understand.

The car keeps moving, the city lights blurring outside the

window, and I can't stand the silence any longer. I inch my hand closer to him, my fingers trembling slightly as they hover near his. It's reckless, stupid, but I can't help myself. I need some kind of connection, some reassurance that he isn't mad at me, although I'm not so sure why I care now when I never have before.

Finally, my hand brushes his, just the lightest touch, but it feels like a spark igniting in my skin. He doesn't move, doesn't acknowledge it, and for a moment, I think he hasn't noticed. But I can feel the tension in the air shift slightly, the weight of his presence tilting toward me in some inexplicable way.

The car slows as we pull up to the hotel, and my stomach twists with something I can't name. Relief, maybe, or disappointment. He opens the door and steps out without a word, waiting for me to follow. I feel a pang of sadness as I slide out of the car. He's still not talking to me. The tension between us is unbearable, and I hate it.

"Say something," I whisper, my voice barely audible as we step into the elevator.

He glances at me, his expression still unreadable. "About what?"

"Anything," I say, my voice breaking slightly. "I'm sorry."

His brow furrows. "What are you apologizing for?"

"If you're not mad," I say softly, my chest tightening, "then why won't you look at me?"

He pauses, his gaze finally shifting to meet mine. His gray eyes are stormy, unreadable, and my breath catches in my throat. "Jenny," he says, his voice low, almost a warning. "You're drunk."

The words should sting, should snap me back to reality, but instead, they make me smile faintly. He's looking at me now, really looking at me, and in the soft light of the elevator, he's even more breathtaking than I remembered. "Maybe," I say, my voice barely above a whisper. "But you still haven't said anything."

He exhales sharply, his jaw tightening as if he's fighting some internal battle. And then, before I can think, before I can second-guess myself, I lean closer. My heart pounds in my chest, my lips parting as I tilt my head up to him. The air between us is charged, electric, and for a moment, I think he's going to pull away.

But he doesn't.

The air between us thickens, heavy with a tension that feels almost tangible. My heart pounds in my chest, each beat louder than the quiet hum of the elevator. He looks at me, his gray eyes intense, searching, as though trying to solve a puzzle he doesn't entirely understand.

Slowly, almost hesitantly, his hand lifts, and before I can fully process what's happening, his fingers brush against my temple. His touch is warm, feather-light, as he tucks a loose strand of hair behind my ear. The gesture is intimate, tender in a way that makes my breath hitch.

"What are you doing?" I whisper, my voice barely audible, the words trembling as they leave my lips.

"What are you doing?" he throws the question back at me.

Neither of us answer, but there's no need for words in this moment. They feel like an interruption…an annoyance.

Instead, his hand moves, grazing the curve of my jaw before sliding to the side of my neck. His palm rests there, his fingers brushing against the sensitive skin just below my ear. The warmth of his touch sends a shiver through me, and I can't help but tilt my head slightly, leaning into him as if pulled by some invisible force.

The elevator stops, the faint ding signaling our floor, but neither of us moves. His thumb strokes the edge of my jaw, his gaze never leaving mine. I feel like I'm standing on the edge of something vast and unknown, and all I can think about is him...the way his hand feels against my skin, the way his eyes hold me captive.

My thighs clench together instinctively, heat pooling low in my belly. My clit throbs with a need so intense it's almost painful, and the ache makes it impossible to focus on anything but the man in front of me. I swallow hard, my breathing shallow, as the moment stretches between us.

His head tilts down, and I feel his breath warm against my lips. Every nerve in my body feels like it's on fire, every ounce of my focus narrowed to the way he's looking at me...like I'm the only thing in the world that matters.

And then, his lips brush mine. It's so light, so fleeting, that I almost wonder if I imagined it. But he doesn't pull away. Instead, he moves closer, his lips returning to mine with more intent. The kiss is deep and slow, unraveling me with every soft, deliberate movement. His hand slides to the curve of my waist, pulling me closer, and I melt into him, my body pressing against his as if we were made to fit together.

The world falls away, and all I can feel is him...the warmth of his lips, the faint hint of whiskey on his breath, the way his chest rises and falls against mine. His other hand moves to the small of my back, steadying me as I lean into him, my fingers tangling in the fabric of his shirt.

Every thought, every worry, every doubt fades into nothingness. All that exists is this moment, this kiss, and the way he makes me feel like I'm burning alive in the most exquisite way possible.

Zack's hands tighten on my waist, pulling me closer until every inch of me is pressed against the hard line of his body. His kiss deepens, consuming, demanding, as if he's trying to draw out every hidden part of me I didn't even know existed. My fingers twist in his hair, the soft strands between my hands anchoring me as my knees threaten to give way.

He pulls back suddenly, his breath hot and ragged against

my cheek. "Jenny," he murmurs, his voice thick with tension. "We should stop."

I look up at him, my chest heaving, my hazel eyes meeting his stormy gray ones. His face is shadowed with conflict, but his grip on me doesn't loosen. "I don't want to stop," I whisper, the words tumbling out before I can think them through. "I can't."

"You're drunk," he says, but his voice lacks conviction, and the way his gaze drops to my lips betrays him. His control is cracking, the sharp lines of his jaw tightening as if he's holding himself back by sheer will.

"I'm not," I insist, though the wine has left me buzzing, my inhibitions stripped raw. "Not enough to not know what I'm doing. Please, Zack."

This is a lie, and the chill that grips my heart at the words makes me know that I am lying to myself. I do not know what I'm feeling, or maybe I know, and it is terrifying, but in this moment, I am completely out of my control because I need to feel, to a greater extent, all of this fire that his mere presence burns me with. Maybe before the end, before we go too far, I will find the courage to stop for the sake of my future with Brett, but this moment is definitely not the moment.

His hand moves to my face, his thumb brushing over my cheek as if he's trying to read me, to find the answer he's searching for. "This is a bad idea," he mutters, almost to himself.

"Maybe," I breathe, my hands trailing down to his chest, the solid warmth of him beneath my fingers sending a shiver through me. "But... just a little more?"

The elevator dings again, the sharp sound cutting through the thick air between us. Before I can process it, the doors slide open, and two women step in, their laughter dying abruptly when they see us tangled together. Their wide-eyed expressions make my cheeks burn, and I pull back from Zack, my breathing ragged as I try to regain some semblance of composure.

He exhales sharply, his jaw clenching as he steps aside to give the women room. They glance at each other, awkward and clearly trying not to stare, as the doors slide shut again. The elevator descends, the silence thick with unspoken tension. My heart pounds in my chest, and I feel Zack's gaze on me, heavy and unrelenting.

When the elevator stops at their floor, the women hurriedly step out, throwing quick, embarrassed glances over their shoulders. As the doors close behind them, I realize we've gone down again, nowhere near our destination.

Zack mutters a curse under his breath, pressing the button for our floor with a sharp jab of his finger. The movement is taut, controlled, but the moment the elevator begins to rise, all control snaps.

He's on me again, his hands finding my waist and grabbing my ass, pulling me flush against him. His lips find mine with a ferocity that makes my head spin, the kiss fierce and unrelenting. My fingers tangle in his hair, holding him to me as if letting go would mean drowning in everything I'm feeling.

The elevator dings once more, the sound barely registering as the doors slide open to our floor. Zack pulls back, his breathing heavy, his hands lingering at my waist as he stares at me with an intensity that leaves me trembling. Without a word, he takes my hand, his grip firm but reassuring, and leads me out.

My legs feel unsteady, my body trembling with adrenaline and something far more dangerous. But his hand is steady, grounding me as we make our way back to the hotel suite. I cling to him, the reality of what's about to happen humming beneath my skin, making every step feel charged.

When we reach the suite, Zack doesn't hesitate. He opens the door to his room and guides me inside, the soft click of the door behind us shutting out the rest of the world.

I reach for him, chest heaving and unable to keep my hands to myself.

My hands are shaking as I undo his buttons one after the other, and then midway through he runs out of patience. He takes the rest of it off himself, and in no time the fabric is flying across the room. The sight of him...broad shoulders, toned chest, the raw power of his physique...makes my breath hitch. He groans softly as I trail my hands over his skin, the muscles beneath flexing at my touch.

His hands slide up my thighs, warm and deliberate, taking my dress with them until the silky fabric bunches around my hips. I shiver at the sensation, his palms gliding over my bare skin, leaving trails of fire in their wake. My breath hitches as I feel the weight of the moment pressing down on me, the tension between us coiling tighter with every second.

Zack pulls back just enough to yank the dress over my head, his movements swift and sure. The cool air brushes against my skin, and I'm left standing in just my bra and panties. My arms instinctively twitch as if to cover myself, but I resist, the thrill of his gaze anchoring me in place.

No man has ever seen me like this before...completely exposed, vulnerable. My heart races as I wonder what he sees, whether he likes it. My bra, delicate and lacy in a soft blush pink, feels suddenly too small, barely able to contain the fullness of my breasts. They're larger than most, over-whelming on my small frame, and for a fleeting moment, insecurity creeps in. I've always felt disproportionate, too much in all the wrong places, and the weight of his silence only amplifies my doubts.

His eyes darken as they rake over me, lingering on every

curve, every inch of bare skin. His gaze pauses at my breasts, his lips parting slightly as if he's momentarily lost himself. The intensity in his expression steals my breath, and my body responds without thought...my back arching slightly, my chest rising as if silently offering myself to him.

"Fuck," he murmurs, the word rough and guttural, sending a shiver down my spine. His hand reaches out, cupping one breast, his thumb brushing over the lace that barely conceals my hardened nipple. The friction makes me gasp, my head tipping back as the heat pools low in my belly.

I'm trembling, overwhelmed by the sheer weight of his attention. My panties...thankfully a matching blush pink... feel soaked against my skin. They cling to me, the evidence of my arousal undeniable, and I'm both mortified and exhilarated. I only wore these because of the shoot earlier today and knew that at some point or the other I would be in my underwear. I couldn't have imagined this was where the day would bring me to.

Otherwise, I would've been in something far less alluring...boxers, maybe, or the plain cotton granny panties I usually wear. The thought makes my cheeks flush even deeper, a tangle of embarrassment and gratitude swirling within me.

Zack's fingers trail down my sides, his touch reverent yet possessive, as if he's memorizing every curve, every freckle, every inch of me. His other hand slips behind me, deftly unhooking my bra. The straps slide down my shoulders, and the garment falls away, leaving me completely bare from the waist up.

I glance up at him, my hazel eyes wide and searching, the anticipation and tension thrumming through me like a live wire. His gaze devours me, his eyes locked on my breasts, full and heavy with each shaky breath I take. My nipples tighten under his scrutiny, the cool air heightening my sensitivity, and I can't help but wonder what he's thinking.

"You're perfect," he says, his voice low and rough, laced with awe. The words hit me like a bolt of lightning, scattering my insecurities and leaving only the raw heat of his approval. His hands slide up, cupping both breasts as his thumbs brush over my nipples, sending jolts of pleasure straight to my core.

I bite my lip to keep from crying out, but a soft whimper escapes anyway, my head falling back as his touch ignites something primal in me. My body leans into his hands of its own accord, desperate for more, the ache between my legs growing unbearable.

I can feel the wetness pooling against my panties, and I know he must see it, the way they cling to me, the darkened fabric betraying just how much I want this. He groans softly, his hands sliding lower, skimming over the curve of my waist and hips before settling on the hem of my panties.

He hooks his hands into the waistband, and he pulls them down slowly, his eyes locked onto mine. The fabric slides over my thighs, then my calves, and finally pools at my feet. I shiver as the cool air brushes against my bare skin, every nerve alight with a mix of anticipation and embarrassment.

When his gaze drops to my exposed sex, my breath catches. I feel completely bare under his eyes, vulnerable in a way that makes my heart pound erratically. No one has ever seen me like this, and the intensity of his stare leaves me trembling. His tongue flicks over his bottom lip, and the raw hunger in his expression sends a jolt straight through me.

"You're soaked," he murmurs, his voice thick and low, more of a growl than a statement. He reaches out, and the moment his fingers slide against my folds, I gasp, my body jolting at the sensation.

"Zack," I whisper, the sound more a plea than a word.

"You're so fucking wet, Jenny," he mutters, his fingers

trailing through the slickness, teasing me, testing me. "It's all for me, isn't it?" His eyes flick up to meet mine, and the intensity in his gaze is enough to steal the air from my lungs.

I can only nod, my hands clutching the edge of the bed for support as his fingers begin to explore me in earnest. His thumb brushes over my clit, slow and deliberate, and my hips buck involuntarily at the surge of pleasure that shoots through me.

"You're so sensitive," he says, his tone laced with something between awe and possession. "You're perfect."

My thighs tremble as he continues, his touch relentless yet achingly precise. My breath comes in short, ragged gasps, and when his finger slips inside me, I freeze. The stretch is new, unfamiliar, and it stings just enough to make my body tense.

Zack notices immediately, his free hand stroking my thigh in a soothing motion. "Relax," he says, his voice softer now, reassuring. "I'll take care of you."

I exhale shakily, forcing myself to release the tension in my body. The sting fades as he begins to move, his finger sliding in and out with measured, deliberate strokes. The discomfort melts away, replaced by a pleasure so sharp it's almost overwhelming.

"That's it," he murmurs, his gaze never leaving mine. "You're doing so good."

When he adds a second finger, I gasp, my hips arching into his touch as the stretch intensifies. The sensation is dizzying, every nerve in my body focused on the way he moves, how he fills me, how he makes me feel like I'm unraveling and coming alive all at once.

He curls his fingers inside me, brushing against a spot that makes me cry out, my hands grabbing into him as a wave of pleasure crashes through me. My thighs tremble uncontrollably, and I feel myself spiraling, unable to keep up with the sensations building inside me.

"Zack, I—" The words die on my lips as his thumb circles my clit again, the combined sensations pushing me closer and closer to the edge.

"That's it," he says, his voice rough, almost unrecognizable. "Let go for me, Jenny."

And I do. The tension snaps, and I shatter around him, my body convulsing as the orgasm rips through me. It's blinding, all-consuming, leaving me trembling and gasping for air. He doesn't stop, his fingers slowing but never leaving me, drawing out every last wave until I collapse onto him spent and trembling.

He pulls his hand away, and I watch through half-lidded eyes as he brings his fingers to his mouth. He licks them clean, his gaze locked on mine the entire time. "You taste incredible," he says, his voice low and almost reverent.

My chest heaves, my mind struggling to process the words, the sensations, the intensity of it all. Before I can respond, my legs give out, and I collapse fully onto the bed, my body still trembling from the aftermath.

Zack doesn't give me time to recover. He moves over me with a predatory grace, his hands spreading my thighs as he lowers himself between them. The heat of his breath against my slick, sensitive sex sends a shiver through me, and before I can catch my breath, his tongue strokes over me, firm and deliberate.

The sensation is electric, sharper than anything I've ever felt. My hands fly to his head, my fingers tangling in his hair as he devours me, his mouth and tongue relentless. Each stroke, each flick sends another jolt through me, the pleasure building faster than I can process.

"Zack!" I cry out, my back arching off the bed as his tongue circles my clit, the pressure perfect, deliberate, maddening. My thighs tremble around him, and my body feels like it's on fire, every nerve alight with a pleasure so intense it borders on pain.

He growls against me, the vibration sending shockwaves through my body. His hands grip my thighs, holding me in place as he buries his face deeper, his tongue working me with a precision that leaves me gasping and shaking.

I lose track of everything...time, space, even my own name...as the sensations spiral out of control. The orgasm hits me like a tidal wave, and I scream, my body convulsing as the pleasure overwhelms me. My vision blurs, my mind blanking out as the waves crash over me, leaving me trembling and utterly spent.

When I finally come back to myself, Zack is hovering over me, his lips glistening, his eyes dark with satisfaction. "You're mine," he says, his voice rough and unyielding. "Every inch of you, Jenny. Mine."

CHAPTER
Twenty~Four

ZACK

"Y ou're mine. Every inch of you, Jenny. Mine."

My voice is raw, the words reverberating through me with a finality that feels like a revelation.

I mean it with every fiber of my being. The claim isn't just a declaration…it's a release, an admission of something I've been denying for far too long. Looking at her now, flushed and trembling beneath me, her hair wild, her lips swollen from my kisses, I feel something shift deep inside me. It's overwhelming, humbling.

Jenny is breathtaking. The faint blush spreading across her cheeks, the way her chest rises and falls with every shaky breath, the softness of her skin, the curves of her body…I've never seen anything like her. She's not just beautiful; she's radiant, glowing from within, her vulnerability only making her more alluring.

I've been with countless women before, but this...this is different. For the first time, I don't care about my own pleasure. All I want is to make her feel good, to give her something unforgettable. Something that no one else ever has or ever will.

I lower myself back to her, pressing a kiss to the center of her chest, just above her pounding heart. She shivers beneath me, and I trail my lips downward, worshiping every inch of her as I go. Her skin is soft, smooth, and warm under my mouth, and the little gasps she makes spur me on, each sound like a spark igniting a fire in my veins.

My lips find her breasts, full and heavy, a perfect contrast to her delicate frame. I take one into my hand, kneading gently as my tongue flicks over her nipple. She arches into me with a soft moan, her hands tangling in my hair as if she can't bear to let go. I suck on her breast, slow and deliberate, and the way her body reacts...her thighs shifting, her hips lifting slightly...makes my cock throb with need.

"Zack," she whispers, her voice trembling, and I glance up at her. Her hazel eyes are half-lidded, glazed with desire, but there's something else there too. Uncertainty. Wonder. She's overwhelmed, caught between the intensity of the moment and her own inexperience, and it makes me pause.

. . .

She moans, arching into me, her fingers tangling in my hair as I give her everything. I move to the other, lavishing it with the same attention, my tongue flicking over her sensitive skin. Her gasps, her shivers…everything about her is intoxicating.

With a sudden burst of boldness, she pushes against me, rolling me onto my back. I let her take control, fascinated by her determination. She straddles me, her bare sex pressing against my hardness through my pants. She begins to move, rocking herself against me, her wetness soaking through the fabric. The sight of her…her head tipped back, her hair cascading over her shoulders, her body moving with instinctual need…makes my cock throb painfully.

"Jenny," I groan, my hands finding her hips, steadying her as she moves against me. "Fuck, you're incredible."

She leans down, her lips capturing mine in a kiss that's all heat and desperation. I roll her back onto the bed, pinning her beneath me as I stand and begin to undress. My shirt is already gone, but my hands are unsteady as I unbuckle my belt, yank down my pants, and finally strip away my briefs and socks. When I stand before her, completely bare, I see her eyes widen.

Her gaze drops to my length, and for a moment, she looks hesitant…shy even…but there's a boldness in her that makes my chest tighten. She sits up slowly; her movements deliberate as she slides off the bed and kneels in front of me.

. . .

"Jenny…" I start, my voice thick with disbelief. She's never done this before…at least, I'm sure she hasn't…but her hands reach out, trembling slightly as she wraps her fingers around me. The touch makes me hiss, my legs nearly buckling as she begins to stroke me.

Her hands are soft, tentative at first, but she watches me closely, gauging my reactions, growing bolder with every movement. My breath catches as she leans forward, her tongue darting out to flick over the tip of my cock. The wet heat of her mouth is almost too much to bear, and when she takes me in, inch by agonizing inch, I throw my head back, a groan ripping from my throat.

"Jenny, fuck," I gasp, my voice hoarse as my hands fist the sheets at my sides. The sensation is unlike anything I've ever felt…her tongue and lips working together with a tentative curiosity that makes my entire body tremble. My thighs tense as her soft, warm mouth wraps around me, and I throw my head back, barely able to process the waves of pleasure crashing through me.

She starts slowly, her lips sliding down my length as far as she can manage. She can't take all of me, but it doesn't matter…the effort alone drives me insane. Her tongue flicks against the sensitive underside as she pulls back, her lips grazing over me with a deliberate slowness that makes my hips jerk involuntarily.

"Jenny," I groan, my voice strained as I fight to stay in control. My eyes flick down to her, and the sight alone is enough to nearly undo me. She's kneeling between my legs, her hazel eyes flicking up to meet mine briefly, her cheeks flushed with heat and determination. My cock disappears into her mouth inch by inch, and when she can't take more, she wraps her small hand around the base, stroking me in time with her movements.

Her grip is tentative at first, her fingers soft and unsure, but then she grows bolder. She tightens her hold, her strokes firm and deliberate, and it's maddening. A sharp groan rips from my throat as I feel the dual sensations of her hand and mouth working together, her tongue pressing against me as her lips slide up and down my shaft.

"Fuck" I hiss, my hands flying to her hair, tangling in the silky strands as my hips buck upward. She moans softly around me, the vibrations sending another jolt of pleasure through my body. I look down again, watching as she takes me deeper, her lips stretched around me, her cheeks hollowing with effort. The sight of her...so beautiful, so utterly focused on me...makes my chest tighten with something I can't name.

Her hand moves faster now, her strokes matching the rhythm of her mouth as she works me with an intensity that leaves me breathless. She pulls back slightly, letting her tongue swirl around the tip before taking me in again, her movements growing more confident with every passing second.

"Jenny, darling," I groan, my voice breaking as my hips move on their own, pushing deeper into her mouth. She adjusts, her fingers tightening around me as her tongue presses against the sensitive underside, stroking in ways that make my vision blur. I feel the pressure building, my entire body tensing as I teeter on the edge.

But then she pauses, pulling back slightly, her lips still wrapped around the tip as her hand strokes me with deliberate precision. The cool air hits the wet skin she's left behind, and I shudder, every nerve alight with the contrast. She glances up at me, her gaze filled with a mixture of shyness and boldness, and it's almost too much.

I groan again, my voice low and desperate. "You're going to…fuck…you're going to make me lose it."

Her lips curve slightly against me, the faintest hint of a smile before she takes me deeper again, her tongue swirling around the tip before sliding down. The sensation is overwhelming, a perfect mix of softness and pressure, of pleasure and need. My legs tremble, my hands tightening in her hair as I fight to hold back, to stop myself from completely unraveling.

But she doesn't stop. Her movements grow faster, more deliberate, her lips and hand working in tandem to push me closer and closer to the edge. My breaths come in sharp gasps, my body trembling as the tension builds to a breaking point.

"Jenny," I rasp, my voice barely audible as I feel myself teetering on the brink. I can't hold on much longer, and the thought of coming undone like this...completely at her mercy...is both terrifying and exhilarating.

Just as I feel myself slipping, I gently pull her away, my hands cradling her face as I guide her up to meet my gaze. Her lips are swollen, her cheeks flushed, and the sight of her like this...her eyes filled with heat and determination...makes my chest tighten all over again.

"Come here," I murmur, my voice rough as I pull her onto the bed. I need her...every part of her. I know I'll never forget this moment for the rest of my life.

Her body trembles in my arms, her cheeks flushed and lips swollen. She climbs over me, straddling my hips again, her sex pressing against the hard length of me. The wet heat of her makes me groan, my hands gripping her waist instinctively as she moves, rocking against me. The friction sends a jolt of pleasure straight through me, but it's more than just that...watching her take charge like this, seeing her confidence grow, leaves me in awe.

Her head tips back as she moves, her hair cascading over her shoulders, her chest rising and falling with each ragged breath. I reach up, cupping her breasts, molding them in my hands as her movements grow bolder. She gasps when my thumbs brush over her hardened nipples, her hips grinding down against me with more urgency.

· · ·

"Zack," she whispers, her voice trembling, and I can feel the tension in her body building. My hands slide down her back, gripping her hips as I roll her onto her back once more, pinning her beneath me.

She looks up at me, her hazel eyes wide and filled with trust, and it nearly undoes me.

For a brief moment, I think about condoms, but there's none in sight.

"I'll take care of you in the morning," I whisper, brushing a strand of hair from her face. She nods, her trust in me palpable, and it hits me like a punch to the chest.

I position myself at her entrance, pressing in slowly. The heat of her is almost unbearable, but she's so tight that I pause, my jaw clenching as I fight to stay in control. "Jenny," I whisper, my voice trembling, "are you okay?"

She nods, her nails digging into my arms as I press in further. The resistance is there, and when I realize what it means, I freeze. "You're a virgin," I say, my voice hoarse with shock.

She blushes, her eyes meeting mine, and I can see the truth written all over her face. "Don't stop," she pleads, her voice soft but firm. "Please, Zack. I want this."

• • •

I swallow hard, my emotions warring inside me. I should stop, give her time, but the look in her eyes...so filled with trust, with need...keeps me anchored. I nod, leaning down to kiss her softly. "I'll go slow," I promise, my voice barely above a whisper.

She blushes, her eyes meeting mine, and I see the truth written all over her face. "Don't stop," she pleads again, her voice still soft but firm. "Please, Zack. I want this."

I swallow hard, the weight of her words anchoring me. I should stop. I know I should. But the trust in her gaze, the raw vulnerability mixed with an undeniable need, makes it impossible to pull away. I lean down, brushing my lips over hers with a softness that feels almost foreign to me.

"I'll go slow," I whisper, my voice barely audible. My forehead rests against hers as I push forward again, inch by agonizing inch, her body yielding to me with excruciating slowness.

She gasps, her hands clutching at my shoulders, her nails digging into my skin as I stretch her, filling her in ways she's never experienced before. I pause, giving her a moment to adjust, stroking her hair and murmuring reassurances against her lips. Her breaths come in short, shallow gasps, her chest rising and falling rapidly as she clings to me.

· · ·

"Zack," she whispers, her voice trembling, and I freeze, ready to stop if she asks. But she surprises me. Her hands slide down my back, her fingers pressing against my skin as she shifts her hips slightly, seeking more. "Don't stop," she murmurs again, her voice stronger now, more certain.

I press forward, my cock sliding deeper into her tight heat, and the sensation is overwhelming. She's so warm, so impossibly tight, and every nerve in my body feels like it's on fire. I grit my teeth, forcing myself to go slow, to give her time, even as my instincts scream at me to take her completely.

"You're incredible," I murmur, my voice rough as I bury myself inside her fully. She lets out a soft cry, her head tipping back against the pillow, her body arching beneath me. I stay still, my forehead pressed to hers, letting her adjust to the stretch.

Her hands tremble as they move to my face, cupping my cheeks as her hazel eyes meet mine. "It's... it's starting to feel good," she says, her voice breathless but tinged with wonder. The tension in her body eases, her thighs relaxing around my hips as she begins to move, testing the rhythm.

I groan, the sensation of her moving against me nearly breaking my restraint. I let her set the pace, my hands gripping her hips as she begins to rock beneath me. Her movements are tentative at first, her body adjusting to my size, but soon, she finds a rhythm, her hips rolling against mine with growing confidence.

. . .

"You're doing so well," I whisper, my voice thick with emotion as I watch her. She's breathtaking, her flushed cheeks, her parted lips, the way her hair spills over the pillow like a halo. Her breasts move with each thrust, the peaks of her nipples hard and begging for my attention. I lower my head, taking one into my mouth, sucking gently as my hands roam over her body.

Her moans grow louder, her nails raking down my back as her body begins to respond to mine fully. She's not holding back anymore, her hips meeting mine with increasing urgency, her gasps turning into cries of pleasure.

"Zack," she whimpers, her voice trembling, and I can feel her body tightening around me, the telltale signs of her approaching release.

I move faster, driving into her with deliberate precision, angling my hips to hit the spot that makes her cry out. "I've got you," I murmur, my voice strained as I fight to maintain control. The way she feels, the way she moves, is driving me to the edge, but I hold back, desperate to make this perfect for her.

Her body arches, her thighs tightening around my hips as the tension inside her snaps. She cries out my name, her body convulsing around me, and the sensation is enough to send me spiraling. My thrusts become erratic, my control slipping completely as I bury myself inside her one last time. My release crashes through me, a wave of pleasure so intense it leaves me trembling.

The tension that's been building inside me snaps, my control shattering as a guttural groan tears from my throat. My hips jerk, my entire body trembling as my release surges through me, hot and unrelenting. I bury myself inside her, my forehead pressed against hers as wave after wave of pleasure crashes over me, leaving me utterly undone.

"Fuck," I rasp, my breath ragged as my body continues to shake with the force of it. Each pulse of my release feels endless, each sensation heightened by the way her body clenches around me, holding me in place as if she doesn't want to let go. My vision blurs, my thoughts scattered, and for a moment, the world ceases to exist outside of this...the heat of her, the sound of our mingled breaths, the way she whispers my name like a prayer.

When the final tremors subside, I collapse beside her, utterly spent, my chest heaving as I try to catch my breath. My arm slips around her waist instinctively, pulling her close as we lie tangled together. Her head rests against my chest, her fingers tracing lazy patterns over my skin, grounding me in a way I've never felt before.

Neither of us speaks, the silence heavy with the unspoken emotions hanging between us. The only sounds are the rhythmic beating of our hearts and the soft hum of her breath against my skin.

· · ·

But as I hold her, something shifts inside me...something I can't ignore. This wasn't just a moment, wasn't just sex. It was more.

It was the culmination of something that's always been there, buried deep, like a quiet undercurrent in my chest. My affection for her has always lingered, subtle and unspoken, but now it's risen to the surface, undeniable and raw. Being with her like this has changed everything. She isn't just someone who's slipped into my life...she's someone who's always been a part of it, whether I acknowledged it or not.

And now that it's out in the open, now that I've felt her, tasted her, claimed her...I know I'll never see her the same way again.

I'd planned for this to be fleeting...something to indulge in for a time, a temporary distraction before letting go. But now, with her curled against me, her breaths soft and even, her warmth pressed into my chest, I feel... unsettled. Weary. Almost threatened by what this could mean, what she could mean.

Jenny shifts, her small hands clutching at my skin as she seeks comfort, burrowing closer as if she's trying to disappear into me. Her vulnerability, the way she trusts me so completely... it forces the walls in my mind to crack, if only for a moment.

· · ·

I sigh, tightening my arms around her and letting my lips brush against the top of her head. For now, I tell myself, I'll stop thinking. I'll stop questioning. This moment...this fleeting, perfect moment...is all I have. And I don't know if it will ever come again. So, I force myself to let go of the weight pressing on my chest and simply hold her, savoring her softness, her presence, and the fragile peace that's wrapped itself around us.

CHAPTER
Twenty~Five

JENNY

The morning light seeps through the curtains, soft and golden, spilling warmth across the room. My eyes flutter open, heavy with sleep, and for a moment, I feel disoriented. My head throbs faintly from last night's alcohol, and my body feels… different. Sensitive. Sore. As though it belongs to someone else entirely.

And then I feel him.

Zack's arm is draped over my waist, his hand resting possessively against my stomach, his chest pressed against my back. Heat radiates from his body, sinking into my skin, and I can feel every inch of him…solid, warm, devastatingly close. My breath catches, the reality of last night slamming into me with vivid, all-consuming clarity.

. . .

His hands had roamed my body like he owned it. I recall the feel of his cock inside of me.

I can still feel the ache, the way he'd moved inside me with unrelenting precision, each thrust pushing me higher, harder, until I'd shattered beneath him.

I remember the way the orgasm had overtaken me…violent, unstoppable, leaving me trembling and clutching at him like he was the only thing anchoring me to reality. My thighs had shaken uncontrollably, my cries muffled against his chest, and he hadn't stopped. He'd kept going, drawing wave after wave of pleasure from me until I was nothing but a trembling, gasping mess in his arms.

My face burns at the memory, a mix of shame and something far more dangerous pooling low in my stomach. I squeeze my thighs together, but the dull throb there only reminds me of how completely he'd undone me.

And now… now I'm lying here in his arms, no longer a virgin, no longer the same girl I was yesterday.

My chest tightens as Brett's face flashes in my mind. Brett, who was supposed to be the one. Brett, who I'd imagined for years as the boy I'd give myself to. Brett, whose name now feels like a distant echo compared to the man lying beside me.

God, what have I done?

•   •   •

I glance over my shoulder, careful not to move too much, and my breath hitches. Zack is still asleep, his face relaxed in a way I've never seen before. His dark hair falls in messy waves across his forehead, his jawline sharp and dusted with stubble. The sheet rests low on his hips, revealing the hard planes of his chest, and I feel my pulse quicken.

He looks... devastatingly handsome. Untouchable. Like something out of a dream I'm not yet sure I want to have.

The worst part is, I can't stop staring at him. Last night, in the dim lights of the club, he'd looked like a force of nature... fury and power incarnate as he defended me. And then later, in this bed, he'd become something else entirely. Tender. Consuming. Irresistible. The way he'd whispered my name, the way his body had moved against mine, the way he'd looked at me like I was the only thing that mattered...it's all imprinted on me, and I know I'll never forget it.

But how can I feel this way about Zack when my heart is supposed to belong to Brett?

The thought sends a sharp pang through me, and I carefully lift Zack's arm, sliding out of the bed as quietly as I can. My dress is crumpled on the floor, a stark reminder of the reckless decisions I made last night, and I grab it hastily, pulling it on with trembling hands. My panties are nowhere to be found, and the realization sends another jolt of embarrassment through me.

I glance at Zack one last time before I reach the door. I shouldn't. But I do.

And the sight of him nearly undoes me.

. . .

He's sprawled across the bed, the sheet tangled around his hips, his arm stretched across the space I've just left. The sunlight streaming through the window catches in his hair, painting him in gold, and his face is serene in sleep. Soft. Beautiful. Devastating.

My chest tightens, and for a moment, I can't move. My heart races as I take in the sight of him, my pulse thundering in my ears. He looks like everything I've ever wanted…everything I didn't know I needed. And the realization terrifies me.

How can I feel this way about Zack? How can I feel anything for him when it's supposed to be Brett?

Tears prick at the corners of my eyes, and I force myself to turn away, to shut the door quietly behind me. But as I step into the hallway, the ache in my chest only deepens, and I know one thing for certain.

Nothing will ever be the same again.

The morning feels like a whirlwind, my head still spinning as I rush to pull myself together. The haze of last night clings to me.

. . .

The memories are vivid, too vivid, and they're making it impossible to focus.

I force myself into the shower, letting the cool water wash over me as I scrub away the remnants of sleep and something deeper...something raw and dangerous that has settled under my skin. My legs feel weak, my body sore in places I've never felt before, and I can't stop thinking about how I'd given him everything.

And then there's the gnawing worry about protection. I hadn't even thought about it last night, lost in the heat of the moment, but now it's a steady thrum in the back of my mind. I push the thought away as I dry off quickly, wrapping the towel tightly around me as I glance at the clock.

There's no time to wallow. My schedule today is packed, starting with a photoshoot for Tod's at Castel Sant'Angelo.

I dress quickly, pulling on a simple but elegant outfit for the day...high-waisted trousers, a fitted white blouse, and sleek flats. My hair is still damp as I gather my essentials, shoving my phone and lipstick into my purse with shaking hands. Just as I sling the strap over my shoulder, there's a knock.

The sound startles me, freezing me in place. My heart leaps into my throat, and for a moment, I don't move, listening intently. The knock comes again, softer this time, and I realize it's not coming from the main door. It's the adjoining door between Zack's room and mine.

Panic flares in my chest. I can't face him. Not now, not after everything. My heart pounds as I step back from the sound, trying to pretend I haven't heard it. If I stay quiet, maybe he'll go away.

But then my phone buzzes in my purse, the shrill tone breaking the silence. My hands fumble as I grab it, silencing the noise. Too late. He knows I'm here.

"Jenny," Zack's voice comes through, low and clipped. "Answer."

I hesitate, my thumb hovering over the screen. Slowly, I lift the phone to my ear. "H-hi," I manage, my voice hoarse and shaky.

"Where's your first shoot today?"

The question catches me off guard, his tone devoid of anything that hints at the intimacy of last night.

"Um.. why?" I ask, my chest tightening.

"The morning-after pill. I'll have it sent to your location as soon as possible."

My cheeks flush hot, a mix of embarrassment and something else I can't quite name. His words are practical, responsible, but they still leave me feeling exposed, vulnerable.

"Oh okay, Thank you. I'll be at Castel Sant'Angelo."

"Okay," he says simply. "I'll take care of it."

"Thanks," I manage finally, my voice barely audible. I hang up quickly, my hands trembling as I shove the phone into my bag.

There's really no need for me to be this nervous and on edge, but I can't help it. I find myself nearly tiptoeing out from my room into the foyer, and only when I shut the door to the suite behind me do I finally breathe.

The shoot at Castel Sant'Angelo is already in full swing, but I can barely focus. The setting is breathtaking…the ancient fortress rising against the clear Roman sky, a perfect backdrop for the sleek luxury of Tod's. The photographer barks directions, his voice cutting through the buzz of the crew, but his words barely register. My mind is a mess, my body still reeling from the night before.

As I pose in the soft leather jacket and ankle boots they've styled me in, I catch myself stealing glances at the entrance, wondering if Zack will show up. My stomach flips at the thought, and I curse myself for letting him invade my head like this.

The heat of the midday sun is almost oppressive, and I excuse myself to grab some water. Just as I reach for a bottle, my phone buzzes insistently in my bag. I pull it out, seeing Zack's name flash on the screen.

"Hello?" I answer, my voice barely above a whisper.

"Did the driver find you?" His voice is calm but direct, laced with something that sounds suspiciously like concern.

I glance around, spotting the sleek black car parked discreetly near the set. "Yeah, he's here."

"Good." There's a pause, and I can almost picture him on the other end, his jaw tight, his gray eyes focused. "Make sure you take it, Jenny. Don't forget."

The clinical nature of the reminder makes my cheeks flush, but there's no mistaking the care beneath his words. "I know," I reply quickly, wishing my voice sounded steadier. "I will."

"Good," he says again, softer this time. "What time do you finish?"

. . .

"Probably around two," I say, my fingers tightening around the bottle of water. "Why?"

"I'll be close by. Let's grab lunch after," he says, his tone leaving no room for argument.

The casualness of his suggestion, the way he acts like this is perfectly normal, throws me. "You don't have to—"

"I'll see you then, Jenny," he cuts me off gently, but firmly, before ending the call.

I stare at the screen, my heart racing. The phone feels heavier in my hand as I shove it back into my bag, the weight of his words settling over me like a lead blanket.

The driver approaches me with the small, discreet package. My cheeks burn as I take it, muttering a quiet thanks before slipping it into my bag. The other girls on set notice, their eyes darting between the car and me, their whispers carrying just enough for me to catch.

"So you do have connections," one of them says. "How lucky."

I ignore them because my insides are churning for completely different reasons.

. . .

At two we wrap up earlier than expected but to my surprise, I spot the car waiting for me again.

For a brief, irrational moment, I think he's inside, but when the door opens, it's only the driver.

"Mr. Jackson asked me to take you to him," the driver says, his tone polite but professional. "He's nearby."

My pulse quickens as I climb into the car, my mind racing. Lunch. It's just lunch, I tell myself, trying to tamp down the flurry of emotions. But when I see him waiting outside the small café, looking impossibly put together in a navy button-up that makes his gray eyes even sharper, I know it's not just lunch. Not for me.

It's about Zack...the way he makes my heart race and my knees weak, the way he's managed to slip under my skin without me even realizing it.

As I step out of the car, Zack's gaze locks onto mine, his expression unreadable but intense. He holds the door open for me, his fingers brushing mine briefly, and the simple contact sends a shiver down my spine.

"You're early," he says, his voice low, almost teasing.

. . .

"They finished ahead of schedule," I reply, trying to keep my voice steady.

"Good," he says, his lips quirking into the faintest smile. "I'm starving."

I follow him inside, my heart pounding with every step. There's an air of casualness to him, but I can feel the tension simmering just beneath the surface. It's in the way he pulls out my chair, the way his eyes linger on mine just a second too long.

CHAPTER

Twenty-Six

ZACK

I chose La Pergola, a three-Michelin-starred restaurant perched on a hill overlooking Rome. The dining room is bathed in soft golden light, and the glass walls offer sweeping views of the Eternal City. The domes and spires of ancient Rome shimmer against the azure sky, while manicured terraces below us frame the scene with a painterly elegance. It's the kind of place that demands your attention, but my focus remains squarely on Jenny.

She's sitting across from me, her fingers nervously tracing the rim of her water glass. The soft curls of her hair frame her face, and the afternoon sun dances across her skin, making her look almost ethereal. She looks different due to the styling from the photoshoot, but it just makes me all the more realize just how gorgeous she is.

There is however something off...her usual brightness is dimmed, and she's quieter than I expected.

After last night, I'm not surprised, but I do want to

know…more than anything…what is now going through her head.

"How was the shoot?" I ask, my voice even, measured.

Jenny glances up at me, offering a small smile. "It went well."

Simple and curt, and it sets me on edge, I'm worried, all other concerns aside, that I might have hurt her.

The waiter arrives with our first course…delicate plates of handmade ravioli drizzled with truffle oil. I nod my thanks, but the sight of the food barely registers. My mind is elsewhere.

Just like me, she's distracted. It's obvious. And I'd be lying if I said I wasn't too. Last night lingers between us like smoke…thick, impossible to ignore. I lean back slightly, my fingers brushing the edge of my glass.

"How do you feel about last night?" I ask, my voice steady.

Jenny stiffens, her fork hovering mid-air before she sets it down. Her hazel eyes meet mine briefly before darting away. "I… I don't know," she says softly, her voice almost drowned out by the distant murmur of other diners.

"I don't mean to put you on the spot," I say, leaning forward slightly. "But it's important to me that you're okay, especially since it was your first time."

"I'm okay," she says as she tries her best to seem engaged with her food.

I clear my throat, the tension in the air thick as I try to approach the subject delicately. "Have you thought about… birth control?" The words feel heavier than I anticipated, even as I keep my tone neutral.

Her head snaps up, her hazel eyes widening like I've just asked something far more intimate. She's startled, maybe even embarrassed, and for a second, I wonder if I've overstepped.

"I..." she starts, but her voice falters. She looks down quickly, her fingers fidgeting with the napkin in her lap. Her cheeks flush, and I can see how much the question has thrown her off. "I've never really thought about it before," she admits, so quietly it's almost a whisper.

I nod, keeping my expression composed even though her vulnerability hits harder than I expect. It's not just the situation...it's her. The way she's trying to process everything while still grappling with the enormity of last night.

"If it would make you more comfortable," I say gently, keeping my voice as steady as I can, "I can help you arrange something. I don't want this to be another thing you have to worry about."

She shakes her head slightly, her fingers tensing around the edge of her napkin. "There will be no need for that," she says finally, her voice steady but distant, the implication sharp and deliberate.

Her words settle over me like a weight. There will be no need for that.

I sit back slightly, my gaze fixed on her face as she avoids my eyes, her attention resolutely on her plate. It's not the words themselves that sting...it's the implication beneath them. She doesn't expect...or want...this to happen again. My chest tightens in a way I wasn't prepared for, and I realize just how much last night had meant to me, against all logic, against all my better judgment.

I take a sip of water, letting the cool liquid ground me. "I see," I say finally, my voice steady, though the air between us feels heavier now. "I just... didn't want you to feel alone in dealing with this. That's all."

Jenny's eyes flicker up to mine for a moment, but she quickly looks away again. "I appreciate it," she murmurs, her tone soft but evasive. She's retreating, pulling back into herself, and it sets my teeth on edge...not because I blame her, but because I don't know how to reach her right now.

The waiter interrupts, clearing away our plates and replacing them with the next course...a beautifully plated sea bass with a delicate citrus glaze. Normally, I'd savor a meal like this, but right now, it might as well be cardboard. I barely register the aroma as I pick up my fork and knife, cutting into the fish mechanically.

"I know this is complicated," I say after a moment, my voice quieter now. "And I don't want to make it harder for you. But I think we should talk about it...about us."

Her fork stills mid-cut, and she looks up at me, her expression guarded. "What is there to talk about?" she asks, her voice carefully neutral. "We both know this was... complicated from the start."

I exhale slowly, setting down my utensils. "Jenny, last night wasn't just some random mistake. At least, not for me."

Her eyes widen slightly at my admission, and for a second, I think I see a flicker of something...uncertainty, maybe even longing. But it's gone as quickly as it appears, replaced by the same guarded expression she's been wearing since we sat down.

"It's just..." She hesitates, struggling to find the words. "You're Brett's brother, Zack. And I don't know what I'm supposed to feel about that. Or about any of this."

"You're not cheating on him," I say firmly. "Brett is with Elizabeth. They're in a relationship. What happened between us doesn't change that."

Her lips press into a thin line, and she looks away again, her gaze drifting toward the panoramic view outside the window. The domes and spires of Rome glimmer in the sunlight, but her focus seems distant, lost in her own thoughts.

"Are you trying to discourage me from him or encourage

me toward you?" she asks suddenly, her tone sharp but not unkind. She's testing me, searching for something, and I'm not sure what.

"Which would you prefer?" I counter, leaning forward slightly, my voice steady but edged with something I can't quite name. "I don't want to push you into anything, Jenny. Last night... it meant something to me. But if it didn't mean the same to you, I won't—"

"I didn't say that," she cuts in quickly, her cheeks flushing. She looks down at her plate, her fingers gripping the edge of the table. "I just... I don't know what to do with it."

I hesitate, the vulnerability in her voice striking something deep within me. " "You don't have to do anything with it. Last night, you were tipsy," I say carefully, gauging her reaction.

Her eyes snap up to meet mine, sharp and unyielding. "But you weren't," she says pointedly, her tone carrying a weight that leaves me momentarily stunned.

I sit back, caught off guard by the directness of her words. "So... you regret it," I say slowly, the words tasting bitter as they leave my mouth.

She exhales shakily, her hands twisting together in her lap. "No," she whispers finally, so softly I almost don't hear her. Her cheeks flush deeper, and she looks away again, her voice trembling. "I don't regret it. It happened. That's it. Full stop. It shouldn't happen again."

"It shouldn't happen again, or you don't want it to happen again?" I counter, my tone calm but deliberate.

She doesn't respond, her silence lingering between us like a heavy weight.

"Okay," I say finally, leaning back slightly. "Like you said, it happened. That's it. Full stop. It's not a secret, but if you insist specifically on keeping it as one, then no one will hear about it from me."

She resumes eating, her movements slow and deliberate. It takes a while before she speaks again, her voice quiet but steady. "I'd appreciate that. Thank you."

I decide then and there to completely remove any emotional weight from the conversation. If this is what she wants, I can match her resolve.

"Since it is a secret, and just between us," I say, setting my fork down, "I don't see why it can't continue during our time here. We expect nothing from each other. No rules are being broken, so… keep your mind open."

At this, I pick up my flute of wine and don't stop until I've completely drained the glass. The burn is satisfying, but not nearly enough to distract me from the fire simmering between us.

CHAPTER
Twenty-Seven

JENNY

I watch as Zack lifts his glass of wine, the deep crimson liquid sliding down his throat. My eyes betray me, fixating on the movement of his Adam's apple as he swallows, the faint tension in his jaw as he drains the glass. He doesn't rush, and the deliberate way he drinks feels like some kind of quiet provocation. My chest tightens, heat pooling low in my belly despite the resolve I'm desperately trying to hold onto.

Damn him. Damn him for being so composed, so unshakable, while I feel like I'm coming apart at the seams. He sets the empty glass down, his fingers brushing the stem lightly, and I tear my gaze away, forcing myself to focus on anything else...the plate in front of me, the soft murmur of the other diners, the breathtaking view of Rome outside the window. But it's useless. He's all I can think about.

I need space. Perspective. Something to keep me from drowning in this confusion. As soon as we return to the hotel, I slip into my room, shutting the adjoining door behind me as though I can physically block Zack's presence out. My heart is still racing, my skin humming with leftover tension.

I grab my phone, needing an anchor to steady me, and type out a quick message to Brett. We've rarely spoken since I arrived, although I have been trying to get in touch with him. As usual, he is slow to respond, but now more than ever, it slowly fills me with fury.

What happened between me and Zack was supposed to be between us, and now I am more confused than I have ever been.

Just before I toss the phone aside, however, my phone's screen lights up, and I dive for the device.

"Hiya Jenny," he replies. "Yeah, I'm fine. Thanks for asking," Brett replies.

"Thanks for asking?" I'm immediately irritated, but this is better than complete silence, so I reply.

"That's really good to hear. I've been worried about you. I'm in Rome now for work."

"Yeah, I heard," he replies back to my excitement. "Zack is in Rome as well. Hope he's taking care of you. Don't be too intimidated by him. He comes off a bit stern, but he's someone to feel extremely safe around. You know how close we are."

"Safe?" My entire body is immediately dying to protest at this, but ultimately, I have to admit that this is the truth. He is safe…he's always been kind, protected me, even up until last night, and then everything changed.

"Yes, I know," I reply, feeling even sadder. "What are you up to these days?" I proceed to ask. "Can you take a quick phone call?"

The seconds stretch into minutes, and the silence on his end feels deafening. I bite my lip, staring at the screen, willing him to say something more. Another minute passes. Then two. Nothing.

My chest tightens, anger bubbling beneath the surface. Zack's words from earlier echo in my mind: "Brett is with Elizabeth."

"Yes, he is. But still... if he just paid attention long enough, he would be able to give us both a chance. But he never did, and he never does."

My emotions are spiraling out of control, and I recognize this, but it is too difficult to stop. Not when Zack is next door, not when more than anything, I'm now very aware of the alternative, and it is brighter and shinier than what I had imagined with Brett.

However, I cannot stop thinking of Brett and Elizabeth. What if he's with her right now? What if he's ignoring me because she's there, smiling, laughing? What if they're... what if they're being intimate just like Zack and I were last night?

Zack is right. Brett is with Elizabeth, and it astounds me now that I had been so undeterred by this on my return. I understand that this is because he has always felt like mine, and everyone else...and the many...had always felt like a passing inconvenience, a distraction for him until it was time for him to really see me.

But what if... what if he never will?

The thought hits me like a punch to the gut, and I sink onto the edge of the bed, my phone clutched tightly in my hands. A wave of frustration washes over me...at Brett for being so distant, at Zack for planting the seed of doubt, and at myself for letting either of them get under my skin.

And then there's the memory of last night...Zack's hands on my body, his lips trailing fire across my skin, the way he made me feel like I was the only thing that mattered in the world. The shame should outweigh the pleasure, but it doesn't. I close my eyes, the vivid recollection of his touch sending a fresh jolt of heat through me. God, I hate how good it felt.

How could I have let this happen? How could I crave it even now, when I'm supposed to be thinking about Brett?

I type another message to Brett, my fingers trembling over the keys: "I really wanted to talk to you more. Let me know when you're free."

I hit send, the message as much a plea as it is a test. The response, or lack of it, will tell me everything I need to know. But deep down, I already know the answer. Brett doesn't care…not the way I want him to. If he did, I wouldn't be here, reeling from Zack's words and touch, craving something I have no right to want.

I throw the phone onto the bed and bury my face in my hands, trying to steady my breathing. But the anger doesn't fade. If Brett had taken me seriously…if he'd seen me as more than just a convenient fixture in his life…I wouldn't have been in Zack's arms last night.

The anger twists into something darker, something I don't want to name. I want to hate Zack for how easily he's undone me, but all I can think about is the way his gaze burned into mine, the low rasp of his voice, the undeniable pull between us. My fingers grip the sheets, my body trembling with the need to let go of the tension coiling inside me.

I hear a faint knock from the adjoining door, and my heart lurches, a mix of dread and anticipation flooding through me. For a moment, I freeze, staring at the door as though it's alive, as though Zack himself might come through it.

But the knock doesn't come again, and I force myself to breathe. I can't do this…not tonight, not now. I need clarity, not more confusion. Yet as I lie back on the bed, staring at the ceiling, all I can think about is him…the way he looked at me across the table, the warmth of his hand on mine, the heat of his body against mine last night.

And despite myself, I know I'll never truly forget it.

The days pass in a haze of photoshoots and perfectly curated schedules, but they do little to quiet my restless mind. The work is demanding yet somehow not enough, leaving me with too much time in the evenings to think. Too much time to listen for Zack.

Even when I tell myself not to, I do it anyway. Every time I'm in the room, scrolling aimlessly through social media or staring at the breathtaking view from my window, my ears are attuned to the faintest sound from the adjoining room. A door opening, footsteps, the low murmur of his voice…it's become a habit I can't seem to shake. And it makes me feel ridiculous.

We haven't crossed paths since the last time we spoke, and I've done everything in my power to keep it that way…or so I tell myself. In truth, I might have been trying a little too hard to create opportunities for us to meet, all while pretending I wasn't. Either way, he's been keeping his distance, and he's done a much better job of it than I have.

Part of me feels relieved. After all, the space is what I need to clear my head, to focus on why I'm really here. But another part of me…the part I try to bury…is undeniably sad. No matter how much I try to throw myself into work or the city around me, I can't stop thinking about him.

Today, especially since for the first time since arriving in Rome, I have a day off. No work, no photo shoots, no carefully scheduled appearances. I should be excited, thrilled even, to explore the city, to immerse myself in its history and culture. But instead, I find myself sitting in the room, staring out at the sprawling view of Rome and feeling paralyzed by indecision.

The golden rooftops and ancient ruins seem to mock me. Rome is a city for lovers and dreamers, and all I feel is this unrelenting tug of confusion and desire. My fingers hover

over my phone, scrolling past images of scenic ruins and quaint countryside villages. A thought strikes me: maybe I should take a day trip. I could visit the ruins, lose myself in history, or drive out to one of those charming little villages where the tables are set with red-checkered tablecloths, and the food tastes like someone's grandmother made it.

The idea lifts my mood, even if only slightly. But then reality sinks in. I'd need a car. And while I could figure out the way there, getting back? That's another story. The buses would be a nightmare, and renting a car feels daunting. The solution hits me as quickly as the anxiety: I'll need Zack's car.

It's not just an excuse to talk to him. Okay, maybe it is. But I genuinely need it. And if I don't want to spend another day moping in this room, I have to muster the courage to ask.

After a few minutes of further thought, I decide. Getting up I hurry over to the wardrobe and start getting dressed.

A little while later, I stand in front of the mirror, tugging the hem of my sundress nervously. It's light and flowy, perfect for a day trip, though the slight chill in the air has me draping a soft sweater over my shoulders. I adjust the fabric around my neck, hoping it looks effortless rather than planned. My heart pounds as I step into the foyer and head to his door.

Knock, knock.

The sound is too loud in the quiet space, and I nearly bolt right then. But before I can second-guess myself, the door swings open, and there he is.

Zack stands in the doorway, shirtless, with only a pair of slacks hanging low on his hips. His hair is slightly messy, and there's a faint crease on his forehead like he's been deep in thought…or maybe stress. His presence is overwhelming, and for a moment, I forget how to breathe.

"Jenny," he says, his voice low and smooth but tinged with surprise. His gray eyes sweep over me briefly before his expression shifts to something unreadable. Then I notice his phone in his hand and realize he must have been in the middle of a call.

"I—" I start, but my words catch in my throat. Damn it. Why does he always have this effect on me? "I'm sorry. I didn't mean to interrupt. I just—"

He holds up a hand, silencing me as he steps back inside, motioning for me to follow. I do, hesitantly, my nerves buzzing. He resumes his call, his voice low as he speaks in clipped, professional tones. I glance around his room, trying to distract myself. Papers are strewn across the desk, and his laptop screen glows with spreadsheets or emails…something that looks far too important for my intrusion.

As he paces to the desk, the scene feels almost cinematic. The warm light filtering through the window catches the angles of his face, the defined muscles of his back, the way his hand runs through his hair as he concentrates. He's beautiful. Effortlessly, painfully beautiful. And I hate how much I want him.

I linger by the door, unsure what to do. Should I sit? Leave? He glances at me once, his gaze flickering briefly over my face before returning to his call. The weight of his presence is stifling, and yet I can't tear my eyes away. There's something mesmerizing about the way he moves, the way he commands the space around him without even trying.

Finally, he ends the call, setting the phone down on the desk with a soft thud. He looks at me, his brow lifting slightly. "What's up?" he asks, his tone casual, but there's a faint edge of curiosity beneath it.

I clear my throat, trying to gather my thoughts. "I, um… I wanted to ask you something."

His gaze sharpens, and he leans back against the desk, crossing his arms over his chest. "Go on."

"I was thinking of taking a day trip," I blurt out, my

words tumbling over each other. "To see some ruins, maybe visit a village or two. But I need a car, and I don't... I mean, I don't want to get lost on the buses, so I thought—" I pause, flustered, my cheeks burning. "Could I borrow yours?"

I feel bad asking now that I'm staring straight him. I can very clearly see the stress etched on his face and the faint shadows under his eyes betraying just how much he's carrying. He looks exhausted, like he's been shouldering the weight of the world and refusing to let anyone share it. And I don't want to just announce my plans for the day and bounce out the door so selfishly.

"Also.." I add. "I mean if you're not too busy maybe we could go together. You've been working so hard, and I thought—" I pause, feeling my cheeks heat up again. "Maybe it'd be good for you. For both of us."

"Today is your day off right?" he asks and I nod in response.

"Yeah."

He leans back in his chair, studying me with an intensity that makes my heart race. The silence stretches, and I find myself needing to grab onto something but finding nothing but air.

Finally, he responds. His lips curve into a small, almost reluctant smile, and he lets out a quiet sigh. "Alright," he says, standing up and setting his phone down. "I'll get dressed and meet you downstairs at the reception."

Relief floods through me, mingled with something deeper, something warmer. As he moves to the side of the room, I find myself watching him again, just before I ultimately turn around and take my leave, my heart pounding at the thought of the day ahead. Whatever happens, I know one thing for certain...this day trip just got a whole lot more interesting.

CHAPTER

Twenty-Eight

ZACH

The car I rented for the day is a vintage convertible… a cherry-red Alfa Romeo Spider. It's not the most practical choice for a day of exploring ruins and villages, but practicality wasn't exactly what I had in mind when I booked it. Something about the car felt… right. Maybe it was the idea of driving through the countryside with the top down, the sun warm on our skin, and the wind tangling our thoughts into knots we couldn't ignore.

Jenny stands by the curb when I pull up to the hotel entrance, her sundress fluttering faintly in the breeze. She looks hesitant, almost shy, but when she sees the car, her face lights up. That smile…damn, that smile could power a city.

"Wow," she says, trailing her fingers along the polished red hood as she circles to the passenger side. "This is… unexpected."

"Good unexpected or bad?" I ask as I step out to open her door. The old-fashioned gesture earns me a raised eyebrow, but she slips into the seat without a word.

"Good," she admits, glancing around the interior with wide eyes. "Definitely good."

As soon as we hit the road, I regret leaving the top down. The wind kicks up, tossing her hair into a chaotic storm that she keeps trying to bat out of her face. It's distracting...not just for her, but for me. Her laugh bubbles up every time she loses the battle, light and unrestrained, and I have to grip the wheel tighter to keep my focus on the road.

"Do you want me to pull the top up?" I ask, already reaching for the latch. "It's going to drive you crazy."

"No!" she says quickly, pushing my hand away. "It's fine. I love it."

Her fingers brush against my arm for barely a second, but it's enough. The heat of her touch lingers, igniting something I've been trying so damn hard to suppress. I stay stoic, my hand falling back to the wheel, but inside, I feel the crack forming in my resolve.

I don't care that the original goal was to get her to forget about Brett. That doesn't matter anymore. All that matters is her...her boundaries, her comfort. I won't do anything to make her uneasy again, not after the way she looked at lunch the other day. She'd seemed so dejected, her shoulders hunched, her gaze avoiding mine at all costs. And since then, she's done everything in her power to avoid me altogether.

Even now, as she grins and tries to wrestle her hair into submission against the wind, I can't ignore the distance she's carefully built between us. But her laugh, her touch...even brief...remind me that the distance isn't unbridgeable. I just have to tread lightly, even if it means denying myself the pull I feel toward her.

"Are you sure?" I press, glancing at her as another strand of hair whips across her cheek. "You're going to end up with it in your mouth."

She shakes her head, grinning as she wrestles it back again. "I'll manage."

I hesitate, then pull my baseball cap off and hold it out to her. "Here. Use this."

She blinks, surprised by the offer, but takes it without comment, sliding it onto her head. The cap is too big for her, the brim casting a shadow over her face, but it works. Her hair settles, the wind no longer able to tug it free, and she leans back into the seat with a contented sigh.

"Thanks," she says softly, adjusting the brim slightly.

I nod, keeping my eyes on the road, but once again there is that strange warmth in my chest I can't quite push away. It's ridiculous, really…handing over a damn hat shouldn't feel like anything. But it does. And that's exactly why I shove the feeling aside and focus on the drive.

The ruins are everything I hoped they'd be: quiet, sprawling, and steeped in history. Jenny steps out of the car first, her sneakers crunching on the gravel as she takes in the massive stone archways and crumbling columns. Her awe is infectious, and I find myself watching her more than the ruins themselves.

"This is incredible," she murmurs, turning in a slow circle. "It's like stepping back in time."

I gesture to a small map of the site I grabbed at the entrance. "There's a trail that leads to the amphitheater. You want to check it out?"

She nods eagerly, and we fall into step together, the gravel crunching softly beneath our feet.

Around us, the air hums with the chatter of other visitors, the occasional laughter of children, and the murmur of tour guides explaining the ruins. But the energy of the crowd only seems to amplify the magic of the place…the ancient stone arches, weathered walls, and the faint scent of wildflowers carried on the warm breeze.

Jenny's eyes dart from one structure to another, her curiosity evident in the way she pauses to take in the details...the carvings on a crumbled pillar, the way sunlight filters through the gaps in a ruined roof. I find myself watching her more than the scenery, the way her expression lights up, the faint furrow in her brow when she's reading a plaque.

"It's incredible, isn't it?" she says, her voice filled with awe as she gestures toward a towering archway ahead of us.

I nod, though my gaze lingers on her instead of the structure. "It is. Makes you wonder how they managed to build something so massive without modern tools."

"Right?" She glances at me, her excitement contagious. "But you should know though, since you're in construction."

"I'm an investor, and my involvement is more on the real estate side," I reply, and she nods at the clarification.

We step closer to the archway, and the guide's voice carries over to us as he describes its history in a mix of Italian and English. Jenny leans in slightly, her shoulder brushing mine as we listen. It's a fleeting touch, but I feel it down to my core. I shove my hands into my pockets, trying to focus on the guide's words instead of the warmth of her skin.

The path winds around to a small courtyard surrounded by more ruins, with a few benches scattered under the shade of ancient trees. A couple sits on one, sharing a quiet moment, while others mill about, snapping photos or examining the stonework.

Jenny points toward a shaded corner with a small fountain, its water trickling softly. "Can we stop there for a bit? I just want to take it all in."

"Sure," I say, following her lead. As we settle onto the low wall near the fountain, she tilts her head back, letting the dappled sunlight play across her face. The breeze lifts her hair slightly, and I resist the urge to reach out and tuck it behind her ear. Instead, I let my gaze linger, the sight of her etched into my mind like a memory I don't ever want to fade. I can't remember the last time I allowed myself to be this idle...to simply exist without the weight of my responsibilities pressing down on me. There's always something to do, some deal to close, some problem to solve. My life is a constant forward march, with no time to stop and savor anything.

But here, with her, all of that fades into the background. The world narrows to just this moment...the sound of her laughter mingling with the rustle of leaves, the way the light catches in her hair, the soft curve of her lips when she's lost in thought. I don't want to leave. Not the ruins, not the serenity of this place, and definitely not her.

It's unsettling, how much I want to stay. How much I want to see her smile like this forever, unburdened and free. The realization creeps up on me like a quiet storm, and I can't decide if it's comforting or terrifying. Because I know this feeling won't last. It can't. And yet, for the first time in a long time, I find myself wishing it could.

"Have you ever been here before?" she asks suddenly, breaking the quiet. Her voice is soft, like she's afraid to disturb the peace around us.

"Once," I reply. "Years ago, for business. I didn't have time to actually see much of it."

Her eyes light up, and I know she's about to ask me more. "And now?"

"Now," I say, glancing at her, "I suppose I have the time to actually take it in."

Her smile widens, but she doesn't press further.

Jenny's smile lingers as she stretches her legs out in front of her, crossing one ankle over the other. The soft fabric of her sundress shifts with the motion, catching my attention briefly before I look away, forcing my focus elsewhere. A couple strolls by with ice cream cones, the faint scent of vanilla and citrus wafting on the breeze.

She glances at me, a flicker of something playful in her eyes. "I feel like a drink. Something cold and sweet. Do you think they have anything here?"

I nod toward a small kiosk nestled near the edge of the courtyard, shaded by a colorful awning.

"Looks like they might. Want to check it out?"

"Absolutely," she says, hopping to her feet with an enthusiasm that makes me want to smile. I follow her to the kiosk, scanning the handwritten chalkboard menu listing an assortment of drinks...freshly squeezed juices, Italian sodas, and local wines.

She takes her time reading through the options, her fingers brushing her lips as she decides. "Limonata," she declares finally, her tone light. "I've never had a real Italian lemonade before."

"Good choice," I say, stepping up to the counter to order. "And I'll have a—" I glance at the menu again and point. "Aceddu Verde."

Jenny raises an eyebrow as the server nods and begins preparing our drinks. "Green bird?" she asks, amusement dancing in her tone.

"It's a mix of fresh herbs and lime," I explain. "Should be refreshing."

She laughs softly, shaking her head. "I should've guessed you'd pick something... sophisticated. You just can't help yourself, can you?"

I want to tease her back, to say that of course, I'd expect her to go for the sweetest thing, but I hold back. It's too easy to slip into a rhythm that feels friendly again, too easy to act as though there isn't a boulder of tension walking beside us, looming over every word. I don't know how to resolve this, and whenever I'm in this state...even in business...all my guards go up. I can't help but slightly detach myself, toning down any expression of my enjoyment of this current moment with her.

It helps that she's trying to mask her discomfort too, though she doesn't realize how easily I can read her. Maybe it's the countless moments of quiet, unintentional observation over time, moments I never consciously acknowledged but seem to have etched her subtleties into my mind. The realization sends a strange thrill through me, sweet and unexpected.

The server hands us our drinks, and we begin walking toward a quiet corner of the courtyard. Just as Jenny turns to step onto the gravel path, I notice her shoe...a sleek pair of white tennis shoes with thin laces...has come undone. The loose ends flap against the stones as she steps, and before she can trip, I step forward.

"Wait." I hold out my hand. "Hold on to my drink for a moment.."

She blinks, startled, but complies, accepting my juice with a quizzical tilt of her head. I crouch down, gripping the ends of her laces and tying them into a secure knot. My fingers work quickly, but the act feels oddly intimate, the proximity grounding me in a way I don't expect.

"You could trip" I say, standing and brushing off my hands. "And falling here would be especially dangerous."

For a little while, she's quiet, which makes me wonder if I've done or said something wrong.

"Thanks," she says softly, her voice quieter than before.

She hands me back my drink, her fingers once again brushing mine briefly.

I glance down at her, and our eyes meet for just a second. Her cheeks flush slightly, and she glances away, clutching her cup. I tell myself it's nothing, but I can feel the phantom warmth of her touch on my skin, the lingering electricity between us that no amount of rationalizing can deny.

CHAPTER

Twenty~Nine

JENNY

My heart nearly stops in my chest. Zack crouching down to tie my tennis shoes is the sweetest, most unexpected thing anyone has ever done for me. I can't stop processing it, the simplicity of the act making it all the more profound. And now, as I stare at him...taking in the sharp lines of his jaw, the way his dark shirt fits perfectly under that leather jacket, and those jeans...I can't seem to stop thinking about him. About us. About every single moment we've shared.

His words from a few days ago echo in my mind: "Since it is a secret and just between us, I don't see why it can't continue on for our time here. We expect nothing out of each other. No rules are being broken, so keep your mind open." At the time, I hadn't allowed myself to even consider what he was really saying.

But now, being here with him, his quiet presence impossibly close, every word from that conversation feels heavier than before. His suggestion had been simple on the surface...

almost too casual. A way to put the weight of what had happened between us into a neat, manageable box. A way to let it exist without overtaking us.

Yet, the more I think about it, the harder it becomes to ignore the storm he's unleashed inside me. How can I compartmentalize this? The way his touch lingers in my mind, the way his voice draws me in, the way his presence seems to bend the very air around us.

It's impossible to separate the man in front of me now... calm, collected, quietly breathtaking...from the one who made me feel things I never thought I could. The way he looks at me, even when he's trying not to, sends my thoughts tumbling into places they shouldn't go.

"I was thinking," I say, breaking the silence as we begin walking again. "Maybe we should stop somewhere in the village for lunch. You know, something authentic."

He raises an eyebrow, clearly intrigued. "Not a bad idea. I saw a few places on the way here that looked promising."

"Perfect." I nod quickly, hoping my enthusiasm doesn't give away just how badly I need the distraction. "Somewhere with wine," I add with a small laugh.

Zack gives me a sidelong glance, his smirk faint but unmistakable. "Wine, huh? Feeling indulgent?"

I shrug, trying to appear nonchalant. "We're in Italy. It'd be rude not to."

His chuckle is low, and it sends a ripple of warmth through me. "Fair enough. I'll find us a place."

We continue down the path, passing through a series of ancient archways and open courtyards.

Finally, we make our way back to the car, the vintage convertible gleaming in the sunlight like something out of a movie. Zack holds the door open for me again, and I slide into the passenger seat, grateful for the momentary reprieve from my thoughts.

As we drive toward the village, the countryside unfolds around us in a stunning panorama of rolling hills, olive groves, and terracotta rooftops. The wind tangles my hair again, but this time, I don't bother fighting it. Instead, I lean back and let the breeze carry away some of the tension I've been holding onto.

"There's a place up ahead," Zack says, nodding toward a small cluster of buildings in the distance. "Looks promising."

I squint, catching sight of a quaint trattoria with wooden tables set up under a vine-covered pergola. It's charming, the kind of place that feels hidden from the world. "That's perfect," I say, my excitement bubbling over. "Let's stop there."

He pulls the car into a small gravel lot, and we step out into the warm midday sun. The air is fragrant with the scent of herbs and freshly baked bread, and my stomach growls in anticipation. Zack places a hand lightly on the small of my back, guiding me toward the entrance, and the simple gesture makes my pulse quicken.

We're seated at a table near the edge of the pergola, overlooking a sprawling vineyard that stretches toward the horizon. The server brings us menus, and I can't help but smile as I scan the offerings...fresh pasta, wood-fired pizza, and an impressive selection of local wines.

"What are you thinking?" Zack asks, his voice low and steady as he studies the menu.

I skim the menu quickly, barely registering the words. My focus flickers between him and the faint hum of desire stirring in my chest. The truth is, I don't care what I order. I don't care about this lunch. All I want is an excuse to let go of the tension between us, to feel him against me again, to stop pretending I don't remember every second of that night.

"Would you like red or white wine?" he asks, his gaze lifting to meet mine.

I glance at the drink section and spot something that makes me smile...a Long Island iced tea. Perfect. Strong enough to blur my thoughts and sweet enough to mask the alcohol. "Actually," I say, feigning nonchalance, "I'll go with this." I tap the menu, showing him my choice.

He raises an eyebrow. "A Long Island iced tea? You know that's a little... aggressive for lunch, right?"

"It's what I want," I say lightly, brushing off his concern. "I can get things I want, can't I?"

The question is layered with a double meaning, one I hope he can read in my eyes. Exactly what I want right now...and how it has nothing whatsoever to do with lunch or this restaurant.

His lips press into a thin line, but he doesn't argue. Instead, he closes the menu and signals the waiter. As he places our orders, I lean back in my chair, satisfied with my small victory. The waiter disappears, and Zack folds his hands on the table, his eyes steady on mine.

"You've been busy lately," he says, breaking the silence. "How are you feeling about everything? The contract? The shoots?"

I know he's trying to steer the conversation into safer territory, but his measured tone only makes me want to push back. "It's fine. Busy, but good. The contract will give me a solid cushion, so I'll probably take a break after this run."

His brow furrows slightly. "A break? Back to New York?"

I nod, swirling the water in my glass absently. "Yeah, for a little while. But it might not be for long. They're moving the shoot location to Paris soon, so when I come back, that's probably where I'll be heading."

"Paris." He repeats the word like he's testing its weight, something in his expression shifting subtly. "What about the apartment you planned to get in New York? You mentioned moving out."

"Yeah," I reply. keeping my tone casual. "I don't think that's possible anymore. I'll be traveling too much to settle anywhere right now."

The waiter returns with our drinks, setting the tall glass of iced tea in front of me and a glass of sparkling water in front of Zack. I don't miss the way his eyes narrow slightly when he sees my drink, but he doesn't say anything as the waiter leaves.

I lift the glass, the condensation cool against my palm, and take a sip through the straw. The sweetness hits first, followed by the slow, warm burn of the alcohol. It's exactly what I need.

"You should take it slow," Zack says, his voice low but firm. "That's not exactly a light drink."

I smile at him over the rim of my glass. "Are you always this concerned about what I do?"

"Yes," he says without missing a beat, leaning back in his chair. "Especially when you're making choices that might lead to regret."

My grip on the glass tightens, and I tilt my head, feigning innocence. "Regret? Like what?"

"Like the last time you got drunk." His gaze locks on mine, steady and unyielding. "Remember what happened?"

Heat rushes to my cheeks, but I refuse to look away. "I remember everything, Zack. You don't have to remind me."

"Then don't make me," he says simply, his voice soft but laced with meaning.

The tension between us feels like a living thing, curling around the table and pulling us closer. I take another sip of my drink, slower this time, the straw a convenient distraction. When I glance back at him, his expression is calm, but his eyes express something deeper...something I can't quite name.

"I'm fine," I repeat firmly, leaving no room for doubt. "I have no regrets."

"Alright," he says, his tone even as our food is delivered. I welcome the reprieve from being the sole focus of his attention, but the lingering discomfort pushes me to drink more… and faster…than I had intended.

CHAPTER
Thirty

ZACK

The moment the waiter clears away our plates, Jenny leans back in her chair, her glass of iced tea nearly empty. She glances toward him with a gleam in her eye that doesn't sit quite right with me. Before I can say anything, she signals the waiter.

"I'll have another one," she says lightly, motioning toward her drink.

The waiter hesitates, glancing at me briefly before nodding. Before he can leave, I speak up. "Actually, no, she won't." My tone is firm, leaving no room for argument.

Jenny stiffens, her lips parting in disbelief. "Excuse me?" Her voice is sharp, but there's a hint of vulnerability beneath it.

I keep my eyes on hers, steady and unflinching. "You've had enough."

She glares at me, her cheeks flushing. "I really don't appreciate you doing that. I can decide for myself."

The waiter awkwardly lingers, unsure of whether to leave

or stay. I nod toward him, dismissing him with a polite but firm, "Thank you."

Jenny's eyes narrow as the waiter walks away. "You don't get to tell me what to do, Zack."

I lean forward slightly, lowering my voice. "You're going to have a raging headache tomorrow, and you'll have to work. It'll be hell."

She smiles, crossing her arms. "Your concern is much appreciated but I can handle my liquor, thank you very much."

"No," I counter, my tone calm but unwavering. "You can't."

Her eyes flash with defiance, but there's something else there too…a flicker of uncertainty.

"Maybe I don't want to handle it," she says softly, her voice dropping to almost a whisper.

Her words hit harder than I expect, the weight of them settling between us like a storm cloud. I lean back in my chair, studying her carefully. The defiance in her gaze falters slightly, giving way to something raw, something honest.

I know what she's referring to, and I cannot believe it. But at the same time, I wonder if I'm just reading incorrectly into the situation. This has to be the case, right?

I take a slow breath, choosing my next words carefully. There is no need to guess or pretend. It has never been my style to do that, and I'm not about to start now.

"Are you saying what I think you're saying?" I ask.

Her gaze lowers as she stirs the empty drink glass before her. Then she lifts her eyes, staring up at me from beneath her lashes.

"Yes," she replies, though her voice is quite shaky. "It's what I want."

At this confirmation, to say that I'm dumbfounded is the least of it. It takes me a while to weigh the pros and cons of following through with her request, but in the end, I throw all of it out and speak directly to the woman in front of me.

I take a slow breath, choosing my next words carefully. "If that's what you want, Jenny..." I pause, letting the silence stretch just long enough to feel heavy. "Then you don't need to get drunk to make me give it to you."

Her lips part as if she's about to protest, but no sound comes out. Her hands tighten around the edge of the table, her knuckles white. I can see the war raging inside her, the push and pull of her emotions as she processes what I just said.

Finally, she exhales shakily and nods, her voice barely audible. "Yes. That's what I want."

For a moment, the world around us seems to fade. The chatter of the other diners, the clinking of glasses, the soft strains of music from the speakers...it all disappears as I hold her gaze. Her vulnerability is palpable, and it hits me harder than I care to admit.

I let the silence linger for just a moment longer before I nod and signal for the check. The waiter approaches quickly, sensing the tension but wisely saying nothing as he places the bill on the table. I pull out my wallet and pay, sliding the leather folder back toward him with a quiet, "Thank you."

Then, I stand, tapping the table lightly with my knuckles. "Let's go."

Jenny hesitates for a split second before rising to her feet. She smooths her dress, avoiding my gaze as we leave the restaurant. But I can feel her beside me, her presence charged with an energy that's impossible to ignore.

As we step out into the warm afternoon sun, I place a hand lightly on the small of her back, guiding her toward the car. The touch is brief, almost automatic, but it's enough to send a jolt through me...a reminder of everything that's waiting for us in just a little while.

I waste no time in getting us back to the hotel, and soon we get on the elevator. There are others amongst us, but still, they might as well have been invisible because she is all I can feel and sense.

The moment the elevator empties out, the tension between us becomes nearly unbearable. I can feel her hesitating, lingering just a little too long, her hand brushing the panel behind her as if delaying the inevitable. Her breathing is shallow, and though her face is turned slightly away, I can see the faint flush creeping along her neck.

Without warning, she steps closer to me, lifting herself onto her tiptoes. Before I can process what's happening, her lips brush mine in a featherlight kiss, startling me into stillness. It's fleeting...just the barest hint of her warmth... before she pulls back, her wide, nervous eyes searching mine.

"I..." she begins, her voice barely audible, her cheeks flaming with embarrassment.

But before she can step away or say something to fill the awkward silence, I react. My hand finds the side of her neck, fingers pressing lightly against her skin, and I pull her closer. There's a moment where she freezes, caught between hesitation and surrender, but then her body softens against mine as I kiss her back.

It's deeper this time. My lips claim hers, slow and deliberate, a quiet ignition to the fire building between us. She makes a soft sound, half gasp, half sigh, and it shoots straight through me, unraveling every restraint I've tried to maintain.

She responds in kind, her fingers gripping the lapels of my jacket, pulling me closer until there's no space between us. The taste of her is intoxicating, and I don't want to stop. I don't think I could, even if I tried.

By the time we stumble out of the elevator, still locked in each other, everything else fades into the background. The hallway is quiet, but I barely register it because all I can feel is her...her lips, her hands, her urgency.

At the door to her room, she pauses just long enough to fumble with the keycard. My lips trail down her neck as she presses it to the reader, and the soft sound she makes nearly undoes me. The door clicks open, and we're inside before it even swings fully shut.

She pushes me back against the door, her hands already sliding under my shirt, exploring the planes of my chest. The sheer hunger in her touch surprises me, leaving me breathless.

"Jenny," I manage, my voice rough as I try to catch my breath. "Wait...are you sure—"

"I'm sure," she cuts me off, her voice firm yet trembling with emotion. "Zack... I've been thinking about this. About you. I can't stop."

Her confession leaves me speechless, a quiet thunder that roars through my chest. Before I can respond, she moves closer, her lips finding mine again with a desperation that ignites every nerve in my body. Her hands press against my chest, pushing the leather jacket off my shoulders as she kisses me with a hunger that leaves no room for hesitation.

Her lips trail from my mouth to my jaw, down the column of my neck, leaving a scorching path in their wake. I stand frozen, caught between the sheer force of her desire and my own unraveling restraint. When she pulls back just enough to grip the hem of my shirt, her eyes meet mine, blazing with something I can't quite name.

"Jenny," I whisper, my voice low and strained, though I don't even know what I'm trying to say.

She doesn't wait for me to finish. Her hands slide under my shirt, her fingers tracing over the planes of my abdomen, and then she lifts it higher. I help her, yanking the shirt over my head and tossing it aside, only to feel her lips return to my skin instantly. The cool air brushes against my bare skin, but I barely notice. All I feel is her…the heat of her mouth, the softness of her lips, the sheer intensity of her focus as she devours me like I'm the only thing that matters.

She kisses her way down my chest, her mouth pressing against every inch she can reach. When her hands smooth over my arms, her lips follow, leaving soft, urgent kisses along my biceps, my forearms. It's reverent and ravenous all at once, and it makes my head spin.

"Jenny," I say again, my voice rougher this time as I grab her wrists, trying to still her for just a moment. I'm looking for an explanation, on why she is so ravenous, and she understands. I feel the same way too, but it stuns me that the hunger is mutual.

She looks up at me, her eyes dark with need, and her lips part as though she's about to speak. But instead of answering, she leans forward, pressing her lips to my collarbone, then lower, her kisses trailing down my torso until I can't think, can't breathe.

"Jenny," I rasp, my voice hoarse and trembling as I cup her face, forcing her to meet my gaze. I'm trying to hold on to some semblance of control, but the way she looks at me makes it impossible. "Are you sure about this?" I ask one more time before we reach the point of no return.

She nods, and I believe her.

Her hands tremble only slightly as she unbuttons my pants, sliding the zipper down with deliberate slowness. My breath catches, the anticipation coursing through me as her fingers brush against me through the fabric. Even that minimal touch sends a jolt straight to my core, and I bite back a groan.

When she leans forward, her lips pressing tentatively

against me through the fabric, the sensation is maddening. She's testing, teasing, and it's driving me insane. My cock aches, straining against the confinement, and when she glances up at me, the determination in her eyes is enough to undo me entirely.

"Jenny," I rasp, my voice thick with desire and a hint of restraint. But she doesn't stop. Instead, she tugs down the waistband of my briefs, freeing me completely. The cool air hits me first, but then her warm hand wraps around me, and the contrast is staggering.

She takes a moment to study me, her gaze dropping to my cock, and I feel a surge of heat under her scrutiny. Her lips part slightly, and then she leans in, her breath warm against the sensitive skin. When her tongue darts out to trace a slow line along the underside, my head falls back, and a guttural sound escapes me.

Her lips close over the head, soft and deliberate, and she sucks gently, her tongue swirling in a way that makes my hips jerk involuntarily. I can't stop the groan that follows, my hand moving to tangle in her hair. She doesn't pull away. If anything, her confidence grows, her pace quickening as she takes more of me into her mouth.

Her tongue presses firmly against the underside, and she moves with a rhythm that's calculated to destroy me. She pulls back slightly, her lips dragging along my length before she takes me deeper again, her cheeks hollowing as she sucks. The sensation is overwhelming, her mouth hot and wet and perfect.

"Fuck," I groan, my voice low and ragged as I fight to keep some semblance of control. My fingers tighten in her hair, guiding her gently, but she's already moving with an intensity that leaves me breathless.

Her hands grip the base of my cock, stroking in time with the movement of her mouth, and the combination is devastating. She takes me deeper, her lips brushing against her hand as she moves, and I can feel the pressure building, coiling low in my abdomen.

"Jenny," I manage, my voice strained. "You don't—"

She pulls back slightly, her lips glistening as she looks up at me. "I want to," she whispers, her voice low and breathless. The raw sincerity in her words leaves me speechless.

She takes me back into her mouth, and this time, she doesn't hold back. Her movements are faster, more deliberate, her tongue pressing and swirling as she takes me deeper. My hips jerk forward instinctively, and she takes it all, her lips sliding down my length until she's nearly at the base.

The sight of her like this...on her knees, her cheeks flushed, her lips stretched around my cock...sends me spiraling. I can't stop the groans that slip from my lips, the way my body reacts to every touch, every movement. She's relentless, her focus absolute, and it's enough to make my vision blur.

"I'm close," I warn her, my voice rough and uneven, but she doesn't stop. If anything, she goes deeper, her tongue pressing harder as she takes me in completely. The tension in my body snaps, and I come with a shuddering groan, the release blindingly intense.

I try to pull back, but she holds me in place, her lips sealed around me as she swallows everything. The sensation is too much, almost unbearable, but she doesn't falter. When she finally pulls back, her lips are swollen, her cheeks flushed, and her gaze is heavy-lidded as she looks up at me.

She licks her lips slowly, deliberately, and it's the most erotic thing I've ever seen. My knees nearly give out as I reach down to pull her to her feet, my hands cupping her face as I crash my lips against hers. The kiss is frantic, all-consuming, as I press her back against the door, the taste of her mixed with my release only fueling the fire between us.

"Jenny," I murmur against her lips, my voice hoarse and

filled with everything I can't put into words. Her response is a soft moan, her hands gripping my shoulders as she pulls me closer.

CHAPTER
Thirty~One

JENNY

My head spins as he kisses me, his lips fierce and commanding, yet somehow tender. My heart pounds so hard I can feel it in every inch of my body, matching the heat that surges through me. His hands cup my face as if I'm something precious, something he can't let go of, and the intensity in his gaze as he pulls back to look at me steals what little breath I have left.

My lips tingle from the force of his kiss, and the taste of him lingers, rich and addictive. I feel a thrill as I press closer, my hands wandering over the firm muscles of his chest and shoulders. God, he feels so solid, so real, and every touch sends a shiver of excitement through me.

I glance up into his eyes, and for a moment, I wonder if he's as undone as I am. His expression is raw, unguarded, and it makes my heart twist. I try to push the thought away, telling myself this is just the heat of the moment, but the way he looks at me...it feels like something more.

His hands find the zipper at the back of my dress, his movements slow and deliberate as he draws it down. The sound of the zipper is impossibly loud in the charged silence between us, the only other sound, my unsteady breathing. The fabric loosens and slips from my shoulders, gliding down my body until it pools at my feet.

His gaze roams over me, dark and unyielding, taking in every inch as though committing the moment to memory. The intensity in his eyes sends a shiver racing through me. I feel exposed, yes, but not vulnerable...his attention makes me feel powerful, desired in a way that steals my breath.

He steps closer, his hands finding my waist, warm and firm as they slide upward. When his palms cup my breasts, his thumbs graze over the peaks, drawing a soft gasp from my lips. The fullness of them fills his hands completely, and the reverence in his touch makes my knees weaken. He squeezes gently, almost testing the weight of them, before rolling his thumbs again, igniting heat that pools low in my belly.

I can feel the hardness of his erection pressing against my stomach, the heat of his arousal, an undeniable presence against my bare skin. It's almost too much, the way his body speaks to mine without words, the silent promise of what's to come making me tremble. I tilt my head back, meeting his eyes, and the hunger there makes me ache for him even more.

. . .

"Jenny," he murmurs, his voice rough as gravel, a whisper of restraint in the depths of his desire. His hands slide down my sides, skimming over the curve of my hips before his fingers hook into the sides of my thong. He hesitates for a moment, as though waiting for permission, but when I don't stop him, he slides the delicate fabric down, letting it fall to the floor alongside my dress.

I shudder as his hand moves between my thighs, his fingers grazing over the slick heat there. The touch is light at first, exploratory, but when I gasp, his movements grow bolder. His fingers stroke me, finding the rhythm of my breath and the tilt of my hips as I press into his touch.

"God, you're perfect," he mutters, his voice low and reverent, and the words unravel me completely. I clutch at his shoulders, my nails digging into the firm muscle as waves of pleasure course through me. His fingers move with precision, his other hand sliding up to cradle the small of my back, steadying me as my knees threaten to buckle.

I can't think, can't breathe, can't do anything but feel him... his touch, his heat, the way he's learning every inch of me as though it's a language he was born to speak. My hands move instinctively, trailing down the hard planes of his chest, over the ridges of his abdomen, and lower still. When I wrap my fingers around him, his breath hitches, and for a moment, he stills.

. . .

Our eyes lock and the raw intensity there leaves me trembling. I stroke him slowly, savoring the weight of him in my hand, the way his body reacts to my touch. His head falls back slightly, a guttural sound escaping his lips, and the pure, unrestrained response sends a thrill coursing through me.

When he looks back at me, his eyes are darker than before, the storm inside them matching the one in my chest. Without a word, he lifts me effortlessly, guiding me toward the bed, his lips brushing against my shoulder, my collarbone, every inch of skin he can reach as he lays me down. The cool sheets meet my back, but his weight soon replaces the chill, blanketing me in warmth as he covers me completely.

Zack leans over me, his body is a masterpiece of strength and precision, yet somehow soft in the way it molds perfectly to mine. His weight grounds me, and the heat of his skin against mine sets every nerve alight. His eyes search mine, a question lingering there...an unspoken need for permission or reassurance. I answer by wrapping my legs around his hips, drawing him closer.

He dips his head, his lips capturing mine in a kiss that steals what little breath I have left. It's slow at first, exploratory, but soon deepens, his tongue sweeping against mine in a rhythm that makes my toes curl. His hand trails upward, finding my breast again, his palm warm and firm as he squeezes gently. His thumb brushes over my nipple, teasing it into a hardened peak, and a soft moan escapes me before I can stop it.

• • •

"Jenny," he murmurs against my lips, my name a prayer on his tongue. His mouth moves lower, his kisses trailing down my neck, over the curve of my shoulder, and along the swell of my breast. When he takes my nipple into his mouth, his tongue swirling around the sensitive peak, I arch into him, a gasp slipping from my lips. His teeth graze lightly, just enough to send a jolt of pleasure racing through me, and I clutch at his shoulders, needing something to anchor me.

"You're driving me insane," I whisper, my voice trembling as his hand moves to my other breast, giving it the same reverent attention. He hums against my skin, the sound low and vibrating through me, and I feel the tension building deep inside me.

His kisses continue their journey downward, slow and deliberate, as if he's savoring every inch of me. When his lips reach the curve of my hip, he pauses, his hands sliding down my thighs to part them gently. The vulnerability of the moment should terrify me, but the way he looks at me…like I'm something sacred…melts away every ounce of fear.

"Zack…" My voice falters, his name barely more than a whisper as his lips press against the sensitive skin of my inner thigh. He doesn't rush, his mouth teasing, his hands firm yet tender as they hold me open for him. The anticipation coils tightly in my belly, every second stretching endlessly until I feel his breath against me, warm and tantalizing.

When his tongue finally finds my sex, a broken cry escapes my lips. He moves with precision, his strokes slow and deliberate, exploring every inch of me as though he's learning what makes me come undone. His hands grip my thighs, holding me steady as I writhe beneath him, the pressure building with every flick of his tongue, every gentle suction that sends sparks shooting through me.

"Zack, please…" I'm not even sure what I'm begging for, but the words spill from me anyway, desperate and raw. He responds with a hum, the vibration sending a shockwave of pleasure through me, and I grip the sheets, my back arching as the tension becomes almost unbearable.

His name falls from my lips like a mantra, over and over, as he takes me higher and higher, his mouth working me with a skill that leaves me breathless. When he slides a finger inside me, curling it just right, the sensation is too much

The stretch is slow and unrelenting, and the heat in my core ignites into a blaze. My hips shift instinctively, seeking him, and he matches my rhythm. I can't stop the gasp that escapes me, high and needy.

"Is this what you want?" he murmurs, his voice rough, darkened with desire. His free hand comes to rest on my hip, holding me steady as his movements grow rougher, faster, more deliberate.

I've never been finger-fucked this way before. I can't respond, not coherently. My body answers for me, tightening around him, trembling as he pushes me closer and closer to the edge. His finger strokes me deeply, each motion slow and deliberate, building a rhythm that has me unraveling, piece by piece.

When he adds another, the fullness is almost too much, but it's exactly what I need. I grip the sheets tighter, a low moan spilling from my lips as my body adjusts, welcoming the sensation.

"Zack," I manage, my voice breaking on his name. It's a plea, a thank-you, a prayer, all rolled into one. He watches me, his gaze heavy-lidded and burning with something that feels dangerous, electric. His thumb brushes against my most sensitive spot, adding a pressure that sends a burst of pleasure rocketing through me, and I lose all semblance of control.

"Look at me," he commands softly, and the weight of his voice pulls me from the haze of sensation. My eyes flutter open, meeting his, and the intensity there steals my breath. His fingers continue their relentless rhythm, and the combination of his touch and his gaze is my undoing. I feel like I'm breaking apart yet somehow being put back together in ways I never thought possible.

"Don't stop," I beg, my voice trembling with need. He doesn't, his pace steady, unrelenting, as he drives me higher. The tension inside me builds, coiling tighter and tighter, until it feels like I might shatter from the sheer pressure of it. My body trembles, my breaths coming faster, shallow and uneven.

"You're so beautiful like this," he murmurs, his voice reverent, and his words push me even closer to the edge. His free hand slides up my side, brushing against the swell of my breast, his thumb grazing the peak just as his fingers curl inside me again, hitting a spot that sends white-hot pleasure rippling through me.

I cry out, the sound raw and unrestrained, as the wave crashes over me. My body clenches around him, every muscle tightening as I'm consumed by the intensity of my release. It's blinding, consuming, a pleasure so sharp it borders on pain, and I cling to him like he's the only thing anchoring me in the storm.

He doesn't stop, guiding me through the aftershocks with gentle, precise movements, his touch softening as the tension slowly ebbs away. My body trembles in his arms, utterly spent, yet more alive than I've ever felt.

When I finally collapse back onto the bed, my chest heaving with each ragged breath, he rises above me, his fingers glistening with the evidence of my release. His gaze is dark, almost possessive, and when his lips curve into the faintest hint of a smile, I feel the heat pooling in my core again.

"You're incredible," he says softly, brushing a strand of hair from my face. His voice carries the weight of truth, and in that moment, I feel seen...fully, completely. And as his lips capture mine in a slow, searing kiss, I realize I never want this moment to end.

CHAPTER
Thirty-Two

ZACK

Her body jerks beneath me, trembling as if the pleasure still hasn't fully let her go. I can see it in the way her abdomen contracts in shallow waves, in the soft hitch of her breath. She looks utterly spent, yet radiant, her skin glistening with a sheen of sweat that makes her even more irresistible. I can't stop myself...I lean down, pressing my lips to her stomach, tasting the salt of her skin as I trail soft kisses along the curve of her hip.

The scent of her surrounds me, sweet and musky and wholly hers. It fills my lungs, and for a moment, I just breathe her in, trying to ground myself in the reality of this moment. I've never felt anything like it...like her. She smells like she's meant to drive me insane.

. . .

I shift, rolling onto my back, pulling her with me until she's draped across my chest. She's so light, fitting against me like she belongs there, her skin soft and warm against mine. My cock, still hard and pressed against her, is slick with her release, the undeniable evidence of what just happened between us. It sends a jolt of arousal through me, even as I try to slow my breathing.

She tilts her head up, her hair falling over one shoulder as her cheek rests against my chest. I slide a hand down her back, savoring the feel of her beneath my fingers. The curve of her spine, the dip of her waist...it's perfect. She stirs slightly, shifting her hips, and the friction makes me groan, low and guttural.

"I can feel you," she murmurs, her voice still heavy with exhaustion and something deeper...satisfaction, maybe.

Her words make me exhale sharply, my hands tightening against her sides. "You're driving me insane," I admit, my voice rough as gravel. "I don't think I'll survive this."

She laughs softly, a sound that sends warmth curling through my chest. But then she shifts again, her hips pressing deliberately against me this time, and my breath catches. Her sex is hot and slick against me, and I can feel every movement, every subtle grind of her hips.

"You're playing with fire," I warn her, my hands gripping her waist. But she only smiles, leaning up slightly so her breasts press against me, her nipples brushing my skin. My hands move instinctively, sliding up her sides to cup her breasts, my thumbs grazing over the taut peaks.

Her breath hitches as I knead them gently, marveling at their fullness, the way they fit so perfectly in my hands. Her skin is so soft, so warm, and the sounds she makes...soft little moans that escape her lips unbidden...are enough to undo me completely. I lean up, taking one nipple into my mouth, sucking gently, and the way she arches against me, the way she whispers my name, is a reward in itself.

"Zack..." Her voice is a plea, her hands threading into my hair as she presses closer. I let my tongue flick against her, savoring the way her body reacts, the way she trembles in my arms.

When I release her breast and look up, her face is flushed, her lips parted as she breathes heavily.

"Do you want to try something?" I ask, my voice low and measured, though my heart feels like it's hammering against my ribs.

She blinks at me, her expression caught between curiosity and nervousness. "What?"

I smile, sitting up slightly and guiding her hips against me. "Ride me," I say simply, watching her cheeks flush an even deeper shade of red. "If you want to."

She hesitates, biting her lip, and for a moment, I wonder if I've pushed too far. But then she nods, her hands resting on my chest as she adjusts herself, lifting her hips slightly. I guide her, my hands firm on her waist, positioning myself against her entrance. The head of my cock brushes against her, and we both shudder at the contact.

Slowly, she lowers herself, her breath catching as I begin to stretch her. "Take your time," I murmur, my hands steadying her as she takes me in, inch by inch. The slick heat of her surrounds me, her body gripping me so tightly it feels like I'm losing my mind.

When I'm fully seated inside her, she pauses, her hands splayed against my chest as she adjusts to the stretch. "God, Jenny..." I groan, my head falling back against the pillow as the sensation nearly overwhelms me. "You feel... incredible."

Her breath is unsteady, her nails digging into my chest as she moves experimentally, a slow grind of her hips that makes us both gasp. She feels perfect...better than I ever could have imagined...and I can't stop my hands from roaming, sliding up her thighs, over the curve of her hips, and back to her waist.

She begins to move, her rhythm slow and tentative at first, but it quickly grows more confident. I lean up, capturing one of her breasts in my mouth again, my hands gripping her hips as I guide her movements. The sound of her moans, the way she whispers my name with every roll of her hips...it's intoxicating, and I know I'll never be able to get enough of her.

· · ·

Her rhythm grows surer, the hesitancy melting away with every shift of her hips. I watch her, utterly entranced...the way her head tilts back, exposing the elegant curve of her neck, the soft flush spreading down her chest, the rise and fall of her breasts as she moves. Every detail of her is etched into my mind like a brand, unforgettable and searing.

"Jenny..." Her name leaves my lips in a gasp, low and hoarse, my voice breaking under the weight of the pleasure coursing through me. I grip her waist tighter, feeling the slick heat of her surrounding me, gripping me so perfectly that it takes every ounce of restraint not to let go too soon.

Her hands slide up my chest, her fingers splaying over my shoulders for balance. Our eyes meet, and the intensity in her gaze steals what little air I have left. She doesn't look away, and neither do I. It's like time has stopped, the world narrowing to just us...her soft gasps, my ragged breaths, the electric connection binding us.

She moves faster now, her hips rolling fluidly, and I can't help the way my own hips meet hers, driving deeper into the tight heat of her. The sensation is indescribable...her warmth, her slickness, the way her body molds to mine. Every grind of her hips sends a jolt of pleasure through me, each one more intense than the last.

"God, you're so beautiful," I murmur, my hands sliding up her back to cradle her face. I pull her down to me, capturing her lips in a kiss that's as desperate as it is tender. She tastes like salt and sweetness, of everything I've ever wanted, and when she moans into my mouth, it nearly undoes me.

. . .

Her legs begin to tremble, the strain of holding herself upright evident, but she doesn't falter. If anything, she presses harder against me, her movements becoming erratic as she chases her release. I slide one hand down to where we're joined, my thumb finding the sensitive bundle of nerves at her center. She gasps, her whole body jerking as I circle it in time with her movements.

"Zack..." Her voice is a broken plea, her nails digging into my shoulders as her rhythm falters. She's so close...I can feel it in the way her walls tighten around me, the way her breath hitches, coming in shallow, uneven bursts. It's enough to drive me insane.

Without a word, I move instinctively, flipping us over in one smooth motion until her back meets the mattress. She gasps softly, her body sinking into the plush bedding, her hair fanning out like a halo. The sight of her, flushed and trembling beneath me, is enough to steal my breath.

I lean over her, my hands on either side of her head, holding her gaze as I lower myself between her thighs. My hands slide down her sides, finding her hips, and I spread her legs apart, the movement deliberate and reverent. She's soft and yielding beneath me, her body pliant, her eyes dark with desire.

. . .

When I press into her again, she arches her back, a sharp cry escaping her lips as I sink into her heat. Her walls clench around me, so tight and slick that I have to grit my teeth to keep from losing it right then. I start slow, my thrusts measured and deliberate, savoring the way she feels, the way her body reacts to every movement.

She trembles beneath me, her hands gripping the sheets as soft whimpers spill from her lips. I press kisses along her jawline, down her neck, to the sensitive curve of her shoulder. Each kiss is a silent worship, a way to ground myself in her. I want to remember every inch of her, every sound she makes, every look in her eyes.

"Zack," she breathes again, her voice a soft cry as her hips rise to meet mine. Her hands find my back, her nails leaving faint trails of heat against my skin, urging me deeper, harder. I oblige, my control slipping with every thrust, the need to be closer to her, to feel all of her, overtaking me.

Her moans grow louder, more desperate, mingling with the sound of our bodies moving together...the wet heat, the soft slap of skin against skin. The bed creaks beneath us, but it's drowned out by her gasps and cries, by the way she whispers my name like it's the only thing keeping her tethered.

I kiss her lips, her cheeks, the soft line of her collarbone, unable to get enough of her. My hands roam her body, sliding up to cup her breasts, kneading the soft curves, my thumbs brushing over her hardened nipples. She arches into my touch, her cries turning into incoherent murmurs that drive me wild.

. . .

I feel her tightening around me, her thighs trembling against my sides as I fuck her. She's so close, and the thought sends a surge of heat through me. I bury myself deeper, my rhythm quickening, my thrusts harder now, rougher, as the last of my control slips away. I groan, low and guttural, as her nails dig into my back, anchoring herself against the onslaught.

Her cries reach a crescendo, her head tipping back as she comes undone beneath me. Her body shakes, her walls fluttering around me, and the sight of her, completely lost in pleasure, pushes me over the edge.

"Fuck," I groan, thrusting up into her one last time as the tension in my body snaps. The pleasure is blinding, all-consuming, every nerve alight as I spill into her. My hands tighten on her waist, holding her close as we ride out the waves together.

I collapse against her, her body trembling and slick with sweat, her head resting on my shoulder. I wrap my arms around her, pulling her close, feeling her heart pounding in sync with mine. For a moment, neither of us moves, our bodies slick with sweat, our breaths mingling as we try to catch them. The room is filled with the sound of our ragged breathing, the air thick with the scent of sex and something deeper...something unspoken.

I press a kiss to her temple, my hand sliding up her back to tangle in her hair. "You're perfect," I whisper, the words spilling out before I can stop them. And it's true. She's everything I didn't know I needed, everything I'll never be able to let go of.

I turn around with her until she's nestled into the curve of my body. I should let her go. Tell her to return to her room, maintain the distance I know we should have, but I might as well cut my arm off than do this. And so, we remain in place, basking in each other's warmth in total disbelief of the extent and intensity of our connection.

She fits perfectly, her body curving into mine like she was made to be here. I reach for the blanket, pulling it over us as I press another kiss to her hair.

The room is silent save for the sound of our breathing, and I feel a fierce protectiveness settle over me. I'll keep her safe, from everything and everyone. No matter what.

CHAPTER
Thirty~Three

JENNY

I wake up to the steady rise and fall of his chest beneath my cheek, his heartbeat a quiet, reassuring rhythm in the sunset silence. His arm is still draped over me, the weight of it grounding and protective. For a moment, I let myself sink into the warmth of him, my eyes tracing the curve of his jaw, the faint shadow of stubble catching the soft light filtering through the curtains. His beauty is staggering, almost unreal. He looks at peace, so different from the intensity he radiates when awake.

But then the reality of what just happened crashes over me, and my chest tightens. This is too much. Too close. Too raw. I tell myself it's just the afterglow, the lingering haze of pleasure blurring my thoughts, but deep down, I know better. This isn't just about the sex…though that was unlike anything I've ever experienced. It's about him, and the way he makes me feel. Vulnerable. Exposed. Seen.

I can't let that happen.

Sliding carefully out from under his arm, I move as quietly as I can, trying not to wake him. My dress is crumpled on the floor, a stark reminder of how this night started, and as I slip it back on, I feel the weight of every decision pressing down on me.

When I turn back to look at him, he's awake, his eyes dark and watchful. He props himself up on one elbow, the sheet slipping down to reveal the planes of his chest. His gaze pins me in place, and for a moment, neither of us speaks.

"Leaving already?" His voice is low, rough from sleep, and it sends a shiver down my spine.

I force a smile, hoping it hides the turmoil churning inside me. "I should go. I need to… think."

He sits up fully now, the sheet pooling around his waist, his expression unreadable. "About what?"

"About this," I say, gesturing vaguely between us.

"And what about this?" he asks.

I actually think of an answer for this, but an entire minute passes, and nothing forms in my brain except cobwebs.

And so, I just state exactly what I want to.

"I… I'm thinking that this is okay because we're both adults, Zack. And w-we have… needs. So… this can work as just what it is. It doesn't have to mean anything more than that."

My stomach twists so painfully at this, but I console myself with the fact that this is the truth. I tell myself I'm just getting emotional and lost in the intensity of the current moment, which is why I'm being this blunt…so clear lines can be drawn for both me and him. It will be better for everybody.

The way he stares at me, though, makes me want to dig a hole and slide myself into it forever. But I strengthen my resolve to go this route.

I want Brett, and this has been a conviction of mine since I was too young to even know what love was. Zack, though alluring, is cold, while Brett…with his warmth…has been what I've been drawn to from the very start. So, I have to test myself and not get distracted by someone like Zack.

Plus, I imagine Zack should be comfortable with this arrangement. He's someone who especially deals with transactions, so he should take this as one as well.

His jaw tightens, but he nods slowly, his gaze never leaving mine. "Is that what you want?"

"It's what makes sense," I say, my voice firmer than I feel. "We can keep things simple. No strings. Just… this."

There's a long pause, the tension in the room thick enough to choke on. When he finally speaks, his tone is calm, almost detached, but there's an edge to it that I can't quite place. "Alright. If that's what you want."

Relief floods through me, but it's short-lived as he adds, "But if this is going to be just sex, Jenny, then it goes both ways. No rules. No boundaries. If you're going to use me, I'll do the same to you."

My breath catches, and I blink at him, stunned. "What… what does that mean?"

"It means you don't get to deprive me when you feel like it," he says, his gaze sharp and unyielding. "You can't decide when or where this happens. If you want this arrangement, then you have to be all in."

His words hang in the air like a challenge, and I can feel my pulse racing. The idea of giving up that kind of control terrifies me, but the thought of walking away from him completely terrifies me even more.

"That sounds… dangerous," I say quietly, my voice wavering despite my best efforts to sound composed.

A faint smile tugs at the corner of his lips, but it doesn't reach his eyes. "It is. But it's not. It's just business."

I'd thought setting this agreement in place would make me feel better and more in control, but instead, it suddenly feels like all the warmth in my chest rushes out of my body, replaced by a frightening chill.

I don't know what to say to that, so I don't say anything. I just nod, my throat tight, and turn to leave. But as I reach the door, something makes me pause. The sight of him, bathed in the golden glow of the setting sun, his bare chest rising and falling with every breath, is enough to make my heart stutter. He looks unguarded, achingly beautiful, and for a moment, I wonder if I'm making a mistake.

"Jenny," he says softly, and the sound of my name on his lips is enough to break me.

I turn back to face him, my resolve wavering. "Alright," I say finally, the words feeling like a surrender. "I'm in."

The smile he gives me then is slow and deliberate, and it makes my stomach flip. "Good," he says. "See you later, then."

And just like that, he settles back into the bed, adjusts his position, and closes his eyes to sleep.

The next few days, I truly begin to understand what he'd meant, and even though, in the moment, it's everything I want, that feeling of losing complete control creeps back in, stronger and more unsettling.

The first instance comes a few days later, on the balcony.

The air was crisp, tinged with the scent of rain lingering from earlier in the evening. The city lights below twinkled like scattered jewels, indifferent to what was about to unfold. I had been sitting inside, trying to read to allay my anxiety over when and if he would ever talk to me again.

And then he'd come over and tugged the book from my hands, setting it aside without a word. His presence loomed over me, commanding without effort, and when he held out his hand, I took it…hesitantly at first. I wasn't sure where this would go, but before I could think too much about it, he guided me toward the open balcony doors. The cool wind kissed my skin as I stepped out, the night enveloping us in its quiet intimacy.

"Zack…" I started, unsure of what to say, but he silenced me with a look. That dark, smoldering gaze of his had me pinned, and my breath hitched when he turned me around to face the railing.

"This is what I want," he'd murmured, his voice low and rough against my ear. His hands settled on my hips, firm but not forceful, as if giving me a chance to stop this before it started. But I didn't. I couldn't.

Before I knew it, I was bent over the cool metal of the railing, the city sprawling below us, both thrilling and exposing. The wind swept my hair across my face, and I barely noticed when his hands pushed up the hem of my dress, his touch leaving a trail of fire against my skin. My pulse raced as the fabric bunched around my waist, and the first press of his body against mine stole my breath.

"Relax," he whispered, his lips brushing the shell of my ear. But there was no relaxing…not with him, not like this. Every nerve in my body was alive, hyperaware of his every movement.

When he slid into me from behind, the stretch was slow, deliberate, and utterly consuming. I gasped, my fingers gripping the railing for support as he filled me completely, his hands anchoring my hips to his. The sensation was overwhelming, the angle perfect in a way that made me tremble. The world around us seemed to blur, the sounds of the city fading into nothing as he plain and simple started to fuck me out of my mind.

Each thrust was measured at first, his control evident in the way he seemed to savor every inch of me. But it didn't last. Soon, his rhythm grew rougher, more desperate, his hips slamming into mine with a force that sent shocks of pleasure spiraling through me. The railing dug into my stomach, grounding me, as my body met his in perfect synchronization.

The wind whipped against my skin, cool against the heat building inside me, and I couldn't hold back the cries spilling from my lips. He leaned over me, his chest pressing against my back, and the sound of his ragged breaths in my ear made me clench around him, drawing a guttural groan from deep in his throat.

"Jenny," he growled, his voice raw and broken. One of his hands slid up my side, gripping the curve of my waist before moving to cup my breast. His fingers teased the sensitive peak, sending jolts of pleasure coursing through me as his pace quickened.

The intensity was overwhelming, the pleasure sharp and unrelenting. My legs trembled beneath me, the railing the only thing keeping me upright as he drove into me, each thrust deeper and harder than the last. The combination of his heat, his strength, and the cool night air was dizzying, intoxicating.

When my release finally hit, it was explosive, ripping through me in waves so powerful they left me shaking. My body tightened around him, and his rhythm faltered as he followed me over the edge, his groan echoing in the night as he buried himself inside me one last time.

I couldn't fall asleep that night because, for some reason, I needed him. Needed the warmth he had offered me initially by holding me in his arms and soothing me. Instead, he'd turned and left, even smacking my ass on his way out, and I'd never felt colder. Still, I told myself it was better this way because it made me hate him…just a little, though…since this was what I had asked for. To simply be fucked, with no emotions left intact.

And so, eventually, I fell asleep thinking of Brett and how much warmer he was. But it felt like cheating because that affection and warmth...if I were honest...Zack had offered me first.

The next time was in the shower.

It had been a long day, the kind that left my body tense and my mind racing. Every moment of stress, every lingering frustration, clung to me like a weight I couldn't shake. And as the sound of water running filtered through my door late at night, I felt an ache that wasn't just physical...it was deeper, clawing at my insides, begging for release.

I didn't think...I acted. My feet carried me to his bathroom before my mind could catch up. The air was thick with steam, curling and rising like smoke, wrapping around me as I stepped inside. The heat kissed my skin, easing some of the tension in my shoulders but stoking something even more consuming within me.

He stood under the cascade of water, his back to me, broad shoulders glistening under the dim light. The sight of him stirred a fire that had been simmering since that night on the balcony, where he had been as cold and unyielding as the wind biting at my skin. He had taken me without hesitation, his hands rough, his voice commanding, but his heart distant...guarded. Now, I felt no shame, no hesitation about what I needed.

I needed him to fuck the day out of me.

"Jenny," he said, his voice low and rough as he turned to face me. His eyes met mine through the rising mist, and I saw the flicker of surprise before it was quickly replaced with something darker, hungrier.

I stepped forward, my hands trembling, not with hesitation but with the sheer weight of everything I felt. Without a word, I slipped into the stall, the water soaking my hair, plastering my clothes to my skin. His gaze roamed over me, lingering on the places where the wet fabric clung, and I saw the moment his restraint snapped.

"You shouldn't be here," he murmured, even as his hands reached for me, sliding down my arms, his grip firm and possessive.

"I should," I whispered back, my voice steady despite the pounding of my heart. "I need this. I need you."

There was no hesitation then. He pulled me against him, his lips crashing into mine, the kiss fierce and consuming, a battle of need and control. The water poured over us, erasing the day but fueling the fire between us. His hands moved quickly, peeling my wet clothes away, his fingers grazing my skin with a touch that sent shivers down my spine despite the heat.

"Turn around," he growled, his voice thick with desire.

And I did, my palms pressing against the cool tiles as his hands gripped my hips. The tension in my body coiled tighter as he positioned himself behind me, his breath warm against my neck. He didn't rush...he never did. But when he finally pushed into me, the stretch was slow, deliberate, claiming every ounce of control I thought I had left.

The stress of the day melted away with every thrust, his movements deliberate, driving me closer and closer to the edge. The sound of the water hitting the tiles mixed with the slap of our bodies, the soft gasps and moans escaping my lips as he filled me completely.

I lost myself in him, in the heat of his touch, the strength of his body against mine, and for the first time all day, I felt free...alive. Every stroke, every whispered word, was a promise, and as my legs began to tremble and my release crashed over me, I knew he had given me exactly what I needed.

When it was over, he didn't let go. He held me there, his arms wrapped around me as the water washed over us, and for a moment, it felt like nothing else mattered. But the memory of his coldness from before lingered, a quiet reminder of why I couldn't let myself fall too far.

So, I pulled away and returned to my room, shaky. Yet, still needing more. It continued further till I fulfilled my contract, then it was time for us to return to New York.

CHAPTER
Thirty~Four

ZACK

The hum of the airplane engines thrums beneath my feet, a steady, monotonous sound that mirrors the weight pressing down on my chest. I've been staring at the tablet in front of me for the better part of an hour, pretending to focus on emails I've already read twice. The screen blurs, the words meaningless, but I refuse to let my thoughts stray to her.

Not here. Not now.

She was late. Her shoot had run behind, leaving me waiting like some fool, checking the time as if I didn't have better things to do. Now she's here, sitting across from me...a vision of quiet defiance in her tailored travel clothes, arms folded, her gaze fixed on the window.

The sunlight streams in, glinting off the auburn strands of her hair, and I hate the way it catches me off guard. I shouldn't be noticing these things. Not when we're on the way back to New York, and whatever this is...whatever this was...needs to end. For both our sakes.

But her silence presses on me like a weight, and I know she can feel my eyes on her. She shifts slightly, her chin tilting in defiance, refusing to acknowledge my presence. A joke of sorts…this cold detachment. It's exactly what she asked for when she made her conditions clear.

"You're quiet," she says finally, breaking the tension. Her voice is light, teasing, but I can hear the edge beneath it. "Last time we were on a plane together, you talked more."

I didn't even bother lifting my gaze from my tablet as I respond. "You said you had no interest in talking. Only getting fucked."

Her words falter. I can see the surprise flicker across her face before she schools it into composure, but I catch it, and I let it hang between us. She turns back to the window, her hands tightening over her arms as if to keep from reacting.

"That's over now, isn't it?" she says after a beat, her voice clipped. "Since we're heading back."

"Sure," I reply, my tone dismissive as I glance back at the tablet.

"Sure?" she repeats, her voice rising just slightly. She straightens in her seat, her frustration unmistakable now. "That's all. That's all you have to say?"

I don't look at her. "You were the one who suggested the arrangement in the first place. I have no complaints or preferences."

I hear the rustle of fabric as she stands, and before I can stop her, she's moved…standing before me, then straddling my lap. The sudden closeness steals my breath for a moment, but I don't push her away. Her hands settle on my chest, her hazel eyes burning with an intensity I hadn't expected.

"You don't complain, but you're cold," she says, her voice trembling with the frustration she's holding back. "Why are you suddenly so cold to me?"

I meet her gaze, my voice calm but firm. "I'm cold to everyone."

"That's not true," she counters, leaning in, her voice lowering. "You weren't cold to me at first. You were—"

"Warm."

I stare deep into her gorgeous hazel eyes. "Yes, I was. But knowing since then that our relationship would only be transactional, I didn't see the need to put in the effort."

Her breath hitches, and for a moment, she's stunned silent. But I see the emotions flash in her eyes...shock, anger, and something I can't quite name. "Well yeah, I guess."

I sigh and react instinctively, instantly regretting it, but I can't help myself. "Remember, Jenny, this is what you asked for, and I'm just honoring it."

"Yeah," she says again. "Right. Thank you."

Then, slowly, she climbs off me and moves back to her seat, her shoulders rigid, her movements measured. I don't watch her go, but I can feel the space between us growing colder with every passing second.

And yet, in the quiet that follows, I can't stop my mind from drifting back to the night before. The way she'd looked at me in her bed, her expression open, vulnerable...something I hadn't been prepared to see. I remember the way she'd trembled under my touch, how her body had softened against mine, and for once, I'd let myself slow down.

It hadn't just been fucking. I'd taken my time, every movement deliberate, every kiss lingering. It had been something more...something I'd told myself I wasn't capable of giving her.

And I hate that a part of me wonders if she noticed. Because I sure as hell did.

I'm glad, though, about the boundary she set. It keeps me in check. Keeps me from losing my mind because I know that if she'd made this something sweeter, something that felt better than I ever expected, I would've completely lost myself in her.

And so now, I'm glad that I can return to New York with my mind intact. But as for the matter between her and Brett... it worries me. From the boundary she set between us, it's clear she intends to go back to him. I tell myself I don't care, but it bothers me deeply that I'm not exactly sure how I'd react if she didn't.

Sighing again, I glance over at her, still sitting stiffly, her face turned away. The distance between us feels insurmountable now. And it's for the best.

CHAPTER

Thirty~Five

JENNY

The car slows as it approaches the grand estate, the sight of the familiar Jackson mansion looming larger with every passing second. I can feel my pulse quicken as the iron gates swing open, their creak almost ceremonious. The driver pulls into the long driveway lined with perfectly manicured trees, and the sprawling estate comes into full view, every corner polished to its usual perfection.

As the car comes to a stop, the housekeeper, Mrs. Finnigan, rushes out with open arms, her face lit up with unrestrained joy. I barely manage to climb out before she pulls me into a hug, her embrace warm and filled with the kind of genuine affection that makes my chest ache.

"Jenny!" she exclaims, her voice thick with emotion. "Oh, it's so good to see you! Look at you, you're never here anymore. Always traveling in and out I'm so happy you're back, again."

I force a smile, but my eyes dart past her, searching for him.

Zack.

And there he is. Just a few steps away, standing tall and impassive as always, his dark hair catching the soft glow of the afternoon sun. The butler approaches him with a respectful bow of his head, immediately reaching for his luggage. Zack nods, murmuring something I can't hear before turning toward the house, his stride, purposeful and unhurried.

I watch him disappear through the doors, his broad shoulders the last thing I see before he's gone. A sharp, inexplicable pang cuts through me, and I have to remind myself to breathe.

Around me, the housekeeper is still speaking, but her words blur, the excitement of her welcome muted by the chaos in my chest.

Soon, more staff emerge from the house, their smiles warm, their voices full of curiosity and welcome. But I barely hear them. My father isn't here, and I find myself thankful for that. The thought of facing him now, of pretending everything is fine when it feels like my insides are twisted into knots, is too much to bear.

I excuse myself as politely as I can, managing a few distracted words of thanks before making my way to the apartment above the garage. The staff's chatter follows me for a few steps, their warmth lingering in the air even after I've left them behind.

Once inside my room, I close the door and lean against it, exhaling a shaky breath. The familiar space, though comforting, feels foreign now. Everything is as I left it...simple, cozy, untouched by the time I've been away. But I can't shake the sense of being out of place, like I don't belong here anymore.

I drop my bags by the door and sink into the bed, exhaustion weighing me down like lead. My body aches from the long flight, but it's nothing compared to the dull, persistent pain in my chest. I press a hand to it, as if I can will it away, but the ache only deepens.

I got what I wanted, didn't I? I'm back. I'm free.

So why does it feel like I've lost something? Like there's a wound in my heart that won't stop bleeding.

The knock on the door jolts me, and I hastily sit up, brushing my hair back as I call out for them to come in. Mrs. Finnigan enters first, followed by a few of the other staff, their faces lighting up at the sight of me. They pepper me with questions about Rome, about the job, about everything. Their warmth is infectious, and for a moment, I let myself sink into it, grateful for the distraction.

"I brought back a few things for you all," I say, managing a small smile as I pull out the souvenirs I'd packed. Tiny trinkets...keychains, miniatures of the Leaning Tower of Pisa, delicate scarves. They accept them with delighted exclamations, their gratitude genuine and heartfelt.

After a while, they leave me alone, and the room falls silent once more. I let out a breath, sinking back against the pillows as I glance at my phone. The urge to call Zack is immediate and overwhelming, the thought of hearing his voice a temptation I can barely resist. The thought of feeling his hands on me, kissing him, and having his cock inside me is even more haunting.

My thumb hovers over his name in my contacts, but I can't bring myself to press it. I can no longer press it. We're back to the way we were, and nothing can ever change that. It was what I wanted, and I know this is the choice I made so I could get back and still have a chance...somewhat...with Brett.

And so, I do just that. In a way, I feel now more than ever that I have to because, for the first time, I know viscerally what I have given up for this.

I scroll down and find Brett's name. The sight of it stirs

something familiar, something safe. Before I can second-guess myself, I press 'call'.

The line rings twice before he picks up, his voice bright and warm, like a ray of sunlight cutting through a cloudy sky. "Jenny! This is a surprise."

A small, tentative smile creeps onto my face. "Surprise? Didn't you remember I was coming back today?"

There's a brief pause, followed by a soft, sheepish laugh. "I'll admit it slipped my mind for a second, but hey, I was bound to remember eventually."

"Eventually?" I tease, my voice light but edged with just enough accusation to make him backpedal.

"Cut me some slack, Jenny," he says, his tone dipping into something softer, almost conspiratorial. "I've been swamped lately. But I'm glad you called…I missed hearing your voice."

The admission catches me off guard, and for a fleeting moment, I forget everything else. "You missed me?"

"Of course," he says, a playful edge to his tone now. "You've been gone for what feels like forever. Tell me, how was Rome? Did my brother drag you to all those boring meetings?"

The mention of Zack sends a shiver down my spine, but I push it aside, focusing on the easy charm in Brett's voice. "No, no, not at all," I reply, leaning back against the head-board. "I went there for work. I told you, right? I got a contract with Tod's."

"Tods? Is that like… a brand? I've never heard of them."

"Oh," I reply, my enthusiasm deflating slightly. "It's a pretty big brand. Yeah."

"Oh, well, that's great to hear. I hope you had a great experience. Rome is picturesque."

"It is, and it was," I say, my tone light, though my words feel oddly detached. "The experience was… pretty good."

"Nice, nice," he replies, his voice warm but distant, as though filling space more than engaging.

An awkward silence follows before he peaks again. "So.. give me details? How much fun did you have? Did you get swept off your feet by some Italian prince? Should I be worried?"

The question is laced with a teasing flirtation, and I can't help but laugh. "No princes. Just a lot of pasta and wine."

"Good," he says, his voice dropping just slightly, enough to make my breath hitch. "I'd hate to think someone else was stealing your attention."

My heart flutters despite myself, and for a moment, the ache in my chest dulls. "What about you? Have you been behaving while I was away, or is New York full of broken hearts now?"

"Broken hearts? Never," he says, feigning innocence. "But I'll admit, it's been a little dull without you around. You're back just in time to fix that."

"Am I?" I ask, my voice quieter now, tinged with something I can't quite name.

"Definitely," he says, and I can hear the grin in his voice. "When do I get to see you?"

"Soon," I promise, the warmth in his tone seeping into me, easing the tightness in my chest. "Are you at home now?"

"Not yet," he says, a trace of regret in his voice. "I'm out in the city, but I'll come check on you as soon as I'm back. You can count on that."

"I'll hold you to it," I say, my lips curving into a smile despite the lingering heaviness in my heart.

We talk a little longer, his questions easy and his laughter infectious, until the call ends and the room falls silent once more. I set the phone down, staring at it for a moment.

For those few minutes, it had been easy to forget the

weight pressing down on me. Brett's charm had been a distraction, a reprieve. But now, the ache in my chest returns, sharper than before, as if reminding me that it's not Brett I can't stop thinking about.

It's Zack.

CHAPTER
Thirty-Six

ZACK

The steady rhythm of my pen against the desk is the only sound in my office. The morning has been uneventful so far…just as I prefer. My schedule is packed, the hours already blocked out with meetings and reports, but at least here, within these four walls, there's a sense of control. Everything in it's place. Predictable. Or at least it should feel that way.

Instead, my focus drifts, slipping between the cracks of the tasks I've set for myself. The trip with Jenny looms in the back of my mind, casting shadows over my carefully organized thoughts. What was supposed to be a straightforward distraction, a calculated move to steer her away from Brett, had turned into something far more complicated. And now, the aftermath weighs on me like an anchor.

The trip wasn't necessary, I tell myself again for what feels like the hundredth time. It wasn't urgent. I could've left things as they were, let her linger in her infatuation with Brett while the merger fell into place. But no. I had to step in. I had to play my part, the puppeteer pulling strings to control an outcome that's now slipping from my grasp.

My pen stills mid-stroke as the memory of her voice surfaces, unbidden...her laughter, yes, but more than that. The way she spoke to me, her words so effortlessly weaving between sharp wit and unguarded sincerity. It had been too easy to lose myself in those conversations, to forget why I'd orchestrated this charade in the first place. And then there was her body. The way it moved beneath mine, the heat of her skin against my own, the way she unraveled under my touch...it had been intoxicating. Fucking her hadn't just felt good; it had felt inevitable, like I was claiming something I hadn't known I needed until she was there, offering it so completely. Being with her, in every sense, had felt right in a way I couldn't afford to admit.

Each moment we spent together...exploring ruins, sharing meals, even the quiet hours in the suite...chipped away at the walls I've spent years building around myself. Walls that should have remained intact. Impenetrable.

But no. She'd gotten through.

The realization stings, it makes me feel like a monumental failure and it has been a very, very long time since I have felt this way in any aspect of my life. Jenny was supposed to forget Brett. That was the goal. To entice her completely, to shift her focus so entirely that she wouldn't even remember the boy who'd never deserved her devotion. But instead, she hadn't and I'm the one left in emotional straits.

I drop the pen onto the desk and lean back in my chair, pinching the bridge of my nose. The mountain of work before me should feel like a welcome distraction, a chance to reassert control. Instead, it feels like a mockery. The deals and deadlines blur together, insignificant compared to the storm I've unleashed. The thought of her with Brett gnaws at me, a constant, unwelcome presence in the back of my mind.

She's back home now, probably settling into the comfort of familiar surroundings, reconnecting with people who adore her in ways I never could. People like Brett, who'll swoop in with his charm and ease, who'll make her smile with effortless grace. And me? I'm here, drowning in the consequences of my own actions, pretending that everything is fine.

A knock at the door pulls me from my thoughts, and I straighten in my chair, forcing the mask of indifference back into place. Whatever this day throws at me, I'll handle it. I always do. But as the door creaks open, I can't help but wonder if I'll ever be able to untangle myself from the mess I've created. Or from her.

Turns out it's Brett, and my eyes almost can't believe it. Speak of the devil, literally.

He bursts in, grinning like a cat that's just found its next meal.

"Morning, big brother," Brett chirps as he strolls into my office, exuding the kind of confidence that only comes from never facing consequences. He collapses into the chair opposite me with practiced ease, tossing one leg over the other and looking far too cheerful for this early hour. "You'll be thrilled to know I have plans tonight."

I glance up briefly from my desk, masking my irritation. "Should I be worried?"

"Not unless you consider dinner at home scandalous," he says, smirking.

My pen stills against the paper. "At home? Since when do you host dinners at the house?"

His grin widens, the kind that makes me instinctively brace for trouble. "It's just Jenny. Nothing remotely controversial."

Her name hits me like a jolt, though I force myself to maintain a façade of indifference. Leaning back in my chair, I fold my hands together, steepling my fingers. "Jenny," I repeat, keeping my voice measured. "And why, exactly, is this dinner happening at home?"

"Convenience," Brett replies with a nonchalant shrug. "Plus, Elizabeth has been on my case lately, combing through my schedule like I'm some wayward teenager. The last thing I need is her catching wind of me entertaining a 'friend' at a restaurant."

"You're treading on thin ice with her," I say, my voice clipped. "And entertaining Jenny at the house isn't exactly a subtle move."

"She's like family, and she lives there," Brett insists, waving a hand dismissively. "You act like I'm planning an elopement."

Something about the way he minimizes her makes me furious, though I try my very best to hide it. "She's also on track to become a world-renowned model now," I point out, narrowing my eyes. "She's not just the chauffeur's daughter anymore, Brett. The least you could do is take her somewhere befitting that. She deserves it."

"World-renowned?" Brett snorts, leaning forward with that trademark charm that works on everyone but me. "You're joking, right? It's for some brand I've never even heard of. But it doesn't matter…model or chauffeur's daughter…you know I'm soft for her. I didn't see her that way. It's just safer while I try to figure out my own head. You haven't forgotten, have you? About all the extensions before you two left for Rome. I still want the chance to figure it out before it's too late."

I stare at him, not even knowing how to address his comments. I decide, ultimately, to play it safe before the wrong thing comes out of my mouth.

"Tod's is a significant brand," I counter sharply. "I arranged that opportunity for her. It's a solid foundation for her career."

For once, Brett looks momentarily thoughtful. "Well, that's a relief then. Knowing you're looking out for her takes a load off my mind. You'll make sure she's got what she needs, right? She's got a great support system, thanks to you."

The casual praise does little to temper my growing irritation. His interest in Jenny feels too familiar...transient, superficial, just like all the others. It's his pattern: infatuation that burns bright and fizzles out, leaving nothing but a trail of discarded hearts in its wake. But this time, the thought of Jenny being part of that trail gnaws at me, stirring something sharper than I care to admit.

"What's the plan for dinner?" I ask, keeping my tone neutral.

"I told the chefs to whip up something nice...stuff she likes," Brett says, leaning back in his chair, the picture of smug satisfaction. "And for the occasion, I grabbed a bottle of Château Margaux. You know, that ridiculously expensive vintage you keep stashed away in the cellar like it's some kind of holy relic. Figured this was as good an excuse as any to crack it open."

My pen halts mid-stroke. I glance up sharply, my gaze locking on him. "You took the 2005 Margaux?" My voice is calm, but there's an edge to it.

He grins, unbothered by the quiet fury simmering beneath my words. "Yeah. Don't worry, big brother, I'll savor every drop for you. It's not like you were ever going to drink it anyway."

"Generous of you," I mutter, the words clipped as my hand tightens around the pen. That bottle isn't just expensive; it's irreplaceable. A symbol of discipline and patience...qualities Brett has never possessed.

"Oh, and I'll pick her up a little something too," he continues, completely oblivious to my growing irritation. "Maybe a nice Hermès bag. Women like that, right? Something under-stated but elegant. It'll show I pay attention."

I lean back in my chair, studying him. His cavalier attitude grates on me, but what stings more is the ease with which he talks about Jenny, as if she's just another fleeting interest. Another accessory to add to his collection.

"And the dinner?" I ask, keeping my tone neutral.

He shrugs. "Something light but fancy. Chef's got it under control. Maybe some grilled seabass with that citrus glaze she liked last time. Toss in a side of those roasted vegetables she raved about. You know, keep it classy."

"You seem to have it all figured out," I say, my voice heavy with forced indifference.

"Don't I always?" Brett quips, flashing a grin that's too self-assured. But then, as if sensing the weight in the room, his expression shifts, softening into something unfamiliar. "Look, Zack, I know you don't approve of my... let's call them 'adventures', but you don't have to worry about Jenny. I'm not going to screw this up."

I arch an eyebrow, unimpressed. "You'll forgive me if I don't share your confidence."

His grin falters, and for a brief moment, the mask drops. "I mean it," he says, his voice quieter now. "I like her. A lot. I'm not going to mess with her. Like I told you, she's like family. I'm serious about this, and if I find out it's not a good fit, then I'll ensure things end amicably."

"Amicably," I repeat, my voice edged with disbelief. "Is that even possible when it comes to relationships?"

Brett laughs heartily at this, his easy charm shining through. "Probably not, but I'm sure Jenny will be fine."

"Maybe she will, and maybe she won't," I say evenly, my tone hard enough to make him pause.

For the first time, he notices the shift in my demeanor, his grin fading into uncertainty.

"What do you mean?" he asks, his brow furrowing.

"I'm saying," I continue, "I think she deserves someone who tries. Someone who really tries. So, if you're going to do this, then really do it. Don't hurt her."

He nods, but I'm not convinced he understands yet. And I need him to understand…so violently, I almost can't contain myself.

"Jenny loves you, Brett," I say, my voice steady though it feels like shards of glass in my throat. "She has her whole life. If being with you makes her happy, then the merger doesn't matter. I need you to focus all your attention on this…on her…and make it work."

He stares at me, stunned. "Y-you're serious about this."

"I am," I reply firmly.

His eyes narrow, his shock refusing to wane. "Wow… I… I'm shocked. I thought you'd be furious…like before. I still can't believe you're willing to risk the merger. Did I hear you wrong just now?"

"You didn't hear me wrong," I say deliberately. "Not everything is about money."

Again, he looks at me like he doesn't recognize me. "You don't sound like the brother I know. I guess that vacation you took in Rome did something to you."

With a carefree laugh, he stands and pats my shoulder lightly. "Well, I just stopped by to say hello. You've been going to bed early since you got back, so I haven't seen much of you. I'll see you later tonight, though? Let's have a drink by the pool."

"Sure," I reply.

He leaves without another word, but the weight of his presence lingers. The thought of Jenny sitting across from him, smiling, laughing at his charm, twists something deep and unrelenting inside me. I clench my fists, willing the ache to fade, but it only grows worse.

CHAPTER
Thirty~Seven

JENNY

Caroline fusses over me like a proud older sister as she adjusts the halter strap of my emerald- green dress. The fabric hugs my curves perfectly, the fitted waist flaring gently at my knees. It's elegant yet under-stated…exactly what I wanted. She steps back, her eyes lighting up.

"You look incredible," she says, her hands clasped together. "Brett's going to lose his mind."

I laugh nervously, smoothing the fabric at my hips. "You think it's not too much? I don't want to look like I'm trying too hard."

Caroline shakes her head. "Jenny, you look stunning. Besides, this is Brett. The man's been chasing you since he got back. He needs to see what he's up against." She winks.

Her words make me smile, but there's a twinge of some-thing deeper beneath the surface. This is what I've always dreamed of…Brett taking me out, showing me off, treating me like I'm someone special. But now that it's happening, there's a weight in my chest I can't ignore. I should be over-joyed, yet the thought of sitting across from him tonight feels... hollow.

Because no matter how much I've wanted this, I can't stop the flashes of Zack that invade my thoughts...his voice, his touch, the way he looked at me like he saw more than I wanted him to. It's wrong. So wrong. Brett is the one I've loved all my life, so why does it feel like I'm betraying something I can't even name?

Caroline gives me a final once-over, tugging at the hem of my dress before stepping back. "You've got this. Just... be yourself."

I nod, though my chest feels heavy. "Thanks, Caroline."

The knock at the door comes a moment later, startling me out of my thoughts. Caroline grins knowingly and steps aside as I open the door.

Brett stands there, leaning casually against the frame, his golden hair styled just enough to look effortlessly perfect. His tailored blazer clings to his shoulders, and the sight of him makes my breath hitch. He looks every bit the charming prince I used to imagine when I was younger.

"Wow," he says, his grin widening as his gaze sweeps over me. "You look amazing, Jenny."

Heat creeps up my cheeks, and I glance down briefly before meeting his eyes. "Thanks. I thought we were meeting in the kitchen?"

He straightens, stepping back slightly. "Change of plans. I figured dinner at home wasn't good enough for someone like you."

I blink in surprise. "Oh?"

"Yeah," he says, his grin softening. "I've made reservations in Manhattan. Thought it'd be more fitting."

My heart flutters at his words, and I can't help the small smile that tugs at my lips. "You didn't have to do that."

"I wanted to," he says, his voice warm. "Come on, let's go."

He leads me outside, and I follow, trying to ignore the nervous energy coursing through me.

When we reach the car, he opens the passenger door for me with a playful flourish. "Your chariot awaits."

"Thank you, kind sir," I reply, laughing softly as I slide into the seat. He closes the door and circles around to the driver's side, settling in with an easy confidence that only Brett could manage.

The drive to Manhattan is quiet at first, the hum of the car filling the space between us. I play with the hem of my dress, sneaking glances at him as he navigates the city streets.

"So," he begins, breaking the silence. "How was Rome? Zack didn't drive you too crazy, did he?"

I stiffen at the mention of Zack, my fingers freezing mid-fidget. "No, he didn't," I say carefully, keeping my tone light.

Brett chuckles, glancing at me briefly. "Good. Sometimes he can be... intense. Efficient, yeah, but also stuck-up as hell."

I force a small laugh, looking out the window to avoid his gaze. "He was fine."

"Fine, huh?" Brett teases, his tone playful. "I hope he wasn't too intimidating. I mean, the guy's got this whole brooding CEO vibe, but he's not all bad. Mostly."

I don't respond immediately, my mind swirling with images of Zack...his rare, unguarded smiles, the warmth of his touch, the way he made me feel both seen and exposed at once. The thought sends a pang through my chest, and I quickly push it away.

"He was fine," I repeat softly, my voice barely above a whisper.

Brett doesn't push further, and the rest of the drive is marked by small talk that feels forced, like we're both trying too hard to fill the silence. When we finally pull up in front of the restaurant, I exhale, relieved for the change of scenery.

The restaurant is breathtaking…warm lights, soft music, and an air of sophistication that makes me feel like I've stepped into another world. Brett places his hand lightly on my back as we're led to our table, and I let myself relax, just a little. This is what I've always wanted, I remind myself. Brett, charming and attentive, treating me like I matter.

The dinner starts smoothly. He orders a bottle of wine without even glancing at the menu, and I let him take the lead, trying to savor the moment. We talk about my time in Paris, my modeling career, and his usual antics that always seem to leave him unscathed. His laugh is infectious, his stories full of humor and bravado, and for a while, I let myself get lost in the fantasy of it all.

But then he asks about Zack again.

"So, what's it like traveling with him? I imagine it's… intense."

The question catches me off guard, and I hesitate. "It was fine," I say, my tone sharper than I intend.

Brett raises an eyebrow, a knowing smirk tugging at his lips. "Fine again? That's all you've got? Come on, Jenny, don't hold out on me."

I force a laugh, shaking my head. "There's nothing to tell. Zack is… Zack."

"Right," he says, leaning back in his chair. "All business, no fun. Must've been exhausting."

You have no idea, I think, but I keep the words to myself. Instead, I smile tightly, changing the subject to the food. Brett lets it go, but the conversation feels heavier after that, like we're both aware of the unspoken tension lingering between us.

As the night goes on, I do my best to focus on him, to remind myself of all the reasons I've wanted this for so long.

Brett is charming, sweet, and everything I used to dream about. But as he takes my hand across the table and smiles at me, I can't help but feel like something's missing. Like a part of me is somewhere else…somewhere I shouldn't be.

Eventually, we head back home, and just like that, the night I had dreamed of for so long and for so many years comes to an end, and I cannot believe how underwhelmed I am.

I don't even wait for him to get the door for me. I get out myself, trying my best to force a smile, trying my best to convince myself that this was all I've ever wanted.

He comes after me, smiling and excited, and suddenly that playful ease of his is not something I want to be around and fancy. It's not special, I realize as I stop and turn around to wait for him. Zack rarely smiles in this way, and so when he does, the moments he does with me hit like the entire world filled with light.

Now I know the very stark difference between genuine and niceties, and it almost makes me sick to my stomach that I didn't see this from the very beginning.

The front porch feels colder than it should, a sharp contrast to the warmth of the car Brett just stepped out of. He stands before me, his hands tucked casually into his pockets, the faintest smile on his lips as he glances toward the sprawling estate behind me.

"I should head back to my apartment in Manhattan," he says after a moment, his tone light but edged with something I can't quite place. "Long day tomorrow."

I nod, swallowing against the lump in my throat. Relief rushes through me, sharp and immediate, though it brings its own weight of guilt. I'd been dreading the possibility of things escalating tonight, and now that it won't happen, I feel unmoored by how glad I am. But yet and once again I grapple with myself for being so conflicted about this? Worried that

I'm making a mistake. This is Brett. The Brett I've wanted forever. I should want more.

"Did you have a nice time tonight?" he asks, and I work up a smile, nodding.

"I did," I reply. "Thank you for going the extra mile. I truly appreciated it."

He beams, floored by the compliment, and then he comes in a little closer to me.

I want to step back out of instinct, but it takes all the restraint in the world not to.

His hand lifts, brushing a strand of hair away from my face, and then he leans in.

The kiss is soft, measured, like he's testing the waters. His lips are warm and skilled, moving against mine with practiced ease. It's everything a kiss with Brett Jackson should be…sweet, unhurried, and perfectly executed. I kiss him back because it feels like the right thing to do. Because isn't this what I've been waiting for?

Yet as he pulls away and steps back with a grin, something inside me wilts.

"Wow," he comments, seemingly stunned. "You… that was wonderful, Jenny. I can't believe I've waited so long to do that."

I absolutely do not share in this sentiment, but I respond in kind.

"Yeah," I reply. "It was good, thank you."

"I'll see you soon?" he asks, and I nod because what else am I supposed to do?

Beaming once again, he turns around to leave, and I watch him walk to his car, the taillights a fading glow as he drives away, and all I feel is a suffocating wave of disappointment. My heart had barely fluttered.

The realization is a stab to my chest.

The memory of Zack's kiss lingers in my mind, sharp and

vivid. It wasn't sweet or measured. It had been raw, consuming, and so unapologetically him that it had made me feel like I was losing my grip on reality. And now, standing here in the quiet, I miss him so much it physically aches.

I don't go to my room. The thought of sitting alone with these swirling emotions is unbearable, so I turn toward the kitchen instead.

It doesn't take me long to find what I am looking for...one of the opened bottles of wine in the corner. I pick it up, but didn't want to have it here alone in the dark so I head out of the kitchen.

The soft glow of the moonlight spills through the conservatory windows as I step inside. The cool air feels like a balm against the flush in my cheeks, a reminder that I'm no longer in Brett's car, no longer under the weight of a kiss that felt hollow despite its perfection. My hand tightens around the neck of the wine bottle.

Soon I set it down on the coffee table and stare, the label blurred through the haze of emotions swirling in my chest. My fingers brush over the glass, hesitating before reaching for the corkscrew. The silence presses down on me, amplifying my thoughts and concerns.

Why do I feel like this? Why does it feel like I'm breaking apart?

I sink into one of the chairs, the bottle untouched, and rest my elbows on my knees, my head in my hands.

Kissing me under the stars. It should have been perfect. Instead, it felt like I was standing outside myself, watching a moment that didn't belong to me. My lips had moved against his, but my mind... my heart... had been elsewhere.

With him. With Zack.

I press my palms harder against my face, as if I can push the thoughts away. But they linger, growing heavier with each passing second. The sound of the conservatory doors creaking open pulls me from my spiraling thoughts. My head snaps up, and I freeze as a low voice cuts through the quiet.

"You've still not learned your lesson about alcohol, I see."

The words send a shiver down my spine. Slowly, I turn, my breath catching when I see him. Zack stands in the shadows near the French doors, his hands casually tucked into his pockets, the light from the windows casting his face in sharp relief. His expression is unreadable, but there's something in his eyes...something that makes my heart race.

The sight of him is a punch to the gut. I've missed him so much it physically hurts, and now, with him here, the ache only intensifies.

"It makes you tipsy," he continues, his voice low and rough, "and you can barely control yourself afterward."

I stare at him, the words sinking in slowly. My lips part to respond, but nothing comes out. The air between us feels charged, thick with everything unsaid. My hand moves instinctively to the back of the chair for support, and I cling to it, feeling as though the ground might give way beneath me.

The silence stretches, taut and unbearable. Finally, I manage to speak, my voice unsteady. "I... I don't want to control myself."

His eyes narrow slightly, his head tilting just enough to make me feel like he's seeing through me, into me. The corners of his mouth twitch, as if he's about to say something, but he doesn't. Instead, he takes a step closer, and I'm rooted to the spot, unable to move.

"Why is that?" he asks, his tone deceptively calm. But there's an edge to it, something sharp and dangerous that makes my pulse thunder in my ears.

I swallow hard, my grip on the chair tightening. "Because," I whisper, the word barely audible. I don't finish the sentence because I don't know how. How do I tell him that I feel like I'm unraveling, that every thought I have leads back to him? That even sitting across from Brett tonight, all I could think about was him?

He takes another step closer, the distance between us shrinking. "Jenny," he says softly, his voice rough and achingly familiar. My name on his lips is a tether, pulling me toward him even as my mind screams at me to stop.

"I…" My voice cracks, and I shake my head, unable to look at him. "I don't know what I'm doing anymore."

He's silent for a long moment, and when he speaks, his voice is low and steady. "How was your date?"

The question hits me like a slap, and I flinch, my head snapping up to meet his gaze. The intensity in his eyes is almost too much to bear, and I drop my gaze, focusing on the floor instead. "It was fine," I lie, my voice barely above a whisper.

"Fine," he repeats, and there's something in the way he says it that makes my chest tighten. "So that's it, then? Everything you've ever wanted?"

I squeeze my eyes shut, willing the tears back. "I thought it was," I admit, my voice breaking. "But… I don't know anymore. I don't know what I want."

His footsteps are soft against the tiled floor, but I feel every step like a jolt to my system. When I open my eyes, he's standing directly in front of me, so close I can see the faint lines of tension around his mouth. He doesn't touch me, but his presence is overwhelming, like gravity pulling me toward him.

"Jenny," he murmurs, his voice barely more than a whisper. "What do you want?"

The question hangs in the air, heavy and impossible. My lips part, but before I can answer, his hand lifts to cup my cheek, his thumb brushing lightly against my skin. The touch sends a shiver through me, and I tilt my head slightly, leaning into his palm despite myself.

"I don't know," I whisper, the words tumbling out before I can stop them.

He tilts my chin up gently, his eyes locking onto mine. "Yes, you do," he says, his voice low and certain. "You just don't want to admit it."

The room feels too small, the air too thick. Every inch of me screams to answer him, but my voice refuses to cooperate. And then his lips are on mine, slow and deliberate, claiming me in a way that sends my head spinning. This isn't like Brett's kiss...this is something entirely different. Zack kisses me like he's unraveling me piece by piece, like he's pulling down every wall I've built.

The distance between us disappears as his lips brush against mine, slow and deliberate, and the world falls away. The kiss isn't rushed or frantic...it's steady, like he's savoring every second. My hands move on their own, gripping the front of his shirt as I pull him closer, desperate for more.

The world fades away, and all that's left is him...his lips, his hands, the way his body fits against mine. The kiss deepens, slow and sensual, and it's like he's drawing every ounce of tension and longing out of me, leaving nothing but raw need in its place. My fingers grip his shirt, pulling him closer, desperate to lose myself in him completely.

When we finally pull apart, my chest is heaving, my thoughts a jumbled mess. His forehead rests against mine, his hands still cradling my face as he searches my eyes.

"Tell me," he murmurs, his voice rough and barely steady. "What do you want, Jenny?"

I close my eyes, the weight of his question pressing down on me. I don't have the answer...not yet. But in this moment, with his lips still tingling on mine, all I know is that I never want him to stop asking.

CHAPTER
Thirty-Eight

ZACH

I saw them from the window of my bedroom.

Brett's car was parked just outside the house, the headlights cutting through the night as the front door swung open. She stepped out first, her auburn hair catching the faint glow of the porch light, and I felt it...sharp and hot, like a blade twisting deep in my chest. Then Brett followed, leaning in casually as he whispered something to her that made her laugh softly. My hands curled into fists at my sides as I watched him take her hand and pull her close.

And then he kissed her.

It wasn't rushed, not a fleeting brush of lips. It was deliberate, tender, the kind of kiss I'd only imagined giving her. My jaw tightened, my teeth grinding together as I forced myself to look away, to focus on anything but them. The papers on my desk. The ticking of the clock. The steady rise and fall of my own shallow breaths.

But it didn't work.

The jealousy burned so fiercely inside me that I could

barely think straight. Soon enough, he drove off, leaving her there alone, and before I realized what I was doing, I was moving…striding out of my room, down the hall, taking the stairs two at a time. Each step felt heavier than the last, weighed down by the storm raging inside me.

By the time I reached the ground floor, she was no longer there. The front door clicked shut behind her as she stepped inside, and the sound echoed in the silence of the house. I waited and watched, stopping just short of the doorway to the conservatory, my hand hovering over the frame.

What was I doing? What was I going to say? I had no idea. All I knew was that I needed to see her, to say something… anything…to make sense of this mess. The thought of her in Brett's arms, of her lips on his, was unbearable.

A little while later, I watched her reappear with a bottle of wine in hand and couldn't help but shake my head. She was at it again. Stopping here was all the permission I needed, so I headed in.

The kiss had been phenomenal, and the despair I'd seen in her expression afterward changed everything.

But now, as I stare at her, I truly wonder where this will go. Where I want it to go because unless we figure it out, and quickly, the damage to the family will be too grave.

So, I blurt out the words that have been ruminating in my head all day.

"Move to Paris with me," I say.

She blinks hard, flabbergasted. "What?"

"I'll move to Paris with you," I repeat, the words tumbling out before I can come to my senses and stop them. "You said it yourself…you know the city, the language, the work. Tod's wants you there, and I'll keep the business running from there, at least for a little while, till we work things out between us and ascertain that we're both sure about each other."

Her breath catches at my words, her lips parting as she stares at me, wide-eyed. The bottle of wine she holds trembles slightly in her grip, and I can see the storm of emotions flashing across her face…confusion, disbelief, and something deeper. Something raw.

"Zack," she whispers, as though my name is too heavy for her voice to carry.

I step closer, drawn by the undeniable pull between us, and gently take the bottle from her hands. Setting it on the small table, I meet her gaze, letting every barrier I've built crumble before her. There's no use pretending anymore. Not after everything.

"Let's stop pretending," I say, my voice low but steady.

Tears well in her hazel eyes, and she blinks rapidly, trying to suppress them. "I don't understand," she murmurs, her voice trembling. "Why would you…why now? Why so suddenly?"

I reach out, brushing a stray strand of hair away from her face, my thumb lingering against her cheek. "Because I'm tired of fighting this," I admit, my words carrying the weight of every sleepless night, every moment I've tried to convince myself this wasn't real. "I'm tired of pretending I don't want you when it's all I can think about. And I think you feel the same."

Her breath hitches, and a single tear escapes, trailing down her cheek. I catch it with my thumb, wiping it away as gently as I can.

"I'm sorry," she whispers, her voice breaking. "For being so … cold to you in Rome. For giving the stipulation that I did."

"I want you," she breathes against my lips, the words soft but filled with certainty. "I want this."

Her confession ignites something in me. My hands grip her waist as if she might vanish if I let go. Her warmth seeps into my skin, igniting something primal and consuming. I press her against the edge of the table, lifting her slightly as I lean in, my lips capturing hers with a desperation I can't contain. She's all I can think about, all I can feel.

Her hands tangle in my hair, tugging me closer, and I groan into her mouth, the sound raw and guttural. My fingers find the hem of her dress, and without breaking the kiss, I push it up, exposing the smooth, silken expanse of her thighs. My hands glide over her skin, tracing the curve of her hips, the dip of her waist. She gasps against my lips, her breath hot and uneven, and it only fuels the fire roaring inside me.

"Zack," she whispers, her voice trembling but filled with need.

I can't stop. I won't stop. Not now. Not when she's here, pliant and eager in my arms. I lift her onto the table, her legs wrapping around my waist as my hands explore every inch of her body. Her dress pools around her hips, and my palms glide up to her breasts, cupping them through the thin fabric of her bra. She arches into my touch, her head falling back as I kiss my way down her neck, my lips and tongue savoring the taste of her skin.

"You're perfect," I murmur against her collarbone, my voice rough with desire. "Every inch of you."

Her fingers clutch at my shoulders, nails digging into my skin as I lower the straps of her dress, baring her completely to me. The sight of her steals what little breath I have left. I take my time, my hands and mouth worshiping her. I trail kisses down the curve of her neck, over the swell of her breasts, my tongue teasing her sensitive peaks until she's trembling beneath me, her soft cries driving me mad.

When I finally lower my pants, the need to be inside her becomes unbearable. I grip her hips, positioning her at the edge of the table, and with a slow, deliberate thrust, I enter her. She gasps, her body tightening around me as I fill her completely. The sensation is overwhelming…hot, wet, and impossibly perfect. I press my forehead to hers, trying to catch my breath as I pull back slightly, then thrust again, setting a rhythm that makes her cling to me like I'm her lifeline.

The table creaks beneath us, the sound echoing in the quiet of the conservatory, and I freeze, my heart pounding. Her eyes fly open, wide with worry, and I know we can't keep this up here. Not like this. Not with the risk of someone hearing us.

I scoop her up effortlessly, her legs still wrapped around me and carry her to the armchair near the window. Settling into the seat, I position her astride me, her knees on either side of my thighs. She looks down at me, her cheeks flushed, her lips swollen from my kisses, and for a moment, all I can do is stare. She's stunning, absolutely breathtaking, and I can't believe she's here with me.

"Zack," she whispers again, her hands framing my face as she leans down to kiss me. "Please."

I don't need any more encouragement. I grip her hips, guiding her as she lowers herself onto me, taking me in inch by agonizing inch. She throws her head back, her hair cascading over her shoulders as a soft moan escapes her lips. I capture the sound with my mouth, kissing her deeply as she begins to move, her body finding a rhythm that matches mine perfectly.

The chair creaks beneath us, and I realize she's too loud, her cries of pleasure filling the space around us. I reach up, covering her mouth with my hand as I drive into her harder, deeper, my control slipping with every thrust.

"Shh," I murmur against her ear, my voice hoarse. "You're going to wake the whole house."

Her eyes meet mine, wide and glassy with pleasure, and she nods, biting her lip to stifle the sounds. But it's not enough. The way she moves, the way she clings to me, it's like she's trying to consume me, to merge our bodies completely. And God, I want it too. I want to lose myself in her, to forget everything but the way she feels around me, the way she looks at me like I'm the only thing that matters.

I kiss her again, my hand sliding into her hair as I hold her close, my other hand gripping her hip to steady her as we move together. The tension builds and builds, coiling tighter and tighter until it snaps, sending us both over the edge. She cries out against my mouth, her body shuddering around me as I follow her, the release so intense it leaves me trembling.

For a moment, we stay like that, tangled together in the chair, our breaths mingling as we come down from the high. Her head rests against my chest, and I press a kiss to her hair, my hands trailing gently up and down her back.

"We can't stay here," I whisper after a while, my voice soft but firm. "Someone could walk in."

She nods, her body still languid and pliant in my arms. Gently I guide her still shaky legs upstairs with me to my bedroom. When we reach the door, she hesitates, glancing back toward her own room, but I don't let her go. Instead, I pull her inside, closing the door behind us and laying her down on the bed.

As we settle beneath the covers, completely sated, her head resting against my shoulder, I feel an unfamiliar sense of peace. For the first time in a long time, I'm exactly where I want to be.

CHAPTER
Thirty~Nine

JENNY

The days that follow are nothing short of a dream. I wake each morning wrapped in Zack's arms, his touch a quiet promise that this, whatever this is, is real. We've perfected the art of secrecy...or maybe the family just chooses not to notice. If they suspect anything, they say nothing, leaving us in this fragile bubble of intimacy that feels both thrilling and terrifying.

But this morning is different. It's the last full day before I leave for Paris, and the weight of it looms heavy in the air. Zack is seated in the armchair in the lounge area of his suite, a plate of toast balanced on the armrest. I'm moving around the room barefoot and wearing one of his oversized dress shirts. It's crisp and white, and it smells like him...clean and warm, with a hint of the cologne I've come to associate with his presence.

"I can't believe I've lived here all my life and never been in your room," I say, glancing around. The suite is massive, an extension of the man himself. The ceilings soar, the walls lined with dark wood and understated art that speaks of wealth without flaunting it. A floor-to-ceiling window overlooks the estate grounds, and the light streaming through casts a golden glow on everything, softening the sharp edges of the modern furniture.

Zack watches me quietly, his expression unreadable as he butters a piece of toast with precise, deliberate movements. When he finally looks up, his gaze locks on mine, and he holds out the toast with a small, almost imperceptible smile.

"Come here," he says, his voice low and steady.

I cross the room and settle at his feet, folding my legs beneath me. He leans down, offering the toast, and I take a bite. Peanut butter and jelly, the simplest thing, but it feels like so much more when it's from his hand.

Zack sets the toast down as I chew, his gaze never leaving mine. There's a softness there, but also something darker... something I can't quite name. I swallow hard, the weight in my chest suddenly matching the thickness of the air between us.

"I need to leave for Paris tomorrow," I say quietly, my voice betraying none of the ache that claws at my insides. "What's your plan about coming with me?"

For a moment, he just looks at me, and I see the war waging behind his eyes. It's the first time we've talked about it since he made that promise. I've held onto his words, believing in them because Zack isn't the kind of man who breaks promises. But now, something about the way he avoids my gaze tells me this conversation won't end the way I've imagined it.

He sighs, the sound heavy and resigned. "Jenny..." he begins, his voice low, careful. "I've thought about it. Really thought about it. But I can't. I can't leave everything here."

My heart stops. "What?" The word comes out in a whisper, as if saying it any louder might shatter me completely.

"I wanted to make it work," he says, running a hand through his hair, his frustration evident. "But it's not realistic. My life is here, my work, my family. I can't just upend everything."

I stare at him, struggling to process his words. "But you said…" My voice cracks, and I bite down on my lip to keep the tears at bay. "You said you'd come with me."

"I know," he replies, his tone cool now, detached. "But I wasn't thinking clearly. My priority was you…not ruining the merger, not letting Brett get in the way. I was doing what I thought was best at the time."

I'm in shock, but still, I manage to speak. "At the time, but… that was just a few days ago. How can you have changed your mind so drastically?"

Each word cuts deeper, stripping away the fragile hope I'd built around us. I feel like I'm standing on the edge of a cliff, the ground crumbling beneath me. "So… all of it? Paris, us… was it all just a lie?"

His face hardens, the mask of the calculating businessman slipping back into place. "It wasn't a lie," he says evenly. "But I can't give you what you want, Jenny. Not now. Not like this."

I can't breathe. The room spins around me as the enormity of his words sinks in. He doesn't even flinch as he watches me unravel, as I rise to my feet, shaking. "You didn't even try," I choke out, grabbing my clothes from the back of the chair where they're draped. "You made me believe you would, but you won't."

"Jenny, wait," Zack says, his voice low but firm, as though he's trying to maintain control of the situation. His eyes darken, a flicker of something…guilt? …crossing his face. "I didn't mean for it to come out this way."

I wait. Needing to hear this.

"How exactly did you mean for it to come out, Zack? Over

dinner, maybe? Or were you planning to let me find out when I got to Paris alone, waiting for you?"

His jaw tightens, and he exhales sharply. "You don't understand."

"Then make me understand," I demand, my voice trembling. "Tell me why you would lie to me, why you would… would…use me like this."

"I did it for the family," he snaps, stepping closer. "To keep you away from Brett. From all of this. You don't belong in this mess, Jenny. It's toxic, and it's—"

"No," I hold up my hand completely disinterested in hearing anymore. "No. Thanks for playing me like a game Zack. How brilliant. You won."

I instantly start to gather my clothes.

He freezes, his expression hardening into something colder, sharper. "It wasn't a game."

I laugh bitterly, the sound hollow and foreign to my own ears. "Wasn't it? Because from where I'm standing, that's all it ever was to you. A way to win, to control everything around you."

His silence is deafening. I pull on my dress hastily, my hands shaking so much that the fabric slips through my fingers. He watches me, his gaze unyielding, as though daring me to break under the weight of his presence. But I won't. Not this time.

As I reach for my shoes, he finally speaks, his voice steady but devoid of any warmth. "I'll make sure you're taken care of. I've already arranged a first-class ticket to Paris. It will be sent to your room."

I freeze mid-motion, my hands stilling as his words pierce through the silence. He doesn't stop, as if he's rehearsed this, as if delivering this blow with precision will somehow make it easier.

"There's more," he continues, his tone clinical. "I'll

transfer a substantial sum into your account. Enough to give you freedom, independence. You won't have to worry about rent, bills, or anything else. There's a portfolio too...stocks and bonds. Solid investments. They'll give you long-term security."

I slowly straighten, the weight of his words crashing over me like a tidal wave. "You've really thought this through," I say, my voice hollow.

"I wanted to make sure you'd have everything you need," he says. His hands are tucked into his pockets now, his posture stiff.

"This isn't about me, Jenny. It's about you."

"About me?" I repeat, my voice breaking with disbelief. "You think throwing money and stocks at me will make this right? That it'll erase the fact that you lied to me? That you—" My throat tightens, choking off the rest of the sentence.

I stare at him, the man I thought I knew, and feel my heart fracture into pieces I'm not sure I'll ever be able to put back together. "Clean," I whisper, shaking my head. "Efficient. That's how you see this?"

His jaw tightens, a flicker of something...regret? pain?...crossing his face. But he doesn't answer. He just stands there, unyielding, as if willing himself not to break.

"Do you even hear yourself?" I demand, stepping closer. "This isn't a business deal, Zack. This is my life. My heart. And you're standing there, calculating what you think it's worth in stocks and bonds."

The silence that follows is suffocating. My hands tremble as I grab my coat and bag, each movement heavy with the finality of what's happening. I look at him one last time, searching for something...anything...that might tell me this isn't real. That this isn't the end.

But his face is a mask of restraint, his eyes shadowed with the weight of words he refuses to say.

"I don't want your money, Zack," I say, my voice trembling with barely contained emotion. "I don't want your stocks or your bonds or your carefully planned escape route. I just wanted you. But clearly, that was too much to ask."

He doesn't stop me as I walk to the door. He doesn't call out or try to explain. He just stands there, letting me go as if I was never his to keep.

CHAPTER

Forty

ZACK

The door to the car slams shut behind me as I step onto the sidewalk outside Brett's Manhattan apartment.

It's an absurd hour of the morning, and the city is draped in that quiet lull just before the chaos begins. My coat is thrown hastily over my shoulders, the dress shirt I grabbed…the one Jenny wore around my suite…still unbuttoned at the collar. The fabric smells faintly of her, and the scent feels like a taunt, a ghost I'll never exercise.

I grip the ticket in my hand as if it's a lifeline. It was meant to be mine. I'd bought it myself for the first time rather than having my assistant do it, excited despite my doubts, and in the end, I hurt both her and myself irrevocably.

. . .

I'd planned everything. I would have gone with her to Paris. We'd build our own life there for a little while. But when I woke up this morning, that familiar weight crushed me. The reality that I might ruin her all over again. I couldn't bear to take the leap, and now it's too late. She's gone.

And yet, it's not her absence that breaks me. It's her final look, the devastation in her eyes, the way she held herself as if bracing for impact. She didn't crumble. She didn't cry. She just walked away with all the dignity I didn't deserve. Her words echo in my mind, cutting deeper than I thought possible.

You didn't even try.

I should have. God, I should have. I truly do not deserve to have her.

My knuckles rap against Brett's door before I can second-guess myself. The moments stretch, and I hear muffled movement on the other side. When the door creaks open, Brett stands there, disheveled and half-asleep, his shirt tugged over his head at an awkward angle. His face contorts with confusion when he sees me.

"Zack?" He rubs his eyes, his usual smug grin nowhere in sight. "What the hell are you doing here? It's—" he glances at the clock on the wall. "—seven in the goddamn morning."

. . .

"I need to talk to you," I say, my voice quieter than I intended. The words feel foreign, as if someone else is speaking for me. "Now."

He blinks at me, his brow furrowing. "Uh, sure. Come in, I guess."

I step inside, the plush carpet muffling my movements as I pace the living room. My thoughts race, colliding into each other like freight trains, and I feel his gaze on me, curious and concerned.

"You're scaring me a little, man," Brett says, scratching the back of his neck. "Is someone sick? Was there an accident or something?"

I cut straight to the point. "No," I reply, "it's about the merger, and it's about Jenny."

At her name, I stop pacing. My chest tightens, and for a moment, I can't bring myself to look at him. Then I force the words out, raw and unvarnished. "She loves you, Brett. She always has.

She's loved you for as long as I can remember. If that's what makes her happy, then I'm willing to let everything else fall apart."

. . .

Brett stares at me, his confusion deepening. "What the hell are you talking about? Let what fall apart?"

"The merger," I say simply. "If you want her, Brett...if she's what you need to be happy...I'll pull out of the deal with Elizabeth's family."

He looks at me like I've just sprouted another head. "You're serious? You'd kill a billion-dollar merger for her?"

I nod, the motion slow but deliberate. "I'm serious."

His disbelief morphs into something more somber as he watches me. "Zack, I don't know what's going on with you, but this doesn't sound like you. I know you've been lenient with me in still pursuing her, but I know you've been furious and that you never actually expected me to go through with it."

"This isn't about me, Brett. It's about her."

"Did she say something to you?" he asks.

"No," I reply. "I just... I know her. I've watched her grow up, I've cared for her... like family from the beginning, even if no one has noticed. And you... I care deeply for you as well. You both should be happy, and I won't trade that for anything."

. . .

Brett studies me carefully, his eyes narrowing as he pieces things together. "This is too strange," he says. "Do you by chance have feelings for her or something? What is happening?"

"Don't be ridiculous," I say, no longer willing to give him the chance to dig any deeper.

"Okay, okay," he say this hands up in surrender even though suspicion remains in his eyes,

"So … what exactly do you want me to do?" he asks.

I hold out the plane ticket, my hand trembling despite my effort to appear composed. "Go to her in Paris. Far away from here and everyone else's eyes. Be honest and spend time getting to know her. Try to make things work between you two and make her as happy as possible."

Brett hesitates, staring at the ticket as if it's some foreign object. "You're really giving me this?"

"It's yours," I say, forcing myself to let go. "She leaves tomorrow."

He takes the ticket, nodding slowly. "Okay, I'll go."

. . .

I turn away, my chest heavy as I move toward the door. Before I leave, I glance over my shoulder, my voice barely above a whisper. "Don't hurt her, Brett. Please."

He doesn't reply, but his expression tells me everything I need to know. He won't.

As I step out into the cold morning air, I feel the weight of what I've done settle over me. There's no going back now. All I can do is hope that this will somehow lead her to the happiness I couldn't give her. Even if it means losing her forever.

CHAPTER
Forty~One

JENNY

I sit on the edge of my bed, staring at the suitcase I've just finished packing. The room feels hollow, stripped of everything but the essentials I'm leaving behind. It mirrors the emptiness in my chest, the sharp ache I've tried and failed to ignore since this morning.

A knock at my door startles me. My heart jumps, irrationally hoping it's Zack, but when I open it, Brett is standing there. His blond hair is slightly disheveled, his grin a little too crooked to be carefree.

"You're packed already?" he asks, his eyes landing on the suitcase. "Aren't you leaving tomorrow?"

"No," I reply stiffly, my hand tightening on the doorframe. "I moved my flight. I'll be leaving tonight."

His brows shoot up, the grin faltering. "Tonight? That's... sudden."

I, on the other hand, am much more startled than he is because, in all the years I've lived here, he has never been to my father's apartment.

Still, he steps inside, glancing around the room with the ease of someone who's always belonged. His hands stay stuffed in his pockets, but his energy feels restless, like he's holding something back.

"You're really going, huh?" he says, his voice quieter now. "Just like that?"

"I have to," I say firmly, sitting back on the bed. "I have a job to do."

He watches me for a moment, then pulls something from his pocket and holds it out. "Well, you're not going alone."

I frown, staring at the folded paper in his hand. "What's that?"

"A plane ticket," he says, stepping closer. "Zack gave it to me this morning. Said if I was serious about you, I should go with you."

My breath catches, and for a second, the room tilts. "Zack gave you... a ticket?"

He nods, his grin turning softer, almost self-conscious. "Yeah. It's first class too. Looks like he wanted to make sure you were comfortable."

The words twist something deep inside me. The idea of Zack planning this, arranging for Brett to be with me, sends a sharp pang through my chest.

"You're serious?" I manage, my voice barely above a whisper.

"Dead serious," he says, sitting beside me on the bed. "Look, Jenny, I know I've been... flaky in the past. But this isn't about that. I really want to be there for you, to try. Paris could be good for us."

I shake my head, overwhelmed. "Brett... I don't know."

His expression softens further, and he reaches out to take my hand. "You don't have to decide right now, but I need you to know I mean it. Whatever this is, I'm willing to take the leap."

I pull my hand away gently, standing to create some space. "I appreciate it, really. But I've made up my mind. I need to focus on my career, on myself."

His brows knit together, confusion flickering across his face. "Jenny, are you sure? You're not even going to give it a chance?"

I turn back to my suitcase, closing it with trembling hands. "It's better this way," I say softly. "For both of us."

He stands, and I feel his presence at my back. "You two got closer in Rome, didn't you?" His tone is light, almost teasing, but the question hits like a hammer.

I whirl around, startled. "What?"

He chuckles, shaking his head. "I never thought I'd see the day, but it seems my older brother is actually in love."

The words hang in the air, and I stare at him, speechless. "You're wrong," I finally say, but my voice lacks conviction.

"Am I?" he asks, stepping closer. "Think about it, Jenny. Zack doesn't do this. He doesn't sacrifice deals or push people toward someone else's happiness. He's never cared like this about anyone."

I don't say a word at this. I'm completely speechless.

I step back, my legs bumping against the edge of the bed as Brett's words hang in the air, pressing down on me with the weight of something I can't ignore.

"Jenny," Brett says softly, his tone losing its usual playful edge. "You have to see it. Zack wouldn't do this for anyone. Not for me, not for our parents, not for anyone in the world except you. He might not seem to realize that he's in love with you, but he's my brother, and I know him more than anyone, and I can see it clear as day. So... please don't leave. At least not yet. Give me a chance to give you two a chance the way he tried to give us both a chance."

I'm so confused I still don't know what to say.

I fold my arms over my chest, trying to shield myself from the possible truth in his words.

"You're wrong," I murmur, looking away. "His only concern is the family business and the merger."

"If this was true, then why would he tell me to go away with you?" Brett laughs softly, shaking his head. "You really think that? You think Zack, the guy who's been running this family like a goddamn machine for years, would risk it all... hand me a ticket to chase after you...if he only cared about the merger?"

"He cares about you much more than you know, and if you care about him as well, try to give this a shot. My head is spinning right now because you're both running out of time, but I'm sure I can make him see it."

I am instantly turned off.

"No interest," I say and rise to my feet.

I get up and start to walk away toward my bathroom, but he tries to stop me.

"Jenny," he calls, but before he can say anything more, his phone begins to ring.

He glances at the screen, frowning. "It's my dad," he mutters. "Hang on."

He answers, his expression shifting from confusion to surprise. "What do you mean, an emergency board meeting?" he says into the phone, his tone sharp. "I didn't know about this. When?"

A pause. Then his eyes widen, darting to me. "Zack called it?" He runs a hand through his hair, his movements suddenly frantic. "Yeah. Yeah, I'll be there."

He hangs up, his face pale as he looks back at me. "Jenny, I think something's wrong."

"What?" I ask, my chest tightening. "What's going on?"

"I don't know," he says, shaking his head. "But if Zack's

calling an emergency board meeting, it's big. He never does that unless something's about to implode."

Fear coils in my stomach, sharp and unrelenting. "What do you think he's planning?"

"I don't know," Brett says again, grabbing his jacket. "But I need to stop him before he does something stupid."

He turns to leave, but I grab his arm. "Brett, wait—"

"I'll fix this, Jenny," he says, his voice firm but gentle. "Just... don't leave yet, okay? Give me until tonight."

I want to argue, to tell him it's pointless, but the determination in his eyes stops me. I nod reluctantly, letting him go. As the door clicks shut behind him, I collapse onto the bed, my heart pounding.

I don't know what's happening, and whatever it is, I really don't want to be a part of it. I also don't want Zack to return and still find me here, so I hasten to finish my packing and get ready to leave for the airport.

CHAPTER
Forty~Two

ZACK

The boardroom feels colder than usual, though the afternoon sun streams through the tall windows, glinting off the polished surface of the table. I stand at the head, my hands resting on the chair in front of me. Around me, the board members murmur, some flipping through their notes, others casting curious glances my way. My parents sit closest, their expressions a mix of worry and expectation. They know something's coming, though not what. Not yet.

I take a slow breath; the words I've rehearsed rattling in my mind. It's the right decision. The only decision. And yet, the thought of saying it aloud feels like tearing something out of myself.

"I've called this meeting to inform you all of a significant change in our plans," I begin, my voice steady despite the storm raging beneath. "As of this morning, the merger with the Fairchild family is no longer—"

The doors swing open with a bang, cutting me off mid-sentence. Brett strides in, his usual swagger accompanied by an energy that borders on manic. His blond hair is a mess, his suit slightly wrinkled, and he looks like he hasn't slept. Yet somehow, he manages a grin that's both infuriating and triumphant.

"Sorry, everyone," he says, his voice too loud, too cheerful. "But it looks like my big brother's got his facts wrong."

I stiffen, my jaw tightening as he strolls to the table, addressing the room like he's the one in charge. "There's no need to cancel anything," he announces, leaning casually against the table's edge. "The merger is still on, and so is the wedding."

A ripple of confusion spreads through the room. My mother frowns, while my father's brows knit together in a rare display of visible emotion. I glance at them briefly before turning my full attention to Brett.

"What the hell are you doing?" I say, my voice low but laced with barely contained fury.

. . .

"Saving your ass," Brett replies smoothly, his grin widening. "Honestly, Zack, what were you thinking? Throwing away a billion-dollar deal for what? Some girl?"

The air in the room shifts, the tension thick enough to choke on. I take a step closer to him, my fists clenching at my sides. "You have no idea what you're talking about."

"Oh, don't I?" Brett asks, his tone mocking. "Jenny's a sweet kid, sure. But let's be real…she's just a distraction. A pretty face with no business being part of this family."

My vision blurs at the edges, the rage bubbling up faster than I can control it. "You don't know a damn thing about her."

"Don't I?" he says again, his voice turning cruel. "Come on, Zack. She's not one of us. She never will be. And if you're throwing away everything we've worked for because you think I've got some future with her, someone not even worthy enough for us to wipe our shoes with then you've really lost it."

I don't even realize I've moved until my fist connects with his jaw. The sound echoes through the room, followed by the gasps of our parents and the stunned silence of the board. Brett stumbles back, clutching his face, but when he looks up, he's grinning again, blood staining his teeth. I'm confused.

"What is wrong with you?"

· · ·

"I knew it," he says, his voice a mixture of pain and triumph. "I fucking knew it. Do you know, in all our years as brothers, you've never hit me before? And now suddenly, I insult Jenny, and you lose it. You have to see it now, don't you? You can't be this dense. You have to see that you're in love with her."

The words hit like a blow, harder than any punch I could throw. I freeze, my chest heaving, my heart pounding so loud I can barely hear anything else. He's right. Goddamn it, he's right.

Brett straightens, rubbing his jaw as he steps closer. "You've never lost control like this before," he says, his tone softer now, almost understanding. "Not over the company. Not over money. Not over anything. But over her? You're ready to throw it all away."

I turn away, my hands trembling as I grip the back of the chair. The truth I've been running from is now laid bare for everyone to see, and there's no taking it back.

"Look," Brett says, his voice quieter now. "I've got a car and a chopper ready for you. If you leave now, you can still make it to the airport before she leaves."

"What?" I'm shocked. "She's leaving?"

. . .

"Right now," he replies. "She moved her flight to this evening."

I glance back at him, my eyes narrowing. "Why are you doing this?"

"Because I'm your brother," he says simply. "And because for once, you're not being an unfeeling robot. You actually care about something. Someone. And you're too goddamn stupid to see it."

The room is still silent, the board members too shocked to speak. My parents exchange glances, their expressions unreadable. But I don't care about any of them anymore. All that matters is her.

Without another word, I stride toward the door, the weight in my chest lifting slightly with each step. I don't know what I'll say when I see her, but I know one thing for certain: I can't let her leave. Not without a fight.

CHAPTER
Forty~Three

JENNY

The airport is a blur of movement and noise around me, but I'm disconnected from it all. My suitcase sits at my side, untouched, and I can't even summon the strength to check in. My phone is off. I can't face the messages I know are waiting for me, or worse, the silence if there's nothing at all.

This is it. The end. And I'm doing everything I can to hold myself together, to keep my tears from spilling over. I know if I start crying, I won't be able to stop.

I take a shaky breath, staring blankly at the departures board. My flight isn't even listed yet, but it doesn't matter. I just need to get away...to leave this place, this life, and everything that's hurt me behind. I'll never come back. Not to the Jackson Mansion, not to New York, not to him.

The ache in my chest feels unbearable, and I clutch the strap of my bag like it's the only thing keeping me upright. I blink hard, fighting back the sting of tears. I can't fall apart here. Not here, where everyone can see.

"Jenny!"

The sound of my name, loud and urgent, cuts through the fog in my mind. My heart stutters, and I turn on instinct, my breath catching when I see him.

Zack.

He's running toward me, his suit jacket slightly askew, his face flushed and frantic. For a moment, I'm frozen, unsure if this is real or some cruel trick of my imagination. But then he's in front of me, breathless and wild-eyed, and I know it's real.

"What are you doing here?" I manage to choke out, my voice trembling, barely audible over the pounding in my chest.

"I couldn't let you leave," he says, his words tumbling out in a rush, raw and desperate. "Not like this. Not without telling you...without asking you."

. . .

I blink at him, my breath hitching as my heart hammers wildly. "Asking me what?"

He pulls something from his pocket, and my eyes fall on the small, crumpled piece of paper in his hand. It's weathered, as though it's been folded and unfolded a hundred times. My stomach twists painfully as recognition hits.

"That's... that's my letter."

"The one you wrote about Brett," he says softly, his voice thick with emotion. His thumb brushes over the worn edge of the paper as he looks at me, his expression vulnerable in a way I've never seen before. "About how you felt, how much you loved him. I have to know, Jenny. Do you feel even a little bit of that for me?"

My world tilts, the floor beneath me threatening to disappear. "What are you talking about?" My voice is shaky, my throat tight as I stare at him in disbelief.

"Because if you do," he continues, his voice gaining steadiness with each word, "I'll give everything up. The business, the merger, everything. Right here, right now. I'll go with you to Paris, Jenny. Just say the word."

My knees threaten to buckle, and I step back, trying to process the enormity of what he's saying.

. . .

"Zack... I don't understand. Why are you doing this?"

He exhales sharply, running a hand through his hair. His usual calm, composed demeanor is gone, replaced by a raw, unguarded intensity that shakes me to my core.

"Because I've always cared about you," he says, the words spilling out like a confession. "Even when I didn't understand it. Even when I tried to deny it."

I open my mouth to respond, but he doesn't let me. Instead, he takes a step closer, his gaze locking onto mine.

"Do you remember how you felt the night you wrote this letter?" he asks, holding it up. "Do you remember how broken you were?"

I can only nod, the memory flooding back...the pain, the hopelessness, the overwhelming desire to escape.

"I found you that night, Jenny," he says, his voice shaking. "I saw you lying there, so small, so lost, and for the first time in my life, I felt... helpless. I didn't know what to do, but I knew I had to do something."

. . .

I stare at him, stunned, as his words hit me like a wave. He swallows hard, his jaw tightening.

"I arranged your first job in Paris," he admits, his voice dropping to a whisper. "I knew it was what you needed. A way out. A chance to find yourself. I didn't expect anything in return...I just wanted to see you happy. To know you were okay."

Tears blur my vision, and I shake my head, unable to believe what I'm hearing. "Zack..."

"I've loved you for a long time," he continues, his voice breaking. "I just didn't know it. Not until now. Not until I thought I'd lost you forever."

My chest feels like it's caving in, the weight of his words suffocating me. I take another step back, my hands trembling. "You hurt me," I whisper, my voice barely audible. "You lied to me, Zack. How am I supposed to trust you?"

His expression crumples, and he takes a tentative step forward, closing the space between us. "I know I hurt you," he says, his voice thick with regret. "And I'll spend the rest of my life making it up to you, if you'll let me. Just... don't leave. Don't walk away from what we could have."

· · ·

I want to say something, anything, but my throat is too tight. He reaches into his other pocket and pulls out a small black velvet box. My heart stops as he sinks to one knee, flipping the lid open to reveal a massive emerald-cut diamond ring.

My hands fly to my mouth as a gasp escapes me.

"I've had this ring for a week," he says, his voice low but steady. "I thought it was the panic of everything falling apart, but I know now...it's you. It's always been you. These past few hours without you have been hell, Jenny. The worst kind of hell. I've never felt this doomed in my life."

Tears spill down my cheeks, and I don't even try to stop them. My heart is pounding so hard it feels like it might burst.

"Marry me," he says, his gaze never leaving mine. "Please. Give me the chance to make this right. To show you how much I love you."

I'm shaking, my entire world spinning, but when I look at him...his earnest expression, the raw vulnerability in his eyes...I know there's only one answer.

"Yes," I whisper, my voice breaking. "Yes, Zack. I'll marry you."

. . .

His face lights up with relief, and before I can say anything else, he's on his feet, pulling me into his arms. I let out a breathless laugh, wrapping my arms around his neck as he lifts me off the ground. Our lips meet in a kiss that's everything…soft, desperate, and filled with all the emotions we've kept locked away for so long.

"I love you," he murmurs against my lips, his voice trembling. "I love you so much, Jenny."

"I love you too," I whisper back, my hands tangling in his hair. I'm in complete disbelief.

The world around us fades away as we hold each other, our love finally out in the open. In this moment, there's no pain, no doubt…only us, and the promise of everything we will build together.

Epilogue

JENNY

The estate is alive with celebration. Strings of lights hang between the towering oaks, their golden glow casting a magical ambiance over the sprawling garden. Soft laughter and the melodic hum of a live quartet drift through the air, mingling with the clink of champagne glasses. It's a scene straight out of a dream, one I never imagined I'd be part of.

But tonight, I'm not just a guest. Tonight, I'm the reason for the celebration.

Zack's hand rests on the small of my back as we move through the crowd, his touch grounding me amidst the flurry of well-wishers. He's devastatingly handsome in a crisp black suit that fits him like a second skin, the sharp lines and subtle sheen exuding the effortless confidence that drew me to him in the first place. His dark hair is neatly combed, but a rebellious strand falls across his forehead, softening his otherwise commanding presence. I catch a glimpse of his eyes as he leans close to whisper something to me…they're lit with a warmth that sends a shiver down my spine.

"Why are you smiling like that?" he asks, his voice low enough that only I can hear.

"Because I can't believe this is real," I admit, my gaze sweeping over the scene before us. The garden is filled with the elite of society…men and women in designer gowns and tailored suits, their laughter ringing out like music. It's overwhelming, but Zack's steady presence keeps me anchored. "This is all so… perfect."

His lips quirk into a smile as he tugs me closer, his fingers brushing against mine. "It's perfect because you're here."

My cheeks flush, and I glance away, unable to handle the intensity of his gaze. My eyes land on the garage apartment in the distance, its windows glowing softly in the night. Through the curtains, I see my father sitting in his favorite chair, a book in hand. He catches my eye and raises his glass…a silent toast that sends a swell of emotion through me. He refused to leave the apartment, even after Zack offered him a house of his own. "This place has too many memories," he'd said. And I couldn't agree more.

"Jenny!" a voice calls, and I turn to see Camille, weaving her way through the crowd. Her eyes sparkle with excitement as she pulls me into a tight hug. "You look stunning!" she says in French. "And this ring… oh my god, it's massive!"

I laugh, holding out my hand so the enormous emerald-cut diamond catches the light. "Zack has a thing for making statements," I say, casting a teasing glance at him.

"I prefer to think of it as making sure the world knows you're mine," Zack says smoothly, in French, and both Camille's and my eyes pop open in shock, much to his amusement.

"You…" I begin, unable to form the words.

"We'll talk about it later," he says, and I almost collapse

right here. He understands French! How sneaky. But I'm glad, though. Knowing this now, everything makes even more sense to me.

As the evening unfolds, I steal a moment for myself, slipping away from the crowd to stand at the edge of the garden. From here, I can see the grand house bathed in light, its windows glowing with the life within. The sight stirs something deep inside me…a sense of belonging I've never felt before. I glance up at the tree where I used to hide during these parties, the branches now empty. The girl who once sat there, longing to be noticed, is gone.

"You're not drinking," Zack's voice breaks through my thoughts, and I turn to find him standing beside me, his hands tucked casually into his pockets. There's a softness in his expression, a quiet joy that makes my chest tighten.

"I have a reason," I say, my voice barely above a whisper.

His brows lift in curiosity. "Oh? And what's that?"

I take his hand, guiding it to rest on my stomach. His eyes widen, darting from my hand to my face as understanding dawns. "Jenny," he breathes, his voice full of wonder.

"I'm pregnant," I say, the words trembling on my lips. "We're having a baby."

For a moment, Zack says nothing, his eyes searching mine as if trying to ensure this isn't a dream. Then, with a suddenness that takes my breath away, he sweeps me into his arms, spinning me around as laughter bubbles from his lips. "You're serious?" he asks, his voice filled with awe.

I nod, tears spilling down my cheeks. "I found out a few days ago. I wanted to be sure before I told you."

He sets me down gently, his hands cupping my face as he kisses me…a kiss full of love, of promises for the future. "You've made me the happiest man alive," he whispers against my lips.

The sound of applause pulls us back to reality, and we

turn to find the crowd watching us, their faces alight with joy. Someone starts a toast, and soon the air is filled with cheers and well-wishes. My father, Camille, even the housekeeper, Mrs. Finnigan, beams at me from across the lawn.

As Zack pulls me close, his hand never leaving mine, I know this is more than just a celebration. It's a promise. A new beginning. The life I once dreamed of from the branches of that tree is now mine, and I wouldn't trade it for anything in the world.

And happily ever after they lived...

Coming Soon…

THE WRONG BROTHER

Chapter One
Daisy

I walk into the bar where Leah asked us all to meet. It's not somewhere we usually go and pretty much anytime we go out as a group, we start off in Maynard's. Maynard's is a pub owned by Dean, Leah's boyfriend, whose surname, quite confusingly, isn't Maynard but Anderson. He said Anderson's doesn't have the same ring to it and used his mom's maiden name instead. Dean and I don't agree on much, but I have to hand it to him – Maynard's sounds a ton cooler than Anderson's for a pub name.

But the fact we're not going there makes me wonder if Leah has broken up with Dean. Maybe this is her telling us all they are through and then we will spend the night either celebrating her singlehood or drowning her sorrows, whichever way the break up went. Both ways sound like they are going to be filled with lots of shots, cocktails, and bluster.

I look around for the girls. The pub is more of a wine bar than a real pub. It is too trendy to be a pub, with its monochrome colors and chrome and glass bar. Actually, that's probably not glass; just something that looks like it. I hope so anyway. It seems kind of dangerous having an actual glass bar. I'm pleased to see that the place hasn't let its need to be trendy affect the seating. Too many wine bars do something cool with the seating that looks awesome and often futuristic, but that makes it unbearable to sit on. Not here. Here there are normal tables and chairs, a few high stools at the bar and a few booths.

I spot an arm waving at me from one of the booths. I wave back and head over to the excited arm. Leah jumps up when I reach the booth. We hug hello and air kiss each other's cheeks.

We are an unlikely pair to look at and I don't think anyone would say we were best friends if they just saw us together. Leah is pretty and blonde with soft curves and her even softer voice. She has a bubbly personality and an infectious laugh. And then there's me. I've been described as 'pretty in a terrifying way' and I kind of like that. I have gothic-black, shoulder length hair with streaks of electric blue in it. Tonight, I am wearing it in a messy up do. No one has ever called me bubbly. I enjoy a laugh but I'm kind of cynical and, I'm told, a bit standoffish. Meh. I've been called way worse.

Leah is wearing a gorgeous, curve hugging pink dress with spaghetti straps. The dress comes to just above her knee, and she is wearing sparkly gold sandals that have ties that come up halfway up her calves in a complicated lacy pattern. Again, we are opposites. I'm wearing black fishnets, a black tutu style skirt and a black corset top. The corset has lines of metal spikes down the bones, and they match the metal spikes coming out of my heels. While it's not the most girly of outfits, when I wear a corset, I feel like a woman because it gives me breasts and hips, a waistline, all things I seem to lack in my normal clothes.

Funnily enough, in the outfit I'm wearing, pretty much all my tattoos are on show. I have upper sleeves on both arms, red roses across my chest, and various pieces on my thighs and calves. The one hidden away is half of a jigsaw puzzle piece and it's on my hip, a spot chosen by Leah who has the other half of the jigsaw puzzle piece on her and didn't want it to be somewhere visible. Again, we're opposites, but the fact we got a best friends' tattoo tells you how much we love each other.

"I'm so glad to see you, Daisy. It's been way too long," Leah says, ushering me into the booth.

Fucking Daisy. Who had the bright idea to name me after a delicate little flower? Well, my parents obviously, but the name couldn't have been any further from matching my personality.

"Way too long," I agree.

I nod at Harriet, and we exchange greetings and how are you pleasantries and then I move on to Ellie, someone I'm shocked to see here to be honest. Ellie is Leah's sister, younger than her by a year or two, and while the two don't dislike each other, they rarely socialize together outside of family gatherings. Seeing her makes me think I am definitely right about the break up. It would be something Leah would think proper – her sister finding out with her friends rather than after them.

Leah has waved down a waiter and ordered five toxic pond cocktails and five shots of blue Aftershock.

"We're just waiting on Rachel. She messaged me saying she'll be here in a minute," Leah says, explaining why she's ordered five drinks for seemingly four people, not that I expect the waiter to care much one way or the other as long as the drinks get paid for.

The choice of drinks again makes me think I'm right about her and Dean breaking up. They are the sort of drinks you drink when you want to get drunk and pretend you're having fun when your heart is breaking. I'm guessing the announcement won't happen until Rachel is here though.

Leah and I have been friends forever, or so it seems. We actually met at high school, but I guess that covers all of the important years and now, at twenty-five, we're still best friends. We met Harriet and Rachel at college. They too were best friends and the four of us became a foursome, and while we're all fairly close, we are still very much two pairs of best friends that have formed a larger group.

Rachel is a beautiful, tall black girl. She should have been a model, she's seriously that beautiful, but she opted to be an accountant instead. Harriet studied psychology, the same as me, and how we met at college, and neither of us work in fields associated with our degrees. I work in fashion and Harriet is a teacher – and no, she doesn't teach psychology, she teaches geography of all things. Leah is a hair stylist in the most expensive salon I have ever been to.

The irony of that is that Dean's family are old money, and in normal circumstances they would have judged Leah as below them, but somehow, she has managed to make them feel that she is fit to be one of them. Apparently even to one of their big cheese sons who is uber-successful in the finance world. The rich brother, and a total snob, I hear. I wonder what he makes of Dean, who owns a bar, but seems to have no plans on expanding his business into a chain of bars or anything like that. I bet he isn't overly happy with Dean's career choices or his relationship with Leah.

Chapter Two

Daisy

The drinks arrive and alongside the five blue shots are five taller glasses with neon green drinks. A shade I feel should never be ingested. The rim of the glass is coated in green sugar, and it is decorated with slices of kiwi fruit and mint leaves.

"I don't think it's green enough," I say dryly, which gets a round of laughter.

"Well, I don't know about that, but it looks disgusting," Harriet says, reaching for one of the drinks and taking a mouthful. "And yet it tastes fantastic."

I pick up one of the glasses and take a wary sip, but Harriet is right. The drink tastes of lime and lemon with an under taste of mint. It might be a bit on the tart side, but the sugared rim counteracts that and makes it a damned good drink.

"Cheers," I say and raise my glass. The others follow suit, and I take another sip, a bigger one this time, now that I know the drink doesn't taste as poisonous as it looks.

The others try their drinks, and we all agree they are much nicer than they look. By unspoken agreement, we leave the shots until Rachel arrives, which isn't much longer. She comes hurrying over to our table. She's wearing jeans, red satin heels and a red lacy top, and she looks amazing as always. Her hair is down, and she's straightened it. It looks good – sleek and shiny – but I prefer it natural, in the beautiful big afro style curls that look like an explosion around her face.

"Sorry, sorry," she says in the way of a greeting, grabbing a stool and putting it at the end of the table. She could have squeezed in one of the sides with two of us, but this is probably more comfortable for us all.

Now that Rachel is here, and we've all done the small talk,

Leah hands out the shots. We all clink our glasses together and down the small drink. It burns on the way down, but it's a good burn and I savor it for a moment before I sip my normal drink.

"So, I know I said we all needed to catch up, and we do, but I do have an ulterior motive for asking you all here tonight," Leah says. "Dean asked me to marry him. And I said yes."

She excitedly thrusts her left hand into the center of the table and shows off her ring. I'm younger than her by two years, but I'm too shocked to react right now. I was so sure she was about to say she was free and single, but I couldn't have been much further from the truth.

I realize I'm the only person not to have said anything and I can feel the eyes of the group on me, and I smile widely, hoping to hell it looks real. I take in the ring, which actually is lovely and doesn't look cheap, something I would have worried about if I had known in advance Dean was going ring shopping.

"It's beautiful Lee," I say. "Congratulations."

It is beautiful and it's perfect for Leah. The band is platinum gold, and the main stone of the ring is a sapphire, Leah's favorite gemstone. The sapphire is surrounded by a cluster of diamonds, yes, real diamonds, and I know the ring has cost Dean quite a bit.

Even though he got the ring right, I know I don't sound as enthusiastic as the others, and the truth is, I'm probably not. I think Leah deserves better than Dean and everyone knows it. And I'm not one to fake a reaction and get all squealy over something I'm sure is going to end up with my best friend getting hurt. Besides if I had shrieked like the others, they all would have known it was fake. Leah could have been marrying a man I hand picked out as her soul mate and I could be the happiest person in the world for her, but the screaming girlie thing isn't me at all. Instead of trying to be Excited Barbie, I do what I do best in these situations.

"I'll get the next round of drinks," I say.

I shuffle along the booth seat and squeeze past Rachel and head to the bar where I ask for a bottle of champagne. The bartender gives me three choices and I go for the middle one. It's a couple of hundred dollars a bottle, but Leah is worth it and to be honest, I would have been more than happy to get the expensive one, but I don't want to make any of the others feel bad if they can't afford to do the same. I'm still not going to force her to drink the cheap one though. What kind of a best friend would do that?

While the bartender is filling the ice bucket, I sense someone moving up beside me at the bar and I turn my head to see Leah slipping into place next to me.

"Do you want some more shots or something?" I ask.

She smiles and shakes her head. "No. I wanted to talk to you," she says. "Just us."

I nod for her to go on and she does.

"I know you're not Dean's biggest fan," she says. "But I love him, and I really need you to be happy for me Daze."

"I am happy for you," I say.

"Tell your face," Leah jokes.

I snort out a laugh. "Seriously though, I'm happy if you're happy. And it's not that I dislike Dean as a person. I think he's funny and kind and there's no doubt he treats you well. But he lacks ambition, and you want to climb the career path. I'm afraid one day you're going to end up at a point where he resents you for working long hours and you resent him for not doing enough. Basically, I'm worried you're settling because Dean is a safe option."

"I'm not settling. I promise you that. I love Dean and I don't care if he owns a bar or if owns a whole chain of bars. It's a job, that's all. Dean isn't particularly ambitious when it comes to work, but he has dreams and goals that make sense. Like retiring early and seeing the world. Like spending time with loved ones rather than slaving away at work all the time. That probably makes us opposites in some ways, but opposites attract, and I know he will never stand in my way if I want something. He supports me one hundred percent," Leah says.

I force a smile that I hope looks real.

"Well, you obviously know him better than I do and if you say he's for real, then that's good enough for me," I say.

"Good because your opinion matters to me the most," Leah says.

I shake my head, but she nods hers.

"Of course it does. You're my best friend," she says.

The bartender filled the ice bucket, opened the bottle of champagne and set it inside the bucket. He plonks it down on the bar in front of me. I give him my card and he runs it through and hands it back.

"How many glasses?" he asks.

"One," I say with a straight face.

The bartender tries his best not to react, but one eyebrow lets him down and I smile.

"Joking," I say. He looks relieved and he lets out a small laugh. "Five please."

"You think that's bad, when we were at college if she ordered a bottle and they asked how many glasses, she would say just a straw," Leah puts in.

"Yes, but I'm older and classier now," I reply.

The bartender puts five glasses on the tray and makes sure I'm ok to carry it. I say I am, and I go to pick it up.

"Wait," Leah says. "There was one more thing before we go back to the others. Will you be my maid of honor?"

"Of course, I will," I say, and Leah flings her arms around me in an enthusiastic hug.

I'm glad I said I would do it. It doesn't matter what I might think of Dean and the long-term prospects for this relationship. I have voiced my concern and Leah has reassured me all is ok, and even if I don't think it's necessarily the case, she's my best friend and I will be there by her side whatever she wants to do, and I won't risk falling out with her by keep telling her I don't like Dean or don't think she should marry him.

We go back to the table, me carrying the tray, which is a lot heavier than I anticipated it to be. I reach the booth and set the tray down on the table to a round of whoops and cheers.

"Somebody's bringing out the big guns," Harriet says when I lift the bottle from the bucket, and she sees the label. I shrug.

"My bestie is only going to get engaged once and we're going to celebrate it in style," I say.

Leah beams at me and I beam back, and I tell myself that wasn't a lie. Her and Dean are in love, and they are going to stay that way and grow old together. Leah and I get back into our seats and we are all drinking champagne and chatting and laughing. We have toasted several times, and I'm starting to feel a bit tipsy – champagne always goes straight to my head. We finish the champagne and Rachel orders us another round of cocktails. They come quickly and they are fruity and delicious.

"How did Dean propose, Leah? Was it romantic?" Harriet asks.

"Well, it probably won't sound much to anyone else, but to me, it was perfect," she says and everyone except me says "aww". I try to join in and end up sounding like a damned echo. "I was waiting for him to finish work, and when he got rid of the last few customers, I knew he would want to cash up the till and that kind of thing, so I picked a trash bag up and figured I'd make a start on collecting the trash. He tried to get me to stop but I didn't and then he starts playing my favorite song ever …"

She pauses and looks at me and I grin.

"Bed of Roses by the ever-talented Bon Jovi," I reply and Leah nods enthusiastically and then she goes on where she left off as there had been no pause.

"On the jukebox. He told me to come to him because he wanted to talk to me and when I did, he took my hands in his and started to twirl me around. We danced and when the song was nearly finished, I reminded him that wasn't talking and he said, no, but this is. And then he got down on one knee and asked me to marry him."

Another round of "awws", but this time, I'm quick enough to join in so that it doesn't look like an afterthought. Again, Dean has nailed it. Leah has always said if anyone asked her to marry them, she would want a lowkey proposal, just the two of them. And that's exactly what she got. I hope it's because Dean knows her well, not because he couldn't be bothered to do anything more special.

Chapter Three
Daisy

"Are we moving on or should I get another round?" Ellie says, looking around at our glasses and finding them all empty.

"Let's go somewhere we can dance," Rachel says, and she gets nods of agreement from the rest of us.

"Just quickly, before we go somewhere louder, there's something I wanted to say," Leah says. "I've asked Daisy to be my maid of honor, and she has accepted." She pauses for a moment while the others congratulate me. I didn't know that was a thing and I'm still not sure it is, but it's a nice moment and I don't ruin it by pointing out it's not necessary. "And you three, Rachel, Harriet, Ellie, I would love it if you would be my bridesmaids."

More shrieking and cheering fill the air followed by three tearful exclamations of yes. Was I meant to cry? Shit, I don't know. But God if I had cried, Leah probably would have thought she was dying or something. I congratulate the others because I have now learned it's a thing and even if it's not, they said it to me, so it feels only respectful to say it back.

I decide then and there that if I'm seriously going to do this maid of honor thing properly – and I am, Leah deserves that, and I would have said no if I didn't think I could do this – I'm going to stop second guessing myself and do what feels right to me. Leah has been my best friend for long enough to know me and to know what sort of reactions I have to things, and she's always loved me for it, so I am not going to change now.

***

After Leah asked the other three girls to be her bridesmaids and they all agreed, we finished our bottle of champagne and moved on to a club. Everyone was in a good mood, and we drank and danced, even after everyone was moaning their feet hurt, we still danced. By around three am, there was only me and Leah left, the others peeling off one by one over the course of the previous hour or so.

Giggling, Leah took my hand and led me to the bar where she ordered two gin and oranges and then she led me to the chill out area of the club where the music was a bit quieter, and people sat around chatting (or coming down) rather than bouncing around. We sat down at a small table.

"Sorry. Do you mind us sitting down for a minute? My feet are burning," Leah says, and I shake my head.

"Tell me more about the wedding," I say once we are seated.

People tend to assume that because I'm a bit gothy in my clothes and makeup that I have no interest in so-called girly things like weddings. That isn't true at all. Aside from the fact Leah is my best friend so of course I care about her wedding, there's also the fact that I coordinate fashion shows for some big-name designers, and around twenty percent of those shows are for wedding dresses. I probably know and care more about weddings than any of my friends do.

"My colors are going to be burgundy and champagne. So, the bridesmaids would wear champagne, and you would wear burgundy. Or do you want to wear black?" Leah asks.

"It's your wedding Lee. I'll wear whatever you want me to. Burgundy is good," I say.

Of course I would prefer black, but burgundy is a good color and it's not like she's putting me in Barbie pink or something equally horrendous.

"We're going to have the ceremony and the reception in the same place – The Petal Hotel. Do you know it?" Leah asks.

"Yes," I say, nodding my head. It's small by hotel standards, but it's absolutely beautiful and it will be perfect for a wedding. "It's gorgeous."

"I know," Leah agrees. "I wasn't sure at first, but when I saw it, I just fell in love with it. We're going to book our room, rooms for the bridal party and the groomsmen, rooms for both sets of parents and then after that, people can book what's left or not stay over. Most guests will be local anyway and anyone coming from out of state can find a room nearby easily enough if it comes to it."

"Yes, there are a few nice hotels around there," I say. "But don't waste a room on me. Seriously, I'm a few blocks away. Let someone who needs it take it."

"Well, that would be helpful if you're sure," Leah says.

I nod firmly. "I'm sure."

Leah excitedly tells me more about her planned menu, her centerpieces for the reception tables, her flowers, and more. Her face is flushed pink, and she is obviously so happy – happier than I think I've ever seen her. She frowns and for a moment, her excitement seems to fade away, but not for long.

"What's up?" I ask. "What's with the frown?"

She sighs.

"Do you think Ellie will be annoyed because she's not maid of honor?"

Leah shakes her head quickly. "No. Ellie and I were never that close. She probably didn't even expect to be asked to be a bridesmaid to be honest."

"Well, what is it, then?"

"I know I'm getting everything I want, and Dean is being super chill about everything, letting me do what I want, and for that reason, I wouldn't ever ask him to change his mind, but he's asked his brother, Brent, to be his best man."

"What's wrong with that?

"I absolutely hate that guy," Leah admits. "He's some sort of an investment banker – or investment wanker if you ask me – and he makes a shit ton of money, so he assumes he's better than everyone else. He's forever asking Dean when he's going to get a real job, or when he's going to expand on his business and all of this."

I don't really know what to say to that. The only reason I haven't asked Dean when he's going to grow up and start working in the real world or expanding his business is because it's literally none of my business. I've said similar things to Leah about him and she's always just said he's happy how he is. If he was my brother, I would probably be on him to step up, especially if he was getting married.

"He's so smug and condescending, like he's better than us because he has a ton more money than everyone else. Don't get me wrong, I get that money is important to live, but as long as we have enough to live comfortably – and we do – why do we need more? Why should Dean work twenty-hour days and miss out on living his life? What's the point? But Brent doesn't see it that way. For him, work and money are life. I'm not surprised he's single. He prioritizes the wrong things," Leah says.

Ok, put like that, he sounds like an asshole, and I get where Leah is coming from.

"Just avoid him as much as you can, and on your wedding day, you and Dean will be in your own little bubble anyway and he won't be able to ruin it for you," I say.

"Well, you're my maid of honor. It's your job to keep him away from me," Leah laughs.

"I think I can manage that," I say.

"More shots or pizza time?" Leah asks.

I check my watch and see it's close to five am.

"Definitely pizza time," I say, and we leave the club and wander over to the pizza joint down the block.

Chapter Four
Daisy

"Hello," I say, answering my cell phone to Leah.

"Oh Daisy, thank God," she says, and I can hear the panic in her voice, and I'm instantly on high alert.

"What is it? What's wrong?" I demand.

"I need to ask a huge favor of you," Leah says. "I'm stuck in traffic, and I reckon I'm going to be here for at least an hour or two – there's been an accident – and I have a cake tasting booked for six o'clock."

I check my watch. It's five thirty.

"Do you need me to call and cancel for you?" I say, thinking maybe she doesn't have the number on her and she's afraid to be sitting on her cell phone for too long with police officers around her due to the accident.

"No. I need you to go to the tasting," Leah says. "I wouldn't ask, but it's an emergency."

"A cake related emergency," I say, smiling.

"I know how it sounds," Leah says, and I can hear that she too is smiling, but only for a second before the panicky tone is back in her voice. "But this baker is so hard to get an appointment with, and she's already agreed to see me outside of office hours for the tasting. If I cancel on her, I know she won't reschedule and I'll end up with a cake that is fine, but just that – fine. Not special or ..."

"Leah, breathe," I interrupt her, and I wait for her to stop talking. "I'll go to the cake tasting."

"Oh, thank you," Leah says, and she sounds so relieved I almost laugh but I don't because I want her to know I'm taking this seriously. Maybe not as seriously as she is, because no matter how I look at it, I can't view a cake tasting appointment being missed as an emergency, but seriously enough that I'm not laughing about it at least.

"Should I pretend to be the wedding planner?" I ask.

"No. The baker knows the wedding planner. That's the only reason we got an appointment with her in the first place. I haven't met her yet so just pretend to be me. You know better than anyone what I like and dislike anyway," Leah says.

I frown. "Can't I just be me and explain I'm there on your behalf as the maid of honor?"

"No, because then she'll think you don't have any authority," Leah says.

"Fine," I say. "I'll be you. I hope you know this goes way above and beyond maid of honor duties."

"I know it does, and believe me, I'll be eternally grateful. I'll send you the address," Leah says. "Thank you, love you, bye."

She ends the call, leaving me half laughing and half shaking my head. I guess of all of the things she could need me to step in for though, this one isn't the worst one. A bit of time spent eating cake certainly doesn't sound too bad to me, and if the baker is that good, it doesn't matter which one I choose, it will taste good

My cell phone pings, and I see that Leah has sent me the address of the bakery and I check where it is in relation to my apartment where I currently am, and I see I I'm going to have to leave right now if I'm to make it on time and just hope the subway is running on time.

I grab my handbag and throw my cell phone in it. My wallet is already in there and my keys are in the door. I leave my apartment and lock the door, and then I run down the stairs and across the lobby and out into the street. I keep running until I'm in the subway station, and I'm rewarded with an announcement that the subway train I want is coming onto the platform in one minute. It's a good job I ran.

The subway train comes in as promised and I hop on it, and I'm lucky enough to get a seat. As the subway train pulls away, a man sits down beside me, and the sudden thrust of the subway train makes him bump against me.

"Sorry," he says, giving me an apologetic smile.

I feel as though my heart literally misses a beat when I look at him, although I tell myself that's stupid. This is real life, not some sappy movie. He is damned gorgeous though. He has light brown skin and grey eyes, an unusual combination that works well with his high cheekbones and sculpted jawline. He looks freshly shaven and that, coupled with his buzzcut, gives him a slight edge that stops him from moving from handsome into pretty.

"It's ok," I say, realizing I haven't spoken in forever and I've just been sitting, staring at the man. If it worries him, he hides it well. In fact, he is still looking at me now even after I have replied to his apology.

"I would curse the subway train and the driver, but how can I curse something that got the attention of the most beautiful woman on here," he says.

I raise an eyebrow, not ready to fall for such a cheesy line, but despite myself, I feel my stomach swirl. I tell myself to stop being so ridiculous but as much as my head wants that, my body is ignoring my command.

"Oh, come on," the man says, and he smiles at me and his teeth are white and straight and perfect, and his lips are oh so kissable. "Don't tell me you're one of those women who don't know they are gorgeous."

I shrug one shoulder awkwardly. I don't think I'm gorgeous – far from it – but I don't think I look like I've hit every branch of the ugly tree either. I'm just, well, me.

"I'm just teasing you," the man says when it becomes clear to him that I'm not even going to attempt to answer him this time. "You just look confident enough to know how to handle a compliment."

"I am," I say. "But there's a massive difference between a compliment and a cheesy pick-up line."

The man puts his hand to his chest.

"Ouch. I'm hurt," he says with a grin.

"Sure, you are" I grin back.

"You said my pick-up line was cheesy."

"It was. But I didn't say I don't like cheese."

"That's true, you didn't. So, are you saying I have a chance?"

"I'm saying bring on the cheddar," I reply, still grinning at him. I stand up. "This is my stop."

Preorder here:
The Rich Brother

About the Author

Thank you so much for reading!
If you have enjoyed the book and would like to leave a
precious review for me, please kindly do so here:

The Wrong Brother

Please click on the link below to receive info about my latest
releases and giveaways.
NEVER MISS A THING

Or
come say 'hello' here:

Also by Jona Rose

Dream Crusher

Until He Confesses

Insufferable Boss

Strictly Business

Confessing To The CEO

Enemy Boss

The Bride's Brother

The Bet

One Bossy Night

Not Yet Yours

Surviving the Boss

It's Only Make Believe

Hard Boss

Printed in Dunstable, United Kingdom

70890571R00211